D1083911

DATE DUE

The Loners

The Loners
Short Stories About the Young and Alienated

Edited by
L. M. Schulman

The Macmillan Company

The Macmillan Company
866 Third Avenue, New York, New York 10022
Collier-Macmillan Canada, Ltd., Toronto, Ontario
Library of Congress Catalog Card Number: 74–99125
First Printing

ACKNOWLEDGMENTS: "What Every Boy Should Know," by William Maxwell, is reprinted with the permission of Farrar, Straus & Giroux from
Stories, by William Maxwell, Copyright © 1954 by Intercultural Publica-
tions, Inc., © 1965 by Farrar, Straus & Cudahy, Inc., © 1966 by Farrar,
Straus & Giroux, Inc.

"Awakening," by Isaac Babel, is reprinted by permission of S. G. Phillips,
Inc., from *The Collected Stories of Isaac Babel,* Copyright © 1955 by S. G.
Phillips, Inc.

"Bad Characters," by Jean Stafford, is reprinted with the permission of
Farrar, Straus & Giroux from *Stories,* by Jean Stafford, Copyright © 1954
by Jean Stafford, © 1956 by Farrar, Straus & Cudahy, Inc., © 1966 by Farrar, Straus & Giroux, Inc.; first published in *The New Yorker.*

"Philco Baby," by Irvin Faust, from *Roar Lion Roar,* by Irvin Faust,
Copyright © 1964 by Irvin Faust, is reprinted by permission of Random
House, Inc.

"Barn Burning," by William Faulkner, Copyright 1939 and renewed
1967 by Estelle Faulkner and Jill Faulkner Summers, is reprinted from
Collected Stories of William Faulkner by permission of Random House,
Inc.

"The Loneliness of the Long-Distance Runner," by Alan Sillitoe, from
The Loneliness of the Long-Distance Runner, by Alan Sillitoe, Copyright
© 1959 by Alan Sillitoe, is reprinted by permission of Alfred A. Knopf, Inc.

"Sonny's Blues," by James Baldwin, from *Going to Meet the Man,* by
James Baldwin, Copyright © 1948, 1951, 1957, 1958, 1960, 1965 by James
Baldwin, is used by permission of the publisher, The Dial Press, Inc.

"Soldier's Home," by Ernest Hemingway, is reprinted with the permis-
sion of Charles Scribner's Sons from *In Our Time,* by Ernest Hemingway,
Copyright 1925 Charles Scribner's Sons, renewal copyright 1953 Ernest
Hemingway.

"The Secret Sharer," by Joseph Conrad, from *'Twixt Land and Sea,* by
Joseph Conrad, is reprinted by permission of J. M. Dent & Sons Ltd. and
the Trustees of the Joseph Conrad Estate.

"A Tree, A Rock, A Cloud," by Carson McCullers, from *The Ballad of
the Sad Cafe,* by Carson McCullers, Copyright 1955 by Carson McCullers,
is reprinted by permission of the publisher, Houghton Mifflin Company.

Foreword

We are always alone. We are never alone. Even in the center of a crowd of friends, we cannot escape our apartness; even in a locked and darkened room, we cannot cut ourselves off from our sense of the life going on outside.

There are exceptions: moments of love and mystical union, or flights into the perfect solitude of madness. But for the most part, we make our peace with the paradox. We cover over the contradiction in our lives with layers of indifference. There it remains, unseen, unfelt, unhealing.

The young, however, have no such protection. Youth may well be a time of wonder and joy. What is more certain is that it is a time of disillusionment, anger, rebellion and loneliness. For this is when we must discover who we are, what the world is, and the elusive nature of our relationship to it.

The stories in this collection are of such discoveries. They proceed from the first loss of innocence in "What Every Boy Should Know" to the final distillation of hard-won wisdom in "A Tree, A Rock, A Cloud." But they follow no straight line of development, share no single tone; they range over a varied, sharply contrasting human landscape.

Ernest Hemingway's young soldier comes home from a foreign war to find himself a foreigner in his native land. James Baldwin's black musician is caught up in a struggle to the death against the crushing pressures with which a

Negro must contend in America. Alan Sillitoe's incorrigible deliquent is offered entry into respectable society at the price of his self-respect. Joseph Conrad's fledgling ship's officer hesitates on the threshold of power and privilege, suddenly made aware of his kinship with the outcast and the criminal. They and the other characters in these stories—whether Irvin Faust's turned-off, tuned-out embodiment of urban alienation or William Faulkner's terrified Mississippi farm boy, Isaac Babel's Odessa ghetto youth in conflict with his heritage or Jean Stafford's rambunctious tomboy version of a Western outlaw—all stand at individual crossroads, with their own questions, their own answers, their own destinies in the balance. If to be a loner means running the risk of being lost, it also confers the exclusive right to be oneself and no one else. The clearest note sounded in this gathering is not one of anguish: it is defiant pride.

Another quality, too, may be observed—a special degree of involvement on the authors' part. It is no accident that the theme of the outsider is one of the great touchstones of literature. The writer lives on particularly intimate terms with the problem of human isolation: he seeks its answer in the alchemy of the storyteller's art. On these pages, we are led to share another's solitude. And in so doing— strangest paradox of all—we both rediscover and escape our own.

L. M. SCHULMAN

Contents

William Maxwell

What Every Boy Should Know

SHORTLY BEFORE HIS TWELFTH BIRTHDAY, EDWARD Gellert's eyes were opened and he knew that he was naked. More subtle than any beast of the field, more rational than Adam, he did not hide himself from the presence of God or sew fig leaves together. The most he could hope for was to keep his father and mother, his teachers, people in general from knowing. He took elaborate precautions against being surprised, each time it was always the last time, and afterward he examined himself in the harsh light of the bathroom mirror. It did not show yet, but when the mark appeared it would be indelible and it would be his undoing.

People asked him Who is your girl? And he said I have no girl, and they laughed and his mother said Edward doesn't care for girls, and they said All that will change.

People said Edward is a good boy, and that was because they didn't know.

He touched Darwin and got an electric shock: ". . . the hair is chiefly retained in the male sex on the chest and face, and in both sexes at the juncture of all four limbs with the trunk . . ." There was more, but he heard someone coming and had to replace the book on the shelf.

He stopped asking questions, though his mind was teeming with them, lest someone question him. And because it was no use; the questions he wanted to ask were the questions grown people and even older boys did not want to answer. This did not interrupt the incessant kaleidoscopic patterns of ignorance and uncertainty: How did they kncw that people were really dead, that they wouldn't open their eyes suddenly and try to push their way out of the coffin? And how did the worms get to them if the casket was inside an outer casket that was metal? And when Mrs. Spelman died and Mr. Spelman married again, how was it arranged so that there was no embarrassment later on when he and the first Mrs. Spelman met in Heaven?

Harrison Gellert's boy, people said, seeing him go by on his way to school. To get to him, though, you had first to get past his one-tube radio, his experimental chemistry set, his growing ball of leadfoil, his correspondence with the Scott Stamp and Coin Company, his automatically evasive answers.

Pure, self-centered, a moral outcast, he sat through church, in his blue serge Sunday suit, and heard the Reverend Harry Blair who baptized him say solemnly from the pulpit that he was conceived in Sin. But afterward, at the church door, in the brilliant sunshine, he shook hands with Edward; he said he was happy to have Edward with them.

In the bookcase in the upstairs hall Edward found a book that seemed to have been put there by someone for his enlightenment. It was called *What Every Boy Should Know*, and it told him nothing that he didn't know already.

Arrived at the age of exploration, he charted his course by a map that showed India as an island. The Pacific Ocean was overlooked somehow. Greenland was attached to China, and rivers flowed into the wrong sea. The map enabled him to determine his latitude with a certain amount of accuracy, but for his longitude he was dependent on dead reckoning. In his search for an interior passage, he continually mistook inlets for estuaries. The Known World is not, of course, known. It probably never will be, because of those areas the map-makers have very sensibly agreed to ignore, where the terrain is different for every traveler who crosses them. Or fails to cross them. The Unknown World, indicated by dotted lines or by no lines at all, was based on the reports of one or two boys in little better case than Edward and frightened like him by tales of sea monsters, of abysses at the world's end.

A savage ill at ease among the overcivilized, Edward remembered to wash his hands and face before he came to the table, and was sent away again because he forgot to put on a coat or a sweater. He slept with a stocking top on his head and left his roller skates where someone could fall over them. It was never wise to send him on any kind of involved errand.

He was sometimes a child, sometimes an adult in the uncomfortable small size. He had opinions but they were not listened to. He blushed easily and he had feelings hurt. His jokes were not always successful, having a point that escaped most people, or that annoyed his father. His sister Virginia was real, but his father and mother had no existence apart from him, and he was aware of them mostly as generalities, agents of authority or love or discipline, telling him to sit up straight in his chair, to stand with his shoulders back, to pick up his clothes, read in a better light, stop chewing his nails, stop sniffing and go upstairs and get a handkerchief. When his father asked some question at the dinner table and his mother didn't answer, or, looking down at her plate, answered inaudibly, and when his father then, in the face of these warnings, pursued the matter until she left the table and went upstairs, it didn't mean that his mother and father didn't love each other, or that Edward didn't have as happy a home as any other boy.

Meanwhile, his plans made, his blue eyes a facsimile of innocence, he waited for them all to go some place. Who then moved through the still house? No known Edward. A murderer with flowers in his hair. A male impersonator. A newt undergoing metamorphoses. Now this, now that mirror was his accomplice. The furniture was accessory to the fact. The house being old, he could count on the back stairs to cry out at the approach of discovery. When help came, it came from the outside as usual. Harrison Gellert, passing the door of his son's room one November night, seeing Edward with his hand at the knob of his radio and the headphones over his ears, reflected on Edward's thinness, his pallor, his poor posture, his moodiness of late, and concluded that he did not spend enough time out of doors. Edward was past the age when you could tell him to go outside and play, but if he had a job of some kind that would keep him out in the open air, like delivering papers . . . Too shocked to argue with his father (you don't ask someone to give you a job out of the kindness of their heart when they don't even know you and also when there may not even be any job or if there is they may have somebody else in mind who would be better at it and who deserves it more), Edward went downtown after school and stood beside the wooden railing in the front office of the *Draperville Evening Star*, waiting for someone to notice him. He expected to be sent away in disgrace, and instead he was given a canvas bag and a list of names and told to come around to the rear of the building.

From five o'clock on, all over town, all along College Avenue with its overarching elms, Eighth Street, Ninth

Street, Fourth Street, in the block of two-story flats backed up against the railroad tracks, and on those unpaved, nameless streets out where the sidewalk ended and the sky took over, old men sitting by the front window and children at a loss for something to do waited and listened for the sound of the paper striking the porch, and the cry—disembodied and forlorn—of "Pay-er!" Women left their lighted kitchens or put down their sewing in upstairs rooms and went to the front door and looked to see if the evening paper had come. Sometimes spring had come instead, and they smelled the sweet syringa in the next yard. Or the smell was of burning leaves. Sometimes they saw their breath in the icy air. A few minutes later they went to the door and looked again. Left too long, the paper blew out into the yard, got rained on, was covered with snow. Their persistence rewarded at last, they bent down and picked up the paper, opened it, and read the headline, while the paper boy rode on rapidly over lawns he had been told not to ride over, as if he were bent on overtaking lost time or some other paper boy who was not there.

In a place where everybody could easily be traced back to his origin, people did not always know who the paper boy was or care what time he got home to supper. They assumed from a general knowledge of boys that if the paper was late it was because the paper boy dawdled somewhere, shooting marbles, throwing snowballs, when he should have been delivering their paper.

Every afternoon after school the boys rode into the alley behind the *Star* Building, let their bicycles fall with a clatter, and gathered in the cage next to the pressroom. They were dirty-faced, argumentative, and as alike as sparrows. Their pockets sagged with pieces of chalk, balls of string, slingshots, marbles, jackknives, deified objects, trophies they traded. Boasting and being called on to produce evidence in support of what ought to have been true but wasn't, they bet large sums of unreal money or passed along items of misinformation that were gratefully received and stored away in a safe place. Easily deflated, they just as easily recovered their powers of pretending. With the press standing idle, the linotype machine clicking and lisping, the round clock on the wall a torment to them every time they glanced in that direction, they asked What time is the press going to start?—knowing that the printing press of the *Draperville Evening Star* was all but done for, and that it was a question not of how soon it would start printing but of whether it could be prevailed upon to print at all. When the linotype machines stopped, there was a quarter of an hour of acute uncertainty, during which late news bulletins were read in reverse, corrections were made in the price of laying mash and ladies' ready-to-wear, and the columns of type were locked in place. The boys waited. The pressroom waited. The front office waited and listened. And suddenly the clean white paper began to move, to flow like a waterfall. Words appeared on one side and then on the other. The clittering clattering discourse gained momentum. The paper was cut, the paper was folded. Smelling the damp ink, copies of the *Draperville Evening Star* slid down a chute and were scooped up and counted by a young man named Homer West, who never broke down or gave trouble to anyone. Cheerful, even-tempered, he handed the papers through a wicket to the seventeen boys who waited in line with their canvas bags slung over one shoulder and their bicycles in a tangle outside. One of them was Homer's brother Harold, but Homer was a brother to all of them. He teased them, eased the pressure of their high-pitched impatience with joking, kept them from fighting each other during that ominous quarter of an hour after the linotype machines fell silent, and listened for the first symptoms of disorder in the press. When it began chewing paper instead of printing, he pulled the switch, and a silence of a deeply discouraging import succeeded the whir and the clitter-clit-clatter. The boys who were left said I can't wait around here all night, I have homework to do. And Homer, waiting also, for the long day to end and for the time still far in the future when he could afford to get married, said Do your homework now, why don't you? They said Here? and he said Why not? What's the matter with this place? It's warm. You've got electric light. They said I can't concentrate. And Homer said Neither can I with you talking to me. He said It won't be long now. And when they insisted on knowing how long, he said Pretty soon.

The key to age is patience; and the key to patience is unfortunately age, which cannot be hurried, which takes time (in which to be disappointed); and time is measured by what happens; and what happens is printed (some of it) in the evening paper.

Just when it seemed certain that there would be no more copies of that evening's *Star*, the waterfall resumed its flowing—slowly at first, and then with a kind of frantic confidence. One after another the boys received their papers through the wicket, counted them, and with their canvas bags weighted, ran out of the building to mount their bicycles and ride off to the part of town that depended on them for its knowledge of what was going on in the outside world in the year 1922.

After their first mild surprise at finding Eddie Gellert in the cage with them, the other boys accepted his presence there, serene in the knowledge that they could lick him if he started getting wise, and that they had thirty-seven or forty-two or fifty-one customers in a good neighborhood to his thirteen in the poorest-paying section of town. His route had been broken off one of the larger ones, with no harm to the loser, who, that first evening, went with him to point out the houses that took the *Star*, and showed him how to fold the papers as he went along and how to toss them so they landed safely on the porch. After that, Edward was on his own.

The boys received their papers from Homer in rotation, and it was better to be second or third or fourth or even fifth than it was to be first, because if you were first it meant that the next night you would be last. "Pay-er . . ." Edward called, like the others. "Pay-er?"—with his mind on home. His last paper delivered, he turned toward the plate kept warm for him in the oven, the place it would have been so pleasant to come to straight from school. But he was twelve now, and out in the world. He had put the unlimited leisure of childhood behind him. As his father said, he was learning the value of money, his stomach empty, his nostrils burning with the cold, his chin deep in the collar of his Mackinaw.

How much money his father had, Edward did not know. It was one of those interesting questions that grown people do not care to answer. Since his mother was also kept in the dark about this, there was no reason to assume he could find out by asking. But he knew he was expected to do as well some day, and own a nice home and provide decently for the wife and children it was as yet impossible for him to imagine. If all this were easy to manage, then his father would not be upset about lights that were left burning in empty rooms or mention the coal bill every time somebody complained that the house was chilly. Life is serious and without adequate guarantees, whether your mother takes in washing or belongs to the Friday Bridge

Club. Poverty is no joke—but neither is the fear of poverty never experienced. Every evening Edward saw, like a lantern slide of failure, the part of town he must never live in, streets that weren't ever going to be paved, in all probability, houses that year after year the banks or the coal company or old Mr. McIvor saw no need for repainting or doing anything about, beyond seeing to it that the people who lived in them paid their rent promptly on the first day of the month.

On Saturday mornings he came with his metal collection book and knocked and the door was opened by a solemn, filthy child or a woman who had no corset on under her house dress and whose hair had not been combed since she got out of bed. The women gave him a dime and took the coupon he held out to them as if that were the commodity in question. If they asked him to step inside he held his breath, ignoring the bad air and an animal odor such as might have been left by foxes or raccoons or wolves in their lair. The women wadded the coupon into a ball or, if they were of a suspicious turn of mind, saved it for the day when he would try to cheat them, and they could triumphantly confront him with the proof of his dishonesty. If they didn't have a dime (often the case in that part of town) or were simply afraid, on principle, to part with money, they put him off with every appearance of not remembering that they had put him off the week before and the week before that. He turned away, disappointed but trying desperately to be polite, and the paper kept on coming.

Regardless of how many customers paid or put off paying the paper boy, the *Evening Star* claimed its percentage every Saturday morning. Any other arrangement would have complicated the bookkeeping, and the owners of the paper did not consider themselves responsible for the riot that broke out, one Friday afternoon, in the cage next to the pressroom. The boys refused to take the papers Homer held out to them through the wicket, and nothing that he said to them had any effect, because their grievances were suddenly intolerable and they themselves were secure in the knowledge (why had they never thought of this before?) that the *Star* was helpless without them. The word "strike" was heard above the sound of the press, which had started on time, for once, and which went right on printing editorial after editorial advising the President of the United States to take over the coal mines—with troops if necessary, since the public welfare was threatened.

At quarter of five, home was not as Edward had remembered it. There was nothing to do, nobody to talk to except Old Mary, and she said Now don't go spoiling your supper! when all in the world he wanted was company. He went back through the empty uneasy rooms and settled in a big chair in the library with a volume of *Battles and Leaders of the Civil War* on his lap. He didn't read; he only looked at the pictures (a farmhouse near Shiloh, the arsenal at Harper's Ferry) and listened for the sound of a step on the front porch. It was dark outside, and people all over town were beginning to look for the evening paper. His mind was still filled with remembered excitement, triumph that blurred and threatened to turn into worry. But then he turned a page. This had the same effect as when a dreamer, waking, escapes from the nightmare by changing his position in bed.

Virginia came in, and Edward called out to her, but she rushed upstairs, too absorbed in her own world of spit curls and charm bracelets, of what Ossie Dempsey said to Elsie McNish, of TL's and ukuleles, to answer her own brother. And where was his mother?

Mildred Gellert, unable to get along with her husband, unable to bear his bad temper, his nagging, had tried leaving him. Sometimes she took the children with her and sometimes, with her suitcases in the front hall, she clung to them and told them they mustn't forget her, and that when they were older they would understand. The trouble was, they did understand already. For a time it was very exciting, full of subtle moves (she communicated with Harrison through her lawyer) and countermoves (his mother came and kept house for him) like a chess game. The Gellerts' house, no matter who ordered the meals and sat at the opposite end of the dining-room table from Harrison Gellert, had a quality of sadness. This was partly architectural, having to do with the wide overhanging eaves, and partly because the shrubbery—the bridal wreath and barberry—had been allowed to become spindly and the trees kept the sunlight from the lawn. Neither surprised by its own prosperity, like the Tudor and Dutch colonial houses in the new addition to Draperville, nor frankly shabby, like other old houses of its period, the Gellerts' house and yard were at a standstill, having reached their final look, which owed so much, apparently, to accident, and so little to design or intention or thought.

When Edward walked into Virginia's room she was lying on the bed reading a movie magazine, and she implied that she would just as soon he went somewhere else. Not that he cared. He sat slumped in a chair until she said, "Do you have to breathe like that?"

"Like what?"

"With your mouth open like a fish."

Nothing made him so uncomfortable as being reminded of some part of himself that there was no need to be reminded of. It took all the joy out of life. "This is the way you breathe," he said indignantly. "Just let me give you an imitation."

She laughed scornfully at his attempt to fasten on her a failing she did not have, and so he reminded her—a thing he had meant not to do—that she owed him thirty cents. This led to more insinuations and denials, in the heat of which he forgot he was home early until his mother, standing in the doorway with her hat on, said, "If you children don't stop this eternal arguing, I don't know what I will do!" Neither of them had heard her come upstairs. They looked at each other, conspirators, on the same side. "We're not arguing."

Convicted without a hearing (their mother went on to her own room) they drew apart from each other again. Virginia said, "That was all your fault. I didn't ask you in here, and you're not supposed to come in my room unless I ask you in." Which was a rule she made up, along with a lot of others.

Before they even realized they were arguing again, a voice called, "Children, please! please!" Their mother's voice, so nervous, unhappy, and remote after the Friday Bridge Club. It embarrassed them, reminding them of scenes at the dinner table and conversations between their mother and father that floated up the stairs late at night after they were in bed.

Edward went into the bathroom and ran lukewarm water into the washbasin. It takes patience and some native skill to make a pumice stone float. Absorbed in this delicate task, Edward forgot about his grimy hands and also about the hands of the clock. A warning from his mother as she started down the stairs (how did she know he was in the bathroom) woke him from a dream of argosies, and the stone boat sank. He arrived in the dining room out of breath, his blond hair slicked down and wet, his hands clean but not his wrists, and an excuse ready on his tongue. He had decided not to mention the strike but it came out just the same. Halfway through dinner it burst out of him, and he felt better immediately.

"How did it start?" Harrison Gellert asked. The lamp that used to hang low over the dining-room table, with its red and green stained glass, its beaded glass fringe, had been replaced, in the last year or two, by glaring wall brackets, a white light in which nothing could be concealed.

"I don't know," Edward said. He passed his plate for a second helping. The plate was filled and passed back to him, and then his father said, "You were there, weren't you?"

"Yes."

"Well, all I'm asking you to tell me is what happened. Something must have happened. How did the strike get started in the first place?"

"I don't remember," Edward said.

He glanced at his sister, across the table. She had stopped eating and with a lurking smile, as if to say *You're going to catch it*, waited for him to flounder in deeper and deeper. He did not hold this against her. The shoe was often enough on the other foot.

"It seemed like it just happened," Edward said, hoping that this explanation, which satisfied him, was truthful and accurate, would also satisfy his father. "I left my arithmetic book in my desk at school and had to go back and get it."

Pleased to have recalled this detail, he stopped and then saw that his father was waiting for him to go on.

"When did the boys decide they weren't going to deliver their papers, before you got there or after?"

"After."

"But the trouble had already started?"

"Not exactly."

"You mean it was like any other evening."

Edward shook his head. What he could not explain was that the boys were always threatening to strike, to quit, to make trouble of one kind or another.

"What are you striking about?"

"The collection. We're suppose to go around collecting on Saturday morning. And people are supposed to pay us, and we're supposed to pay the *Star*. We pay Mrs. Sinclair seven cents and keep three. Only lots of times when we ask for the money, they—You want to see my collection book?"

"No. Just tell me about it."

There were times when, if it hadn't been for the reassurance of Edward's monthly report card, Harrison Gellert would have been forced to wonder if his son were a mental defective. No doubt he was passing through a stage, but it was a very tiresome one.

"Sometimes we have to wait five or six weeks for the money," Edward said.

"But you get it eventually?"

Edward nodded. "But she takes her share right away, out of whatever we do collect, and it's not fair."

"What's unfair about it?"

"She has lots of money and we don't."

"What else are the boys striking for?"

"When the press breaks down, sometimes we don't get home until after seven o'clock. One night it was nearly eight."

"It isn't Mrs. Sinclair's fault that the press breaks down."

To this Edward made no answer.

"What else?"

"We want more money."

"How much more?"

"Oh, let the poor child alone!" Mildred Gellert exclaimed, raising her wan, unhappy face from her salad and looking at her husband.

"He's not a child," Harrison Gellert said. "And I'm not picking on him. How much did you make this week?"

"Thirty-seven cents," Edward said. "But some of it was back pay. I only have thirteen customers. Barney Lefferts has the most. He has fifty-two. He makes about a dollar and a half a week when he gets paid."

"That's very good, for a boy."

"I guess so," Edward said.

"Did anybody take the trouble to explain to Mrs. Sinclair why you were refusing to deliver the paper?"

"Oh, yes, but she didn't listen to us. She was awful mad. And Homer was standing there, too."

"What did she say to you?"

"She was inside, where the press and the linotype machines are."

"But what did she say?"

"She tried to get us to deliver the papers. So we all went outside and left her."

"And then what happened?"

"The other guys jumped on their bicycles and rode off."

"And what did you do?"

"I came on home."

"Who's going to deliver our paper?" Virginia asked.

"Nobody, I guess. They can't, if we're all on strike." Edward turned back to his father. "Do you think I did wrong?"

"It's something you're old enough to decide for yourself," Harrison Gellert said. Edward was relieved. On the other hand, it wasn't the same thing as being told that he had his father's complete and wholehearted approval to take part in a strike any time there was one. If he hadn't gone on strike with the others, it would have been uncomfortable. He would have had enemies. The school yard would not have been a very safe place for him, and neither would the alley in the back of the *Star* Building, but actually he had wanted to go out on strike and he had enjoyed the excitement.

"They'll have to take us all back, won't they?" he asked. "Since we all did it together?"

"Finish your potato, dear," Mildred Gellert said. "You're keeping Mary waiting." She was not young any more; she had given up searching for her destiny and had come home, for the sake of the children. Acceptance has its inevitable meager rewards. The side porch was now enclosed, and it was generally agreed that the new green brocade curtains in the living room had cost Harrison plenty.

During dessert Edward remembered suddenly that he was saving his money to buy a bicycle, and the rice pudding stuck in his throat and would not for the longest time go down. When the others left the dining room, he lingered until Old Mary finished clearing the table and with her hand on the light switch said, "You figure on sitting here in the dark?"

Edward got up and went into the library, where his mother and Virginia were. His mother was sewing. She was changing the hem on Virginia's plaid skirt. Edward sat down, like a visitor waiting to be entertained. He heard the front door open and close, and then his father came in and sat down in his favorite chair and (quite as if he hadn't understood a word of all that Edward had been telling him) opened the evening paper.

When the paper boys ran out of the building, Harold West got as far as the door when Homer called to him. Homer said, "You stay here, Harold," and Harold stayed. After he had delivered his own papers, he rode back downtown and with a list supplied by the front office, he and Homer started out together. Ever so many houses had no street numbers beside the front steps or on the porch roof; or else the numbers, corroded, painted over five or six times, could not be seen in the dark. Not every subscriber to the *Draperville Evening Star* got a paper that night. The lists were incomplete, and there is not adequate substitution for habit. The office stayed open until ten, and there were a few telephone calls, but most people were not surprised that the evening paper, arriving at such different times every night, should finally have failed to arrive at all.

On Saturday morning, Edward went downtown. He saw a knot of boys standing on the sidewalk in front of the *Star* Building. The riot was over, the strike had collapsed, and though they had counted on him to act with them, they had not bothered to inform him of their surrender. If he hadn't been led there by curiosity, he would have been the only one not now apologizing and asking to have his route given back to him.

Riot, in the soul or in an alley, wears off. It is not self-sustaining. Reason waits, worry bides its time. The recording angel assigned to mark the sparrow's fall took a little extra space in order to record the fact that George Gibbs, Harry Lathrop, John Weiner, Bert Savage, Dave O'Connell, Marvin Shapiro, Barney Lefferts, Edward Gellert, and nine other sparrows were flying and fluttering against a net of their own devising.

One at a time the boys were allowed to go inside.

Through the plate glass window Edward saw Barney Lefferts, sitting in a straight chair beside Mrs. Sinclair's desk, with his eyes lowered, anxiously twisting his dirty old cap while she talked on and on. Once, with an odd gesture of pleading, he interrupted her; he said something that she brushed aside. When Edward looked in the window again, Barney Lefferts was crying. While you are learning the value of money, you learn also—you can't, in fact, help learning—that whoever has it has the right to withhold it. Courage doesn't count, in these circumstances.

When Barney Lefferts came out of the building, all that was behind him and he was triumphant. He said, "Jesus, I got my route back!"

Edward's interview with Mrs. Sinclair was short, and the scolding he got from her was restrained, out of respect for his father's credit and certain social distinctions that both Edward and Mrs. Sinclair were aware of.

"I'm very disappointed in you, Edward," she said. "I know, of course, that you wouldn't have done what you did if you hadn't been led astray by the others. But there was somebody who didn't let himself be led astray. Harold West delivered papers until eleven o'clock, last night, and Mr. Sinclair and I are very grateful to him." She played with a paper clip, and then said, "I know you are sorry, but that isn't the same as if you had behaved in an honorable way, is it? I've decided to let you have your route back, but I want you to promise me, on your word of honor, that if such a thing ever happens again around here, you will be on the side of the Newspaper."

Edward promised, conscious of the fact that her thin, flat chest would not be comforting to put his head on, in time of trouble. He was grateful, but not to her. While he was waiting his turn outside, he had made a bargain: he had offered to give up, from now on, for the rest of his life, the secret, sinful practices that would fill people with horror if they knew and that made God (who did know) sad, if God would give him back his paper route, and God had done it.

"We were thinking of giving you a larger route, Edward," Mrs. Sinclair said, "but I'm afraid, in the light of what happened yesterday . . . Well, we won't talk about it any more. What's done is done. Suppose you go and do your Saturday morning collecting."

The promise to Mrs. Sinclair, Edward never had an opportunity to keep. The promise to God he broke, over and over and over. He prayed, he made new promises, he offered acts of kindness, acts of self-denial, in place of the one renunciation he could not manage. And though he knew it could not be so, it almost seemed at times as if God did not mind what he did as soon as he had the house all to himself; or else were trying to make Edward feel worse, because he did get the larger paper route, with fifty-three customers, in a much better part of town, and the total in his bank book rose higher and higher, with compound interest in red, and finally, on a clear bright windy day in September, Edward went to his father's office after school and a few minutes later they walked around the courthouse square to the bank, and from there they went to Kohler's bicycle shop, where Edward, with his father's solemn approval, parted gladly with his savings and rode off on his heart's delight. The new bicycle was blue and silver, and stood out conspicuously among all the other bicycles in the two long racks in the school yard. It had a headlight and a tool case. He adjusted the handlebars so they were low like the handlebars of a racing bike, and then rode without using them at all, unless it was a matter of keeping the front wheel out of the streetcar track. Boys asked to try his new bicycle out, and rather than get into a fight about it, he let them have a brief ride, but it was agony to him until they jumped off and let him have his Blue Racer again. When the bicycle got rained on, he dried it with a rag he kept in his canvas bag. At night he stood it in the woodshed, out of the dew. He would have taken it into his bed if this had been at all practical.

The bicycle was still new, he had only had it a few weeks, when it was run over. It happened on a Saturday noon. Hungry, in a hurry to get home for lunch, he rode up in front of the *Star* Building. A voice in his head reminded him that the boys were not allowed to leave their bicycles in front of the building, and another voice said promptly She won't see it, and even if she does, this once won't matter . . . He leaned his bicycle carefully against the high curbing and went inside. There were two boys ahead of him. While he was counting the money in his change purse, a boy opened the street door and shouted, "You better come out here, Gellert! Somebody just ran over your new bicycle!"

Without any feeling whatever, as if he were dreaming, Edward went outside, and a man he'd never seen before said, "I didn't know it was there, and I backed over it."

Edward kept right on, without looking at the man, until he reached the edge of the sidewalk and could look down at what ought to have been somebody else's ruined bicycle, not (oh please not) his.

His mouth began to quiver.

The man said, "I'm sorry," and Edward burst into tears. What had happened was so terrible, and he felt such pity for the mangled spokes, the tires torn from their rims.

Mrs. Sinclair, seeing that there was trouble of some kind in front of the building, left her desk and went to the door. She looked at the bicycle and then at Edward standing there blindly, with the tears streaming down his face. "You're not supposed to leave your wheels in front of the building," she said, and went inside. People gathered around Edward, trying to console him. The man who had run over Edward's bicycle got into his car and drove away. Someone told Edward his name, and where he lived.

That night Harrison Gellert backed the car out of the garage and, with Edward in the front seat beside him, drove out to the edge of town and stopped in front of a one-story frame house in a poor neighborhood. "You wait here," he said, and got out and went up the brick walk. A man came to the door, and Edward saw a lighted room. His father said something and the man said something. Then he held the screen door open, and his father stepped inside and the door closed. Edward waited in perfect confidence that his father would tell him that it was all settled and the man was going to buy him a new bicycle. Instead, his father came out, after about five minutes, and got in the car and started the engine without saying a word. They were halfway down the block before he turned to Edward and explained that the man didn't know anything about his bicycle.

"But they *said* it was him!"

"I know," Harrison Gellert said. "He may not have been telling the truth."

Conscious of how quiet it had become in the front seat, he added, "Would you like to drive downtown for an ice cream soda?"

They parked in front of the ice cream parlor, and his father honked and a high school boy came out, with a white apron around his hips, and took their order. A few minutes later he reappeared with two tin trays and two tall chocolate sodas. The soda was as good a comfort as any, if Edward had been allowed to eat it in silence, but Harrison Gellert was genuinely distressed and sorry for his son, and his sympathy took the form (as it had in the past when he tried to comfort his wife) of feeling sorry for himself. "As you get older," he said, "you will find that a great many things happen that aren't easy to bear. Things you can't change, no matter how you try. You have to accept them and go right on, doing the best you can."

"But it isn't right!" Edward burst out. "He ran over it. It's his fault!"

"I know all that."

"Then why doesn't he have to pay for it?"

"If it was his fault, he *ought* to pay for having your bicycle repaired. But you can't make him do it if he doesn't want to."

A year earlier, Edward would have cried out, "But *you* can!" He thought it now, but he didn't say it.

"We'll find out from Mr. Kohler how much it will cost to have your bicycle fixed, and I'll go fifty-fifty with you, when it comes to paying for it."

Edward thanked his father politely, but there was no use talking about having his bicycle fixed. It would never be the same. The frame was sprung, and you could always tell a repainted bike from one that was straight from the factory. His father could go to court if necessary, and the judge would make the man pay for ruining his bicycle, and maybe fine him besides.

"It may be cheaper in the end to get a second-hand bicycle," Mr. Gellert said.

With an effort Edward kept the tears from spilling over.

He didn't want a second-hand bicycle. He wanted not to leave his new bicycle in front of the *Star* Building where it would be run over.

And Mr. Gellert wanted to say and didn't say, "I hope this will be a lesson to you."

It was a lesson, of course, in the sense that everything that happens, good or bad, is a lesson.

Edward Gellert was thirteen going on fourteen when the paper boys went on strike against the *Evening Star*, and he was fourteen going on fifteen when his bicycle was run over. One half the individual nature never seems any different, from the cradle to the grave; the other half is pathetically in step with the slightest physical change. Edward's voice had deepened, hairs had appeared on his body where Darwin said they should appear, his feet and hands were noticeably large for the rest of him, and something would not allow him to kneel in the dark beside his bed and ask God to give him back his new bicycle. People might be raised from the dead, as it said in the Bible, but a ruined bicycle could not by any power on earth or in Heaven be made shining and whole again.

Isaac Babel

Awakening

ALL THE FOLK IN OUR CIRCLE—BROKERS, SHOPKEEPERS, clerks in banks and steamship offices—used to have their children taught music. Our fathers, seeing no other escape from their lot, had thought up a lottery, building it on the bones of little children. Odessa more than other towns was seized by the craze. And in fact, in the course of ten years or so our town supplied the concert platforms of the world with infant prodigies. From Odessa came Mischa Elman, Zimbalist, Gabrilowitsch. Odessa witnessed the first steps of Jascha Heifetz.

When a lad was four or five, his mother took the puny creature to Zagursky's. Mr. Zagursky ran a factory of infant prodigies, a factory of Jewish dwarfs in lace collars and patent-leather pumps. He hunted them out in the slums of the Moldavanka, in the evil-smelling courtyards of the Old Market. Mr. Zagursky charted the first course, then the children were shipped off to Professor Auer in St. Petersburg. A wonderful harmony dwelt in the souls of those wizened creatures with their swollen blue hands. They became famous virtuosi. My father decided that I should emulate them. Though I had, as a matter of fact, passed the age limit set for infant prodigies, being now in my fourteenth year, my shortness and lack of strength made it possible to pass me off as an eight-year-old. Herein lay father's hope.

I was taken to Zagursky's. Out of respect for my grandfather, Mr. Zagursky agreed to take me on at the cut rate
of a rouble a lesson. My grandfather Leivi-Itzkhok was the
laughingstock of the town, and its chief adornment. He
used to walk about the streets in a top hat and old boots,
dissipating doubt in the darkest of cases. He would be
asked what a Gobelin was, why the Jacobins betrayed
Robespierre, how you made artificial silk, what a Caesar-
ean section was. And my grandfather could answer these
questions. Out of respect for his learning and craziness,
Mr. Zagursky only charged us a rouble a lesson. And he
had the devil of a time with me, fearing my grandfather,
for with me there was nothing to be done. The sounds
dripped from my fiddle like iron filings, causing even me
excruciating agony, but father wouldn't give in. At home
there was no talk save of Mischa Elman, exempted by the
Tsar himself from military service. Zimbalist, father
would have us know, had been presented to the King of
England and had played at Buckingham Palace. The
parents of Gabrilowitsch had bought two houses in St.
Petersburg. Infant prodigies brought wealth to their
parents, but though my father could have reconciled himself to poverty, fame he must have.

"It's not possible," people feeding at his expense would
insinuate, "it's just not possible that the grandson of such
a grandfather . . ."

But what went on in my head was quite different.
Scraping my way through the violin exercises, I would
have books by Turgenev or Dumas on my music stand.
Page after page I devoured as I deedled away. In the daytime I would relate impossible happenings to the kids next
door; at night I would commit them to paper. In our family, composition was a hereditary occupation. Grandfather

Leivi-Itzkhok, who went cracked as he grew old, spent his whole life writing a tale entitled "The Headless Man." I took after him.

Three times a week, laden with violin case and music, I made my reluctant way to Zagursky's place on Witte (formerly Dvoryanskaya) Street. There Jewish girls aflame with hysteria sat along the wall awaiting their turn, pressing to their feeble knees violins exceeding in dimensions the exalted persons they were to play to at Buckingham Palace.

The door to the sanctum would open, and from Mr. Zagursky's study there would stagger big-headed, freckled children with necks as thin as flower stalks and an epileptic flush on their cheeks. The door would bang to, swallowing up the next dwarf. Behind the wall, straining his throat, the teacher sang and waved his baton. He had ginger curls and frail legs, and sported a big bow tie. Manager of a monstrous lottery, he populated the Moldavanka and the dark culs-de-sac of the Old Market with the ghosts of pizzicato and cantilena. Afterward old Professor Auer lent these strains a diabolical brilliance.

In this crew I was quite out of place. Though like them in my dwarfishness, in the voice of my forebears I perceived inspiration of another sort.

The first step was difficult. One day I left home laden like a beast of burden with violin case, violin, music, and twelve roubles in cash—payment for a month's tuition. I was going along Nezhin Street; to get to Zagursky's I should have turned into Dvoryanskaya, but instead of that I went up Tiraspolskaya and found myself at the harbor. The allotted time flew past in the part of the port where ships went after quarantine. So began my liberation. Zagursky's saw me no more: affairs of greater moment occupied my thoughts. My pal Nemanov and I got into the habit of slipping aboard the S.S. *Kensington* to see an old salt named Trottyburn. Nemanov was a year younger than I. From the age of eight onward he had been doing the most ingenious business deals you can imagine. He had a wonderful head for that kind of thing, and later on amply fulfilled his youthful promise. Now he is a New York millionaire, director of General Motors, a company no less powerful than Ford. Nemanov took me along with him because I silently obeyed all his orders. He used to buy pipes smuggled in by Mr. Trottyburn. They were made in Lincoln by the old sailor's brother.

"Gen'lemen," Mr. Trottyburn would say to us, "take my word, the pets must be made with your own hands. Smoking a factory-made pipe—might as well shove an enema in your mouth. D'you know who Benvenuto Cellini was? He was a grand lad. My brother in Lincoln could tell you about him. Live and let live is my brother's motto. He's got it into his head that you just has to make the pets with your own hands, and not with no one else's. And who are we to say him no, gen'lemen?"

Nemanov used to sell Trottyburn's pipes to bank-managers, foreign consuls, well-to-do Greeks. He made a hundred percent on them.

The pipes of the Lincolnshire master breathed poetry. In each one of them thought was invested, a drop of eternity. A little yellow eye gleamed in their mouthpieces, and their cases were lined with satin. I tried to picture the life in Old England of Matthew Trottyburn, the last master-pipemaker, who refused to swim with the tide.

"We can't but agree, gen'lemen, that the pets has to be made with your own hands."

The heavy waves by the sea wall swept me further and

further away from our house, impregnated with the smell of leeks and Jewish destiny. From the harbor I migrated to the other side of the breakwater. There on a scrap of sandspit dwelt the boys from Primorskaya Street. Trouserless from morn till eve, they dived under wherries, sneaked coconuts for dinner, and awaited the time when boats would arrive from Kherson and Kamenka laden with watermelons, which melons it would be possible to break open against moorings.

To learn to swim was my dream. I was ashamed to confess to those bronzed lads that, born in Odessa, I had not seen the sea till I was ten, and at fourteen didn't know how to swim.

How slow was my acquisition of the things one needs to know! In my childhood, chained to the Gemara, I had led the life of a sage. When I grew up I started climbing trees.

But swimming proved beyond me. The hydrophobia of my ancestors—Spanish rabbis and Frankfurt money-changers—dragged me to the bottom. The waves refused to support me. I would struggle to the shore pumped full of salt water and feeling as though I had been flayed, and return to where my fiddle and music lay. I was fettered to the instruments of my torture, and dragged them about with me. The struggle of rabbis versus Neptune continued till such time as the local water-god took pity on me. This was Yefim Nikitich Smolich, proofreader of the *Odessa News*. In his athletic breast there dwelt compassion for Jewish children, and he was the god of a rabble of rickety starvelings. He used to collect them from the bug-infested joints on the Moldavanka, take them down to the sea, bury them in the sand, do gym with them, dive with them, teach them songs. Roasting in the perpendicular sunrays, he would tell them tales about fishermen and wild beasts.

To grownups Nikitich would explain that he was a natural philosopher. The Jewish kids used to roar with laughter at his tales, squealing and snuggling up to him like so many puppies. The sun would sprinkle them with creeping freckles, freckles of the same color as lizards.

Silently, out of the corner of his eye, the old man had been watching my duel with the waves. Seeing that the thing was hopeless, that I should simply never learn to swim, he included me among the permanent occupants of his heart. That cheerful heart of his was with us there all the time; it never went careering off anywhere else, never knew covetousness and never grew disturbed. With his sunburned shoulders, his superannuated gladiator's head, his bronzed and slightly bandy legs, he would lie among us on the other side of the mole, lord and master of those melon-sprinkled, paraffin-stained waters. I came to love that man, with the love that only a lad suffering from hysteria and headaches can feel for a real man. I was always at his side, always trying to be of service to him.

He said to me:

"Don't you get all worked up. You just strengthen your nerves. The swimming will come of itself. How d'you mean, the water won't hold you? Why shouldn't it hold you?"

Seeing how drawn I was to him, Nikitich made an exception of me alone of all his disciples. He invited me to visit the clean and spacious attic where he lived in an ambience of straw mats, showed me his dogs, his hedgehog, his tortoise, and his pigeons. In return for this wealth I showed him a tragedy I had written the day before.

"I was sure you did a bit of scribbling," said Nikitich. "You've the look. You're looking in *that* direction all the time; no eyes for anywhere else."

He read my writings, shrugged a shoulder, passed a

hand through his stiff gray curls, paced up and down the attic.

"One must suppose," he said slowly, pausing after each word, "one must suppose that there's a spark of the divine fire in you."

We went out into the street. The old man halted, struck the pavement with his stick, and fastened his gaze upon me.

"Now what is it you lack? Youth's no matter—it'll pass with the years. What you lack is a feeling for nature."

He pointed with his stick at a tree with a reddish trunk and a low crown.

"What's that tree?"

I didn't know.

"What's growing on that bush?"

I didn't know this either. We walked together across the little square on the Alexandrovsky Prospect. The old man kept poking his stick at trees; he would seize me by the shoulder when a bird flew past, and he made me listen to the various kinds of singing.

"What bird is that singing?"

I knew none of the answers. The names of trees and birds, their division into species, where birds fly away to, on which side the sun rises, when the dew falls thickest— all these things were unknown to me.

"And you dare to write! A man who doesn't live in nature, as a stone does or an animal, will never in all his life write two worthwhile lines. Your landscapes are like descriptions of stage props. In heaven's name, what have your parents been thinking of for fourteen years?"

What *had* they been thinking of? Of protested bills of exchange, of Mischa Elman's mansions. I didn't say anything to Nikitich about that, but just kept mum.

At home, over dinner, I couldn't touch my food. It just wouldn't go down.

"A feeling for nature," I thought to myself. "Goodness, why did that never enter my head? Where am I to find someone who will tell me about the way birds sing and what trees are called? What do *I* know about such things? I might perhaps recognize lilac, at any rate when it's in bloom. Lilac and acacia—there are acacias along De Ribas and Greek Streets."

At dinner father told a new story about Jascha Heifetz. Just before he got to Robinat's he had met Mendelssohn, Jascha's uncle. It appeared that the lad was getting eight hundred roubles a performance. Just work out how much that comes to at fifteen concerts a month!

I did, and the answer was twelve thousand a month. Multiplying and carrying four in my head, I glanced out of the window. Across the cement courtyard, his cloak swaying in the breeze, his ginger curls poking out from under his soft hat, leaning on his cane, Mr. Zagursky, my music teacher, was advancing. It must be admitted he had taken his time in spotting my truancy. More than three months had elapsed since the day when my violin had grounded on the sand by the breakwater.

Mr. Zagursky was approaching the main entrance. I dashed to the back door, but the day before it had been nailed up for fear of burglars. Then I locked myself in the privy. In half an hour the whole family had assembled outside the door. The women were weeping. Aunt Bobka, exploding with sobs, was rubbing her fat shoulder against the door. Father was silent. Finally he started speaking, quietly and distinctly as he had never before spoken in his life.

"I am an officer," said my father. "I own real estate. I

go hunting. Peasants pay me rent. I have entered my son in the Cadet Corps. I have no need to worry about my son."

He was silent again. The women were sniffling. Then a terrible blow descended on the privy door. My father was hurling his whole body against it, stepping back and then throwing himself forward.

"I am an officer," he kept wailing. "I go hunting. I'll kill him. This is the end."

The hook sprang from the door, but there was still a bolt hanging onto a single nail. The women were rolling about on the floor, grasping father by the legs. Crazy, he was trying to break loose. Father's mother came over, alerted by the hubbub.

"My child," she said to him in Hebrew, "our grief is great. It has no bounds. Only blood was lacking in our house. I do not wish to see blood in our house."

Father gave a groan. I heard his footsteps retreating. The bolt still hung by its last nail.

I sat it out in my fortress till nightfall. When all had gone to bed, Aunt Bobka took me to grandmother's. We had a long way to go. The moonlight congealed on bushes unknown to me, on trees that had no name. Some anonymous bird emitted a whistle and was extinguished, perhaps by sleep. What bird was it? What was it called? Does dew fall in the evening? Where is the constellation of the Great Bear? On what side does the sun rise?

We were going along Post Office Street. Aunt Bobka held me firmly by the hand so that I shouldn't run away. She was right to. I was thinking of running away.

Jean Stafford

Bad Characters

UP UNTIL I LEARNED MY LESSON IN A VERY BITTER WAY,
I never had more than one friend at a time, and my friend-
ships, though ardent, were short. When they ended and I
was sent packing in unforgetting indignation, it was
always my fault; I would swear vilely in front of a girl I
knew to be pious and prim (by the time I was eight, the
most grandiloquent gangster could have added nothing to
my vocabulary—I had an awful tongue), or I would call a
Tenderfoot Scout a sissy or make fun of athletics to the
daughter of the high-school coach. These outbursts came
without plan; I would simply one day, in the middle of a
game of Russian bank or a hike or a conversation, be pos-
sessed with a passion to be by myself, and my lips
instantly and without warning would accommodate me.
My friend was never more surprised than I was when this
irrevocable slander, this terrible, talented invective, came
boiling out of my mouth.

Afterward, when I had got the solitude I had wanted,
I was dismayed, for I did not like it. Then I would sadly
finish the game of cards as if someone were still across
the table from me; I would sit down on the mesa and
through a glaze of tears would watch my friend departing
with outraged strides; mournfully, I would talk to myself.
Because I had already alienated everyone I knew, I then
had nowhere to turn, so a famine set in and I would have

no companion but Muff, the cat, who loathed all human beings except, significantly, me—truly. She bit and scratched the hands that fed her, she arched her back like a Halloween cat if someone kindly tried to pet her, she hissed, laid her ears flat to her skull, growled, fluffed up her tail into a great bush and flailed it like a bullwhack. But she purred for me, she patted me with her paws, keeping her claws in their velvet scabbards. She was not only an ill-natured cat, she was also badly dressed. She was a calico, and the distribution of her colors was a mess; she looked as if she had been left out in the rain and her paint had run. She had a Roman nose as the result of some early injury, her tail was skinny, she had a perfectly venomous look in her eye. My family said—my family discriminated against me—that I was much closer kin to Muff than I was to any of them. To tease me into a tantrum, my brother Jack and my sister Stella often called me Kitty instead of Emily. Little Tess did not dare, because she knew I'd chloroform her if she did. Jack, the meanest boy I have ever known in my life, called me Polecat and talked about my mania for fish, which, it so happened, I despised. The name would have been far more appropriate for *him*, since he trapped skunks up in the foothills—we lived in Adams, Colorado—and quite often, because he was careless and foolhardy, his clothes had to be buried, and even when that was done, he sometimes was sent home from school on the complaint of girls sitting next to him.

Along about Christmastime when I was eleven, I was making a snowman with Virgil Meade in his backyard, and all of a sudden, just as we had got around to the right arm, I had to be alone. So I called him a son of a sea cook, said it was common knowledge that his mother had bedbugs and that his father, a dentist and the deputy marshal, was a bootlegger on the side. For a moment, Virgil was too aghast to speak—a little earlier we had agreed to marry someday and become millionaires—and then, with a bellow of fury, he knocked me down and washed my face in snow. I saw stars, and black balls bounced before my eyes. When finally he let me up, we were both crying, and he hollered that if I didn't get off his property that instant, his father would arrest me and send me to Canon City. I trudged slowly home, half frozen, critically sick at heart. So it was old Muff again for me for quite some time. Old Muff, that is, until I met Lottie Jump, although "met" is a euphemism for the way I first encountered her.

I saw Lottie for the first time one afternoon in our own kitchen, stealing a chocolate cake. Stella and Jack had not come home from school yet—not having my difficult disposition, they were popular, and they were at their friends' houses, pulling taffy, I suppose, making popcorn balls, playing casino, having fun—and my mother had taken Tess with her to visit a friend in one of the T.B. sanitariums. I was alone in the house, and making a funny-looking Christmas card, although I had no one to send it to. When I heard someone in the kitchen, I thought it was Mother home early, and I went out to ask her why the green pine tree I had pasted on a square of red paper looked as if it were falling down. And there, instead of Mother and my baby sister, was this pale, conspicuous child in the act of lifting the glass cover from the devil's-food my mother had taken out of the oven an hour before and set on the plant shelf by the window. The child had her back to me, and when she heard my footfall, she wheeled with an amazing look of fear and hatred on her pinched and pasty face. Simultaneously, she put the cover over the cake again, and then she stood motionless as if she were under a spell.

I was scared, for I was not sure what was happening, and anyhow it gives you a turn to find a stranger in the kitchen in the middle of the afternoon, even if the stranger is only a skinny child in a moldy coat and sopping-wet basketball shoes. Between us there was a lengthy silence, but there was a great deal of noise in the room: the alarm clock ticked smugly; the teakettle simmered patiently on the back of the stove; Muff, cross at having been waked up, thumped her tail against the side of the terrarium in the window where she had been sleeping—contrary to orders—among the geraniums. This went on, it seemed to me, for hours and hours while that tall, sickly girl and I confronted each other. When, after a long time, she did open her mouth, it was to tell a prodigious lie. "I came to see if you'd like to play with me," she said. I think she sighed and stole a sidelong and regretful glance at the cake.

Beggars cannot be choosers, and I had been missing Virgil so sorely, as well as all those other dear friends forever lost to me, that in spite of her flagrance (she had never clapped eyes on me before, she had had no way of knowing there was a creature of my age in the house—she had come in like a hobo to steal my mother's cake), I was flattered and consoled. I asked her name and, learning it, believed my ears no better than my eyes: Lottie Jump. What on earth! What on earth—you surely will agree with me—and yet when I told her mine, Emily Vanderpool, she laughed until she coughed and gasped. "Beg pardon," she said. "Names like them always hit my funny bone. There was this towhead boy in school named

Delbert Saxonfield." I saw no connection and I was insulted (what's so funny about Vanderpool, I'd like to know), but Lottie Jump was, technically, my guest and I *was* lonesome, so I asked her, since she had spoken of playing with me, if she knew how to play Andy-I-Over. She said "Naw." It turned out that she did not know how to play any games at all; she couldn't do anything and didn't want to do anything; her only recreation and her only gift was, and always had been, stealing. But this I did not know at the time.

As it happened, it was too cold and snowy to play outdoors that day anyhow, and after I had run through my list of indoor games and Lottie had shaken her head at all of them (when I spoke of Parcheesi, she went "Ugh!" and pretended to be sick), she suggested that we look through my mother's bureau drawers. This did not strike me as strange at all, for it was one of my favorite things to do, and I led the way to Mother's bedroom without a moment's hesitation. I loved the smell of the lavender she kept in gauze bags among her chamois gloves and linen handkerchiefs and filmy scarves; there was a pink fascinator knitted of something as fine as spider's thread, and it made me go quite soft—I wasn't soft as a rule, I was as hard as nails and I gave my mother a rough time—to think of her wearing it around her head as she waltzed on the ice in the bygone days. We examined stockings, nightgowns, camisoles, strings of beads, and mosaic pins, keepsake buttons from dresses worn on memorial occasions, tortoiseshell combs, and a transformation made from Aunt Joey's hair when she had racily had it bobbed. Lottie admired particularly a blue cloisonné perfume flask with ferns and peacocks on it. "Hey," she said, "this sure is cute. I like thing-daddies like this here." But very abruptly she got bored and said, "Let's talk instead. In the front room." I agreed, a little perplexed this time, because I had been about to show her a remarkable powder box that played *The Blue Danube*. We went into the parlor, where Lottie looked at her image in the pier glass for quite a while and with great absorption, as if she had never seen herself before. Then she moved over to the window seat and knelt on it, looking out at the front walk. She kept her hands in the pockets of her thin dark-red coat; once she took out one of her dirty paws to rub her nose for a minute and I saw a bulge in that pocket, like a bunch of jackstones. I know now that it wasn't jackstones, it was my mother's perfume flask; I thought at the time her hands were cold and that that was why she kept them put away, for I had noticed that she had no mittens.

Lottie did most of the talking, and while she talked, she never once looked at me but kept her eyes fixed on the approach to our house. She told me that her family had come to Adams a month before from Muskogee, Oklahoma, where her father, before he got tuberculosis, had been a brakeman on the Frisco. Now they lived down by Arapahoe Creek, on the west side of town, in one of the cottages of a wretched settlement made up of people so poor and so sick—for in nearly every ramshackle house someone was coughing himself to death—that each time I went past I blushed with guilt because my shoes were sound and my coat was warm and I was well. I wished that Lottie had not told me where she lived, but she was not aware of any pathos in her family's situation, and, indeed, it was with a certain boastfulness that she told me her mother was the short-order cook at the Comanche Café (she pronounced this word in one syllable), which

I knew was the dirtiest, darkest, smelliest place in town, patronized by coal miners who never washed their faces and sometimes had such dangerous fights after drinking dago red that the sheriff had to come. Laughing, Lottie told me that her mother was half Indian, and, laughing even harder, she said that her brother didn't have any brains and had never been to school. She herself was eleven years old, but she was only in the third grade, because teachers had always had it in for her—making her go to the blackboard and all like that when she was tired. She hated school—she went to Ashton, on North Hill, and that was why I had never seen her, for I went to Carlyle Hill—and she especially hated the teacher, Miss Cudahy, who had a head shaped like a pine cone and who had killed several people with her ruler. Lottie loved the movies ("Not them Western ones or the ones with apes in," she said. "Ones about hugging and kissing. I love it when they die in that big old soft bed with the curtains up top, and he comes in and says 'Don't leave me, Marguerite de la Mar' "), and she loved to ride in cars. She loved Mr. Goodbars, and if there was one thing she despised worse than another it was tapioca. ("Pa calls it fish eyes. He calls floating island horse spit. He's a big piece of cheese. I hate him.") She did not like cats (Muff was now sitting on the mantelpiece, glaring like an owl); she kind of liked snakes—except cottonmouths and rattlers—because she found them kind of funny; she had once seen a goat eat a tin can. She said that one of these days she would take me downtown—it was a slowpoke town, she said, a one-horse burg (I had never heard such gaudy, cynical talk and was trying to memorize it all)— if I would get some money for the trolley fare; she hated to walk, and I ought to be proud that she had walked all the way from Arapahoe Creek today for the sole solitary purpose of seeing me.

Seeing our freshly baked dessert in the window was a more likely story, but I did not care, for I was deeply impressed by this bold, sassy girl from Oklahoma and greatly admired the poise with which she aired her prejudices. Lottie Jump was certainly nothing to look at. She was tall and made of skin and bones; she was evilly ugly, and her clothes were a disgrace, not just ill-fitting and old and ragged but dirty, unmentionably so; clearly she did not wash much or brush her teeth, which were notched like a saw, and small and brown (it crossed my mind that perhaps she chewed tobacco); her long, lank hair looked as if it might have nits. But she had personality. She made me think of one of those self-contained dogs whose home is where his handout is and who travels alone but, if it suits him to, will become the leader of a pack. She was aloof, never looking at me, but amiable in the way she kept calling me "kid." I liked her enormously, and presently I told her so.

At this, she turned around and smiled at me. Her smile was the smile of a jack-o'-lantern—high, wide, and handsome. When it was over, no trace of it remained. "Well, that's keen, kid, and I like you, too," she said in her downright Muskogee accent. She gave me a long, appraising look. Her eyes were the color of mud. "Listen, kid, how much do you like me?"

"I like you loads, Lottie," I said. "Better than anybody else, and I'm not kidding."

"You want to be pals?"

"Do I!" I cried. So *there*, Virgil Meade, you big fat hootnanny, I thought.

"All right, kid, we'll be pals." And she held out her

hand for me to shake. I had to go and get it, for she did not alter her position on the window seat. It was a dry, cold hand, and the grip was severe, with more a feeling of bones in it than friendliness.

Lottie turned and scanned our path and scanned the sidewalk beyond, and then she said, in a lower voice, "Do you know how to lift?"

"Lift?" I wondered if she meant to lift *her*. I was sure I could do it, since she was so skinny, but I couldn't imagine why she would want me to.

"Shoplift, I mean. Like in the five-and-dime."

I did not know the term, and Lottie scowled at my stupidity.

"*Steal*, for crying in the beer!" she said impatiently. This she said so loudly that Muff jumped down from the mantel and left the room in contempt.

I was thrilled to death and shocked to pieces. "Stealing is a sin," I said. "You get put in jail for it."

"Ish ka bibble! I should worry if it's a sin or not," said Lottie, with a shrug. "And they'll never put a smart old whatsis like *me* in jail. It's fun, stealing is—it's a picnic. I'll teach you if you want to learn, kid." Shamelessly she winked at me and grinned again. (That grin! She could have taken it off her face and put it on the table.) And she added, "If you don't, we can't be pals, because lifting is the only kind of playing I like. I hate those dumb games like Statues. Kick-the-Can—phooey!"

I was torn between agitation (I went to Sunday school and knew already about morality; Judge Bay, a crabby old man who loved to punish sinners, was a friend of my father's and once had given Jack a lecture on the criminal mind when he came to call and found Jack looking up an answer in his arithmetic book) and excitement over the daring invitation to misconduct myself in so perilous a way. My life, on reflection, looked deadly prim; all I'd ever done to vary the monotony of it was to swear. I knew that Lottie Jump meant what she said—that I could have her friendship only on her terms (plainly, she had gone it alone for a long time and could go it alone for the rest of her life)—and although I trembled like an aspen and my heart went pitapat, I said, "I want to be pals with you, Lottie."

"All right, Vanderpool," said Lottie, and got off the window seat. "I wouldn't go braggin' about it if I was you. I wouldn't go telling my ma and pa and the next-door neighbor that you and Lottie Jump are going down to the five-and-dime next Saturday aft and lift us some nice rings and garters and things like that. I mean it, kid." And she drew the back of her forefinger across her throat and made a dire face.

"I won't, I promise, I won't. My *gosh*, why would I?"

"That's the ticket," said Lottie, with a grin. "I'll meet you at the trolley shelter at two o'clock. You have the money. For both down and up. I ain't going to climb up that ornery hill after I've had my fun."

"Yes, Lottie," I said. Where was I going to get twenty cents? I was going to have to start stealing before she even taught me how. Lottie was facing the center of the room, but she had eyes in the back of her head, and she whirled around back to the window; my mother and Tess were turning in our front path.

"Back way," I whispered, and in a moment Lottie was gone; the swinging door that usually squeaked did not make a sound as she vanished through it. I listened and I never heard the back door open and close. Nor did I hear her, in a split second, lift the glass cover and remove that cake designed to feed six people.

I was restless and snappish between Wednesday afternoon and Saturday. When Mother found the cake was gone, she scolded me for not keeping my ears cocked. She assumed, naturally, that a tramp had taken it, for she knew I hadn't eaten it; I never ate anything if I could help it (except for raw potatoes, which I loved) and had been known as a problem feeder from the beginning of my life. At first it occurred to me to have a tantrum and bring her around to my point of view: my tantrums scared the living daylights out of her because my veins stood out and I turned blue and couldn't get my breath. But I rejected this for a more sensible plan. I said, "It just so happens I didn't hear anything. But if I had, I suppose you wish I had gone out in the kitchen and let the robber cut me up into a million little tiny pieces with his sword. You wouldn't even bury me. You'd just put me on the dump. *I* know who's wanted in this family and who isn't." Tears of sorrow, not of anger, came in powerful tides and I groped blindly to the bedroom I shared with Stella, where I lay on my bed and shook with big, silent *weltschmerzlich* sobs. Mother followed me immediately, and so did Tess, and both of them comforted me and told me how much they loved me. I said they didn't; they said they did. Presently, I got a headache, as I always did when I cried, so I got to have an aspirin and a cold cloth on my head, and when Jack and Stella came home, they had to be quiet. I heard Jack say, "Emily Vanderpool is the biggest polecat in the U.S.A. Whyn't she go in the kitchen and say, 'Hands up'? He woulda lit out." And Mother said, "Sh-h-h! You don't want your sister to be sick, do you?" Muff, not realizing that Lottie had replaced her, came in and curled up at my thigh, purring lustily; I found myself glad that she had left the room before Lottie Jump made her proposition to me, and in gratitude I stroked her unattractive head.

Other things happened. Mother discovered the loss of her perfume flask and talked about nothing else at meals for two whole days. Luckily, it did not occur to her that it had been stolen—she simply thought she had mislaid it —but her monomania got on my father's nerves and he lashed out at her and at the rest of us. And because I was the cause of it all and my conscience was after me with red-hot pokers, I finally *had* to have a tantrum. I slammed my fork down in the middle of supper on the second day and yelled, "If you don't stop fighting, I'm going to kill myself. Yammer, yammer, nag, nag!" And I put my fingers in my ears and squeezed my eyes tight shut and screamed so the whole country could hear, "Shut *up!*" And then I lost my breath and began to turn blue. Daddy hastily apologized to everyone, and Mother said she was sorry for carrying on so about a trinket that had nothing but sentimental value—she was just vexed with herself for being careless, that was all, and she wasn't going to say another word about it.

I never heard so many references to stealing and cake, and even to Oklahoma (ordinarily no one mentioned Oklahoma once in a month of Sundays) and the ten-cent store as I did throughout those next days. I myself once made a ghastly slip and said something to Stella about "the five-and-dime." "The five and-*dime!*" she exclaimed. "Where'd you get *that* kind of talk? Do you by any chance have reference to the *ten-cent store?*"

The worst of all was Friday night—the very night before I was to meet Lottie Jump—when Judge Bay came to play two-handed pinochle with Daddy. The Judge, a giant in intimidating haberdashery—for some reason, the white piping on his vest bespoke, for me, handcuffs and prison bars—and with an aura of disapproval for almost everything on earth except what pertained directly to himself, was telling Daddy, before they began their game, about the infamous vandalism that had been going on among the college students. "I have reason to believe that there are girls in this gang as well as boys," he said. "They ransack vacant houses and take everything. In one house on Pleasant Street, up there by the Catholic Church, there wasn't anything to take, so they took the kitchen sink. Wasn't a question of taking everything *but*—they took the kitchen sink."

"What ever would they want with a kitchen sink?" asked my mother.

"Mischief," replied the Judge. "If we ever catch them and if they come within my jurisdiction, I can tell you I will give them no quarter. A thief, in my opinion, is the lowest of the low."

Mother told about the chocolate cake. By now, the fiction was so factual in my mind that each time I thought of it I saw a funny-paper bum in baggy pants held up by rope, a hat with holes through which tufts of hair stuck up, shoes from which his toes protruded, a disreputable stubble on his face; he came up beneath the open window where the devil's food was cooling and he stole it and hotfooted it for the woods, where his companion was frying a small fish in a beat-up skillet. It never crossed my mind any longer that Lottie Jump had hooked that delicious cake.

Judge Bay was properly impressed. "If you will steal a chocolate cake, if you will steal a kitchen sink, you will steal diamonds and money. The small child who pilfers a penny from his mother's pocketbook has started down a path that may lead him to holding up a bank."

It was a good thing I had no homework that night, for I could not possibly have concentrated. We were all sent to our rooms, because the pinochle players had to have absolute quiet. I spent the evening doing cross-stitch. I was making a bureau runner for a Christmas present; as in the case of the Christmas card, I had no one to give it to, but now I decided to give it to Lottie Jump's mother. Stella was reading *Black Beauty*, crying. It was an interminable evening. Stella went to bed first; I saw to that, because I didn't want her lying there awake listening to me talking in my sleep. Besides, I didn't want her to see me tearing open the cardboard box—the one in the shape of a church, which held my Christmas Sunday-school offering. Over the door of the church was this shaming legend: "My mite for the poor widow." When Stella had begun to grind her teeth in her first deep sleep, I took twenty cents away from the poor widow, whoever she was (the owner of the kitchen sink, no doubt), for the trolley fare, and secreted it and the remaining three pennies in the pocket of my middy. I wrapped the money well in a handkerchief and buttoned the pocket and hung my skirt over the middy. And then I tore the paper church into bits—the heavens opened and Judge Bay came toward me with a double-barrelled shotgun—and hid the bits under a pile of pajamas. I did not sleep one wink. Except that I must have, because of the stupendous nightmares that kept wrenching the flesh off my skeleton and caused me to come close to perishing of thirst; once I fell out of bed and hit my head on Stella's ice skates. I would have waked her up and given her a piece of my mind for leaving them in such a lousy place, but then I remembered: I wanted *no* commotion of any kind.

I couldn't eat breakfast and I couldn't eat lunch. Old Johnny-on-the-spot Jack kept saying "*Poor* Polecat. Polecat wants her fish for dinner." Mother made an abortive attempt to take my temperature. And when all that hullabaloo subsided, I was nearly in the soup because Mother asked me to mind Tess while she went to the sanitarium to see Mrs. Rogers, who, all of a sudden, was too sick to have anyone but grownups near her. Stella couldn't stay with the baby, because she had to go to ballet, and Jack couldn't, because he had to go up to the mesa and empty his traps. ("No, they *can't* wait. You want my skins to rot in this hot-one-day-cold-the-next weather?") I was arguing and whining when the telephone rang. Mother went to answer it and came back with a look of great sadness; Mrs. Rogers, she had learned, had had another hemorrhage. So Mother would not be going to the sanitarium after all and I needn't stay with Tess.

By the time I left the house, I was as cross as a bear. I felt awful about the widow's mite and I felt awful for being mean about staying with Tess, for Mrs. Rogers was a kind old lady, in a cozy blue hug-me-tight and an old-fangled boudoir cap, dying here all alone; she was a friend of Grandma's and had lived just down the street from her in Missouri, and all in the world Mrs. Rogers wanted to do was go back home and lie down in her own big bedroom in her own big, high-ceilinged house and have Grandma and other members of the Eastern Star come in from time to time to say hello. But they wouldn't let her go home; they were going to kill or cure her. I could not help feeling that my hardness of heart and evil of intention had had a good deal to do with her new crisis; right at the very same minute I had been saying "Does that old Mrs. Methuselah *always* have to spoil my fun?"

the poor wasted thing was probably coughing up her blood and saying to the nurse, "Tell Emily Vanderpool not to mind me, she can run and play."

I had a bad character, I know that, but my badness never gave me half the enjoyment Jack and Stella thought it did. A good deal of the time I wanted to eat lye. I was certainly having no fun now, thinking of Mrs. Rogers and of depriving that poor widow of bread and milk; what if this penniless woman without a husband had a dog to feed, too? Or a baby? And besides, I didn't want to go downtown to steal anything from the ten-cent store; I didn't want to see Lottie Jump again—not really, for I knew in my bones that that girl was trouble with a capital "T." And still, in our short meeting she had mesmerized me; I would think about her style of talking and the expert way she had made off with the perfume flask and the cake (how had she carried the cake through the streets without being noticed?) and be bowled over, for the part of me that did not love God was a black-hearted villain. And apart from these considerations, I had some sort of idea that if I did not keep my appointment with Lottie Jump, she would somehow get revenge; she had seemed a girl of purpose. So, revolted and fascinated, brave and lily-livered, I plodded along through the snow in my flopping galoshes up toward the Chautauqua, where the trolley stop was. On my way, I passed Virgil Meade's house; there was not just a snowman, there was a whole snow family in the back yard, and Virgil himself was throwing a stick for his dog. I was delighted to see that he was alone.

Lottie, who was sitting on a bench in the shelter eating a Mr. Goodbar, looked the same as she had the other time except that she was wearing an amazing hat. I think I had expected her to have a black handkerchief over the lower part of her face or to be wearing a Jesse James waistcoat. But I had never thought of a hat. It was felt; it was the color of cooked meat; it had some flowers appliquéd on the front of it; it had no brim, but rose straight up to a very considerable height, like a monument. It sat so low on her forehead and it was so tight that it looked, in a way, like part of her.

"How's every little thing, bub?" she said, licking her candy wrapper.

"Fine, Lottie," I said, freshly awed.

A silence fell. I drank some water from the drinking fountain, sat down, fastened my galoshes, and unfastened them again.

"My mother's teeth grow wrong way too," said Lottie, and showed me what she meant: the lower teeth were in front of the upper ones. "That so-called trolley car takes its own sweet time. This town is blah."

To save the honor of my home town, the trolley came scraping and groaning up the hill just then, its bell clanging with an idiotic frenzy, and ground to a stop. Its broad, proud cowcatcher was filled with dirty snow, in the middle of which rested a tomato can, put there, probably, by somebody who was bored to death and couldn't think of anything else to do—I did a lot of pointless things like that on lonesome Saturday afternoons. It was the custom of this trolley car, a rather mysterious one, to pause at the shelter for five minutes while the conductor, who was either Mr. Jansen or Mr. Peck, depending on whether it was the A.M. run or the P.M., got out and stretched and smoked and spit. Sometimes the passengers got out, too, acting like sightseers whose destination was this sturdy stucco gazebo instead of, as it really was, the Piggly Wiggly or the Nelson Dry. You expected them to take snapshots of the drinking fountain or of the Chautauqua meeting house up on the hill. And when they all got back in the car, you expected them to exchange intelligent observations on the aborigines and the ruins they had seen.

Today there were no passengers, and as soon as Mr. Peck got out and began staring at the mountains as if he had never seen them before while he made himself a cigarette, Lottie, in her tall hat (was it something like the Inspector's hat in the Katzenjammer Kids?), got into the car, motioning me to follow. I put our nickels in the empty box and joined her on the very last double seat. It was only then that she mapped out the plan for the afternoon, in a low but still insouciant voice. The hat—she did not apologize for it, she simply referred to it as "my hat"— was to be the repository of whatever we stole. In the future, it would be advisable for me to have one like it. (How? Surely it was unique. The flowers, I saw on closer examination, were tulips, but they were blue, and a very unsettling shade of blue.) I was to engage a clerk on one side of the counter, asking her the price of, let's say, a tube of Daggett & Ramsdell vanishing cream, while Lottie would lift a round comb or a barrette or a hair net or whatever on the other side. Then, at a signal, I would decide against the vanishing cream and would move on to the next counter that she indicated. The signal was interesting; it was to be the raising of her hat from the rear— "like I've got the itch and gotta scratch," she said. I was relieved that I was to have no part in the actual stealing, and I was touched that Lottie, who was going to do all the work, said we would "go halvers" on the take. She

asked me if there was anything in particular I wanted—
she herself had nothing special in mind and was going to
shop around first—and I said I would like some rubber
gloves. This request was entirely spontaneous; I had never
before in my life thought of rubber gloves in one way or
another, but a psychologist—or Judge Bay—might have
said that this was most significant and that I was planning
at that moment to go on from petty larceny to bigger game,
armed with a weapon on which I wished to leave no
fingerprints.

On the way downtown, quite a few people got on the
trolley, and they all gave us such peculiar looks that I was
chickenhearted until I realized it must be Lottie's hat they
were looking at. No wonder. I kept looking at it myself
out of the corner of my eye; it was like a watermelon
standing on end. No, it was like a tremendous test tube.
On this trip—a slow one, for the trolley pottered through
that part of town in a desultory, neighborly way, even
going into areas where no one lived—Lottie told me
some of the things she had stolen in Muskogee and here
in Adams. They included a white satin prayer book
(think of it!), Mr. Goodbars by the thousands (she had
probably never paid for a Mr. Goodbar in her life), a
dinner ring valued at two dollars, a strawberry emery,
several cans of corn, some shoelaces, a set of poker chips,
countless pencils, four spark plugs ("Pa had this old car,
see, and it was broke, so we took 'er to get fixed; I'll build
me a radio with 'em sometime—you know? Listen in on
them ear muffs to Tulsa?"), a Boy Scout knife, and a
Girl Scout folding cup. She made a regular practice of
going through the pockets of the coats in the cloakroom
every day at recess, but she had never found anything
there worth a red cent and was about to give that up. Once,

she had taken a gold pencil from a teacher's desk and had got caught—she was sure that this was one of the reasons she was only in the third grade. Of this unjust experience, she said, "The old hoot owl! If I was drivin' in a car on a lonesome stretch and she was settin' beside me, I'd wait till we got to a pile of gravel and then I'd stop and say, 'Git out, Miss Priss.' She'd git out, all right."

Since Lottie was so frank, I was emboldened at last to ask her what she had done with the cake. She faced me with her grin; this grin, in combination with the hat, gave me a surprise from which I have never recovered. "I ate it up," she said. "I went in your garage and sat on your daddy's old tires and ate it. It was pretty good."

There were two ten-cent stores side by side in our town, Kresge's and Woolworth's, and as we walked down the main street toward them, Lottie played with a Yo-Yo. Since the street was thronged with Christmas shoppers and farmers in for Saturday, this was no ordinary accomplishment; all in all, Lottie Jump was someone to be reckoned with. I cannot say that I was proud to be seen with her; the fact is that I hoped I would not meet anyone I knew, and I thanked my lucky stars that Jack was up in the hills with his dead skunks, because if he had seen her with that lid and that Yo-Yo, I would never have heard the last of it. But in another way I *was* proud to be with her; in a smaller hemisphere, in one that included only her and me, I was swaggering—I felt like Somebody, marching along beside this lofty Somebody from Oklahoma who was going to hold up the dime store.

There is nothing like Woolworth's at Christmastime. It smells of peanut brittle and terrible chocolate candy, Djer-Kiss talcum powder and Ben Hur Perfume—smells sourly of tinsel and waxily of artificial poinsettias. The crowds are made up largely of children and women, with here and there a deliberative old man; the women are buying ribbons and wrappings and Christmas cards, and the children are buying asbestos pot holders for their mothers and, for their fathers, suède bookmarks with a burnt-in design that says "A good book is a good friend" or "Souvenir from the Garden of the Gods." It is very noisy. The salesgirls are forever ringing their bells and asking the floorwalker to bring them change for a five; babies in go-carts are screaming as parcels fall on their heads; the women, waving rolls of red tissue paper, try to attract the attention of the harried girl behind the counter. ("Miss! All I want is this one batch of the red. Can't I just give you the dime?" And the girl, beside herself, mottled with vexation, cries back, "Has to be rung up, Moddom, that's the rule.") There is pandemonium at the toy counter, where things are being tested by the customers—wound up, set off, tooted, pounded, made to say "Maaaah-Maaaah!" There is very little gaiety in the scene and, in fact, those baffled old men look as if they were walking over their own dead bodies, but there is an atmosphere of carnival, nevertheless, and as soon as Lottie and I entered the doors of Woolworth's golden-and-vermilion bedlam, I grew giddy and hot—not pleasantly so. The feeling, indeed, was distinctly disagreeable, like the beginning of a stomach upset.

Lottie gave me a nudge and said softly, "Go look at the envelopes. I want some rubber bands."

This counter was relatively uncrowded (the seasonal stationery supplies—the Christmas cards and wrapping paper and stickers—were at a separate counter), and I went around to examine some very beautiful letter paper;

it was pale pink and it had a border of roses all around it. The clerk here was a cheerful middle-aged woman wearing an apron, and she was giving all her attention to a seedy old man who could not make up his mind between mucilage and paste. "Take your time, Dad," she said. "Compared to the rest of the girls, I'm on my vacation." The old man, holding a tube in one hand and a bottle in the other, looked at her vaguely and said, "I want it for stamps. Sometimes I write a letter and stamp it and then don't mail it and steam the stamp off. Must have ninety cents' worth of stamps like that." The woman laughed. "I know what you mean," she said. "I get mad and write a letter and then I tear it up." The old man gave her a condescending look and said, "That so? But I don't suppose yours are of a political nature." He bent his gaze again to the choice of adhesives.

This first undertaking was duck soup for Lottie. I did not even have to exchange a word with the woman; I saw Miss Fagin lift up *that hat* and give me the high sign, and we moved away, she down one aisle and I down the other, now and again catching a glimpse of each other through the throngs. We met at the foot of the second counter, where notions were sold.

"Fun, huh?" said Lottie, and I nodded, although I felt wholly dreary. "I want some crochet hooks," she said. "Price the rickrack."

This time the clerk was adding up her receipts and did not even look at me or at a woman who was angrily and in vain trying to buy a paper of pins. Out went Lottie's scrawny hand, up went her domed chimney. In this way for some time she bagged sitting birds: a tea strainer (there was no one at all at that counter), a box of Mrs. Carpenter's All Purpose Nails, the rubber gloves I had said I wanted, and four packages of mixed seeds. Now you have some idea of the size of Lottie Jump's hat.

I was nervous, not from being her accomplice but from being in this crowd on an empty stomach, and I was getting tired—we had been in the store for at least an hour —and the whole enterprise seemed pointless. There wasn't a thing in her hat I wanted—not even the rubber gloves. But in exact proportion as my spirits descended, Lottie's rose; clearly she had only been target-practicing and now she was moving in for the kill.

We met beside the books of paper dolls, for reconnaissance. "I'm gonna get me a pair of pearl beads," said Lottie. "You go fuss with the hairpins, hear?"

Luck, combined with her skill, would have stayed with Lottie, and her hat would have been a cornucopia by the end of the afternoon if, at the very moment her hand went out for the string of beads, that idiosyncrasy of mine had not struck me full force. I had never known it to come with so few preliminaries; probably this was so because I was oppressed by all the masses of bodies poking and pushing me, and all the open mouths breathing in my face. Anyhow, right then, at the crucial time, I *had to be alone*.

I stood staring down at the bone hairpins for a moment, and when the girl behind the counter said, "What kind does Mother want, hon? What color is Mother's hair?" I looked past her and across at Lottie and I said "Your brother isn't the only one in your family that doesn't have any brains." The clerk, astonished, turned to look where I was looking and caught Lottie in the act of lifting up her hat to put the pearls inside. She had unwisely chosen a long strand and was having a little trouble; I had the nasty thought that it looked as if her brains were leaking out.

The clerk, not able to deal with this emergency herself, frantically punched her bell and cried, "Floorwalker! Mr. Bellamy! I've caught a thief!"

Momentarily there was a violent hush—then such a clamor as you have never heard. Bells rang, babies howled, crockery crashed to the floor as people stumbled in their rush to the arena.

Mr. Bellamy, nineteen years old but broad of shoulder and jaw, was instantly standing beside Lottie, holding her arm with one hand while with the other he removed her hat to reveal to the overjoyed audience that incredible array of merchandise. Her hair all wild, her face a mask of innocent bewilderment, Lottie Jump, the scurvy thing, pretended to be deaf and dumb. She pointed at the rubber gloves and then she pointed at me, and Mr. Bellamy, able at last to prove his mettle, said "Aha!" and, still holding Lottie, moved around the counter to me and grabbed *my* arm. He gave the hat to the clerk and asked her kindly to accompany him and his redhanded catch to the manager's office.

I don't know where Lottie is now—whether she is on the stage or in jail. If her performance after our arrest meant anything, the first is quite as likely as the second. (I never saw her again, and for all I know she lit out of town that night on a freight train. Or perhaps her whole family decamped as suddenly as they had arrived; ours was the most transient population. You can be sure I made no attempt to find her again, and for months I avoided going anywhere near Arapahoe Creek or North Hill.) She never said a word but kept making signs with her fingers, adlibbing the whole thing. They tested her hearing by shooting off a popgun right in her ear and she never batted an eyelid.

They called up my father, and he came over from the Safeway on the double. I heard very little of what he said because I was crying so hard, but one thing I did hear him say was "Well young lady, I guess you've seen to it that I'll have to part company with my good friend Judge Bay." I tried to defend myself, but it was useless. The manager, Mr. Bellamy, the clerk, and my father patted Lottie on the shoulder, and the clerk said, "Poor, afflicted child." For being a poor, afflicted child, they gave her a bag of hard candy, and she gave them the most fraudulent smile of gratitude, and slobbered a little, and shuffled out, holding her empty hat in front of her like a beggar-man. I hate Lottie Jump to this day, but I have to hand it to her—she was a genius.

The floorwalker would have liked to see me sentenced to the reform school for life, I am sure, but the manager said that considering this was my first offense, he would let my father attend to my punishment. The old-maid clerk, who looked precisely like Emmy Schmalz, clucked her tongue and shook her head at me. My father hustled me out of the office and out of the store and into the car and home, muttering the entire time; now and again I'd hear the words "morals" and "nowadays."

What's the use of telling the rest? You know what happened. Daddy on second thoughts decided not to hang his head in front of Judge Bay but to make use of his friendship in this time of need, and he took me to see the scary old curmudgeon at his house. All I remember of that long declamation, during which the Judge sat behind his desk never taking his eyes off me, was the warning "I want you to give this a great deal of thought, Miss. I want you to search and seek in the innermost corners of your conscience and root out every bit of badness." Oh, *him!* Why, listen, if I'd rooted out all the badness in me, there wouldn't have been anything left of me. My mother cried for days because she had nurtured an outlaw and was ashamed to show her face at the neighborhood store; my father was silent, and he often looked at me. Stella, who was a prig, said, "And to think you did it at *Christmas*-time!" As for Jack—well, Jack a couple of times did not know how close he came to seeing glory when I had a butcher knife in my hand. It was Polecat this and Polecat that until I nearly went off my rocker. Tess, of course, didn't know what was going on, and asked so many questions that finally I told her to go to Helen Hunt Jackson in a savage tone of voice.

Good old Muff.

It is not true that you don't learn by experience. At any rate, I did that time. I began immediately to have two or three friends at a time—to be sure, because of the stigma on me, they were by no means the élite of Carlyle Hill Grade—and never again when that terrible need to be alone arose did I let fly. I would say, instead, "I've got a headache. I'll have to go home and take an aspirin," or "Gosh all hemlocks, I forgot—I've got to go to the dentist."

After the scandal died down, I got into the Campfire Girls. It was through pull, of course, since Stella had been a respected member for two years and my mother was a friend of the leader. But it turned out all right. Even Muff did not miss our periods of companionship, because about that time she grew up and started having literally millions of kittens.

Irvin Faust

Philco Baby

"GOOD JUST BARELY AFTERNOON, EVERYBODY," PURRED
the voice in his shirt pocket, and on signal Morty smiled
secretly, brushed his hand inside and, without losing a
beat of the backing and stacking, fondled the warm little
head and whispered back "Good just barely afternoon,
Every." So reliable, so dependable, such truth; the big
hand at the top of the clock was a notch past the little one,
and the actuality of Morty's schedule had been recon-
firmed: He had indeed stacked boxes in the allotted time,
four sets to a box, from the corner of Grossman's stock-
room to the window side and around to the chalkline
halfway back. Straightening up for the first time since
Rambling With Gambling, he looked around and again
carefully checked. And doublechecked. Almost satisfied,
he nodded and looked down and with his thumb and forefinger delicately circled held out his pocket so the little
voice inside could get some well-deserved air. Yeah. The
soft, smooth tones came floating up to him, happy to be
free—"Bob Landers here, you lucky people, and right
now for all you winners and losers and all you in-between-
ers, just this barely minute, *here* is the *Chairman of the
Board*." Standing perfectly still lest he in some way spoil
things, Morty slowly absorbed the granting of his wish,
the all-morning hunch that at good just barely afternoon
a wonderful new surprise might leap out of his pocket.

And (typically) the shrewd little bugger had reached down and was producing, Morty realized with growing certainty, the Chairman of the Board. Himself! Excitedly, but very gently, he fingered the tiny tone dial so the Chairman's voice, all light and zingy, filled the room. Hey now, Chair breezed, they gottan awfullotta coffee in Brazil; and standing respectfully beside his last box, head down, Morty memorized the new fact that coffee beans grow by the zillions way down among brazilians (wherever brazilians was). He stood stiffly, mouthing the words until the Chairman had finished; then, as though the command had been snapped by Mr. Grossman himself, he bent down to finish the line-up to the wall by the first afternoon Robert Hall jingle. The voice next to his ear purring away, the big, filled room, neat and cosy, like his own cosy room. Slowly but precisely he lifted boxes, fitted and closed, feeling the assurance of each familiar position. Pleased that all the while Bob was confiding—anxiously —in him. Not, of course, that Bob had right to worry, for Morty was plenty safe all right, and not just half safe and a little sniff under the arm for Bob and the little geezer was proof positive. Plus, for insurance against offending, the Arrid with Perstop in his own drawer, marked with his own name, Morty J. Aranow.

He worked in his quiet, soothing swing, alone in stock (but not *really* alone), handling all the work Billy and he used to do together until Mr. Grossman patted him on the shoulder and rewarded him with the entire room while Billy worked the truck with Sam. Which was a fine reward since Billy never talked to him anyway, except to say knock down that stinkin noise jocko, and it gave him the final, necessary area to complete his circle of command. This was probably (beside Baby) Morty's most important possession—space to be in charge of. Whether around him as he worked, or in an invisible case as he walked the street with the world (his world) reporting from his pocket, or in the darkness of his West 88th Street room, these manageable areas formed the compartments of his life. Aware of the continuity in this final link, he moved now along his chalkmark, hearing Bob Landers talk of familiar things—the Chairman, his boys, Sammy, Pete and Deano, Lavoris and Chockfullanuts donuts. Listening with the reassuring knowledge that they would check into each life space, he assessed soft little Patti, happy Julius and weisenheimer Bobby Darin, who would try for chairmanship, but fail miserably. Reinforced, he pulled hard for the wall, knowing in a dark, dim way that he was repeating the terrible swim for the dock in the great lake of that special camp mama had sent him to many years ago. Feeling from this safe distance the terror of the dock sliding away no matter how hard he kicked and screamed, demonstrating now how smoothly he could stroke, while the comforting lift in Bob's voice told him the wall was close by and he had once more reached shore with no hard, mocking voices tearing at him. Patting his pocket, flipping sweat off his forehead (not worrying about his armpits, which were parched and burning), he awaited Bobby Hall's commercial message and the 12:30 news, which from dateline Delhi, Moscow, Berlin and New York would converge under his nose. Next to the wall he sat down on his stool and pulled out his first Kent with the Micronite filter of the day. He lit up, inhaled and felt so much better (naturally) about smoking with the taste of Kent. After the news, he repeated station identification and then with a happy puff of surprise welcomed the razor-fine voice of William B., pinchhitting for the vacationing Big Wilson, an extra added bonus, since William was a nightly visitor with the Make Believe Ballroom and now they could walk home together and kick off the evening with no break in the space links. He permitted himself another Kent, pulling deeply on the filtered flavor, and stared happily at the floor, which like his pocket and private compartments was always there.

"Why do you always look down?" the quiet voice demanded; slowly his head swung to the tip of the voice and marked a pair of spiked heels, then it moved to bulging insteps and on to pink, hair-crushing stockings. Up the stockings slowly to the inch of white, the dress, the twisted waist, the puffy chest and the smiling face, which on contact opened and said "You look so sad, always with your head down, why is your head always down?" Miss Mandell. Tiny Miss Mandell, one week in the office, leaning to one side with her hip always stuck out as if it couldn't stand her crooked back, with her hair all frizzed and her nose so small, how could she breathe? She shivered him with a draught in his stomach. Since the time in that class with all the strange, jerking, drooling kids, ugliness had chilled him, then reminded him of his superiority. "You know," Miss Mandell said, "if you look up, way up, you'll feel a whole lot better."

"I feel good," he said; if he got real lucky she would disappear and leave him loose like everyone else, but she stayed harder and laughed as if he had said something so funny. "*Hah.* What in the world are you listening to? You're always listening to the radio."

"The William B. Williams show."

"Do you like that program?"

"Yeah I like it."

"And what else do you listen to?"

"A lotta different things."

She sat down beside him. "Like what?" she said. "What do you like?" Asking it as if she were that picky teacher who always demanded, what, why, which way, how does it make you feel . . .

"A lotta things."

The breath hissed out of her tiny nose holes in the teacher-mama sound. "That is not very real," she said softly while he pulled out a Grossman towel rack and dug into the hard plastic. "Yeah . . ." In and out his nail, bending, cracking . . . "I mean," she said with a push-smile, "it is not exactly flesh and blood."

"Yeah I know."

"It is steel and plastic and the Philco people make a million of them. And a million dollars besides."

"Yeah I know."

His Kent was now down to the white Micronite filter and he was dangerously close to falling off schedule; a fleck of blood stained his nail and he covered his hand. "Morty—if I may be so informal—" she said, "would you like to have lunch with me?"

"Oh, I can't, I *always* eat here," he lied. "I—uh—gotta sangwich." Her frizzy head bobbed up and down. "So this once you break a rule and come out." She leaned close to him. "I'll tell you a secret I wouldn't ordinarily tell," she said. (She sure didn't use Arrid with Perstop, if that was her secret, forget it.) "I don't like to eat with Mildred," she whispered. "She's very loud. I *cannot* stand loud people. I like *sensitive* people, Morty, you know?" That tone, a familiar ping in his belly where the feelings about mama lay, all behaved and sleepy, until a Miss Mandell came along with a nudge . . . 'You can do it dolling, you talk beautiful, just stand up on the stage and talk, sweetheart . . .'

"Well I can't." A thing he had never said to mama; oh

he loved his mama all right, but thank goodness she was dead.

"Not even," she said, "if I say pretty please with sugar and cream on it? You know, Morty, I like William B. Williams. And I like the Make Believe Ballroom too."

He looked. Who would say things he had locked up in his head? Could all that ugly? . . . But wait, that kind said things just to agree, to get you someplace . . . But she *knew* the Ballroom . . . Yeah, well it was *his* Ballroom . . . "No, I can't."

"Leona, aren't you ready yet?" called a whistle-thin voice. Miss Tomack. The heavy body followed the voice and she filled the doorway, thick, tight, spilly and blonde; a cow, a soft cow. Beside her, Billy boy, red and sweating from the morning deliveries. "Come on doll, leave jocko alone," Billy said. "You wanna give him bad dreams? Beside, he gotta be free to do his union bustin." Miss Mandell turned pink, all except her nose which stayed white as if he had pushed his thumb into the middle of her face. "Oh oh," Miss Tomack said, "I didn't know."

"I'll—ah—be right with you," Miss Mandell said. Whispering "I'll take a raincheck," she turned, and with her stuck-out hip holding up her dress, she walked to the door and the three of them dropped away from him like the cellophane off his Kent box. He stood very still and heard Miss Tomack's tough, piercing voice say I bet he *sleeps* with that thing, and then quiet. He roused up and hurried to the back to wash up with Dial for people who like people who like Dial.

The morning was boxed in, so lunch was the next hurdle. He gathered himself and walked downstairs on

the right, walked to Ninth Avenue and crossed at his
corner and proceeding still on the right, with the image of
M. Aranow flitting reassuringly beside him in the windows, walked one block south, where the shape and color
of Roger's Bar and Grille told him he had once again made
a dead reckoning. He entered through the waiting side
entrance and occupied his private space while his stool at
the counter served another customer. When it was
released, he straddled it, felt the smooth old leather under
his behind and knew he was safely at lunch. Good old
Roger winked, came over and gravely shook hands; the
good old guy always shook hands. He always said What'll
it be sport, sticking his jaw out and waiting, which were
important things to do. He said it. He did it. Morty wriggled on the stool. He looked down at the shiny beer taps
and felt the same warmth he always did; his buddies
were in charge of the golden, colden streams that were so
mellow, not sweet, just the dry flavored treat, and if the
beautiful glassful never tasted quite like that, it was *his*
fault, not the golden stream's. Another wriggle; he looked
at Roger and brimming all over with excitement, circled
his forefinger and thumb and propped the other three
straight up like an indian headdress. Roger nodded. "Hey
Charlie," he called, "make it a Ballantine for the sport."
The stiffly held fingers tingled. Oh that Roger . . . Morty
drank the golden brew, savoring the extra two weeks of
mellowing in the cool autumn sun. Roger was beckoning;
he swallowed hard and leaned far over. "Say don't forget
to vote, sport," Roger said confidentially. "Remember last
year you picked a winner." It was the embarrassing truth
and flushing, he looked sideways at the six overpoweringly
radiant Miss Rheingold candidates lined up over the taps.
Their smiles were full on him and he dropped his eyes.

"Who do you like, expert?" Roger said, and Morty felt the bright hot look of one particular candidate, whose voice had followed him from WHN to WVNJ and whose name could be said over and over without losing its sense; he cleared his throat. "Pru Pishney," he said firmly, glancing up. Roger looked thoughtful; he pointed to a smiling, blackhaired girl, Dial-clean, the whiteness behind her neat red lips proclaiming careful brushing after every meal. "Not bad," said Roger, "but she ain't stuff." He caressed a round, strapped-up, spilling-over blonde. A Miss Tomack. Ugh. "That I like," Roger said. "She puts out." Oh no! He looked straight at Pru and caught her need. Whipping out a pencil, right there in front of people, he tore off a ballot and X-ed in under the two capital Ps and jammed the paper into the box; Pru's smile of gratitude burned and he hunched over, away from this public display of feeling. Roger's hand was reaching over and patting. "That's OK sport, you did OK," and he swung his head back and forth, wanting desperately to say something. His hand snaked to his pocket and found the dial and brushed it. Judy's voice poured over the counter and with a deep breath he straightened up and looked straight at Roger. Roger patted again. "Hey there," he said, "how's the baby?"

Now there was something to talk about. "Oh good, Roger," he said. "Last night I went on the roof and she got Boston."

"That a fact? Hey now, how about that. Say Morty, I been thinking about something. You know what you remind me of?"

"What, what, Roger?" Roger wouldn't kid, not Roger.

"I'll tellya. A mother kangaroo. You know what that is?"

"Sure." That picture, tiny head, shriveled little arms. Great flat feet. Why? Oh yes . . . "It's a animal. It jumps."

"That's the ticket, kid. Well the mother kangaroo keeps her baby in a pouch and the kid gets a free ride all over, you can just see her head peeking out. Get it? That's you and Baby."

Hey now, he liked that, he liked it fine, especially him and Baby bouncing over the roofs. Except, well couldn't the father kangaroo have a pouch, too? But don't ask Roger, he might say no. So of all the million things begging to be said, he said "Yeah."

"OK sport, OK. Well Morty," Roger said, shifting to his business voice, "what's your pleasure?" The important question. He patted his pouch and felt the little kangaroo crooning softly; he took a look at Pru Pishney beaming at him. And pop. Into his head where a moment before only clashing thoughts and fuzziness existed came the answer to Roger's question. Clearly and precisely it formed, his nightly dream of lunch that was buried deep until the big question released it. "Oh," he said carelessly, drumming his feet against the counter, while the dream grew handles just for him, "I think I have some Uncle Ben's long grain Spanish Rice Mix."

You take care of an afternoon and it takes care of you. You do this important thing by fitting the afternoon exactly into a beginning and an end, and after a million perfectly fitting afternoons, you do it with a watchful confidence. First the news. That ends. Then gently you switch to lively Murray the K and pay close attention to his hard, demanding voice and his boom boom music and his longer, louder commercial messages, you take that time and split Murray into units of three boom discs and three loud messages and after a floor length of packing cases has used up its units, you take your middle break and get a lot to like with a Marlboro, filter, flavor, flip-top box. OK. Check. You are on the mark, the room is all lined up, and Murray swings into his closing theme and you switch to WNEW and the familiar voice that says "Good evening world," you hustle for the window, fold one, two, three tops down, hit the last case, push, bend, jam it together and the afternoon is shot to hell . . .

For a moment after it was packed up he listened to United Airlines and Golden Coach (with high stepping horses and everything?) to Hawaii, and then he walked back to the john and changed to his good Arrow shirt with long lasting Dart collar. When he came back, Dialed, Gleemed, Vitalised and Murined, Miss Mandell was hitching her hip up to her hand. "My my, but you do a lovely job," she said, sagging toward the window, looking at the cases, all in line with their tops tucked in four-ply. "It's the way I do," he said, itching slightly. "Well," she said, "it is a lovely piece of work. You must be a very conscientious person."

"It's the way I do," he said, the itch spreading. Twisty Miss Mandell was standing in the doorway and if she didn't move he was trapped, and she didn't move. He carefully remembered to forget something and looked around to find it. "Suppose," she said while he glanced in every direction, a funny smile (not ha-ha, the other funny) on her face, "suppose we (him and her?) . . . walk uptown . . . Together." (Yeah him and her.) "You see," she said, still not ha-ha funny, "I know all your pertinent personal background. I know you reside at one-oh-three West Eighty-eighth Street. See how nosey I am?"

"Uh huh."

She gave that hard push-cackle. "Oh that's cute. Now come on. I simply won't take no for an answer."

"I walk *all* the way home. It's a real long walk."

"My my, aren't you the regular health fiend. Well I'll just accompany you to Twenty-third, I'm not so athletic." That stubby thing was her hand poking out at him. "Come on," she said, "I'll let you listen to your precious Make Believe Ballroom. Maybe we'll hear a little Frank Sinatra, he's just right in the early evening." The hand wriggling, waving, snapping. "Come." He walked up and touched it; it closed rough and sweaty around him, badly in need of Campana's Italian Balm, choky and in charge, mama's hand. Thank goodness Billy and Miss Tomack weren't hanging around and Mr. Grossman of course didn't even look up from his books as they passed through the office and walked downstairs. Miss Mandell pressured him to a stop on the sidewalk and pulled in a load of bus fumes through those incredible tiny holes. "I just adore New York on a fall evening," she said and whistled the fumes back onto the street. "Suppose we walk up Ninth Avenue, all right, Morton?"

"Uh huh." Could he not? Of course. Not . . .

They started out into the sort of evening he loved to wander through alone, smelling, looking, listening to the security drifting out of his pocket, but now he had to share and that was a complicated and difficult process. Especially with the Chairman of the Board coming on and winging smoothly over the sidewalk. "Oh look at me now," sang the Chair and Morty's neck ached from its sharp bend down to his pocket, while his outside ear concentrated on Miss Mandell, who was making strange noises on the other side. The noises were turning his face red for Miss Mandell was singing. "Oh look at you now," she was singing in a high, trembling voice into his red face. *"You're* not the guy who thought about love and *you're* not the guy . . . and *you're* not the guy . . . but LOOK AT YOU NOW." Her knife-thin nose wobbling, her stuck-out hip brushing against him, drawing every pair of eyes in New York down onto them, while mama said go on sonny sing a song, go ahead go ahead, SING . . . He pulled away from the eyes of New York, but the tight hand pulled him back fast and hard. "Jack you're *ready,*" she shrilled, the Campanaless hand squeezing. His eyes probed the tongues of his shoes. Silence. Only the Chair. "You quiet thing," she said. "You should express yourself more. You ever try singing? I always sing when I'm lonesome or have problems."

"Yeah." . . . No!

She linked arms and locked her hand. "There, a gentleman always offers his arm." Her voice firm and businesslike, her office-phone voice. "Now you just remember that, Morton."

"Yeah."

"Silly. Say yes, not yeah."

"Yes."

The Chair had made way for William B. who was saying his clever things and Morty couldn't pick up one; his shoulder, receiving signals, began suddenly to hurt, and hunching to his ear was soothing. Ahhh Ann Margret, clear and soft, filled his head. Pru Pishney would have an Ann Margret sound. A hip, a hand, a voice knocked, scraped, pierced; his shoulder rose like a frightened cat's; Miss Mandell was shaking him. "Sill, stop with that thing. I'm *talking* to you."

"Yes Miss Mandell."

"Leona, silly. My name is Leona. Say it."

"Leona."

"Say 'yes, Leona.' "

"Yes, Leona."

She hugged his arm. "That's darling," she said, smoothing his shoulder down. "There . . . Morton . . . do you live alone?"

"Yes, Leona."

"I do too. New York is awfully big when you're alone." A whistle sigh. "Oh I could go out with oodles of people, but I don't know. They're all sex fiends if you know what I mean."

"Yes, Leona." Nah, he didn't know, but hc knew Ann Margret had gone . . .

"What do you do on weekends, Morton?"

This was the complicated part, doing two things at once, listening to Annette Funicello, dealing with Miss Mandell, figuring out her questions; that one, what was she leading up to, she was leading up to something, why else ask, Annette never made such demands . . . and Miss Mandell was waiting, so it was an important question, to be answered carefully, like what'll he have for lunch . . . Annette was resting, William B. was back on and Morty strained toward his pocket for help . . . Albany? Forty minutes to Albany, oh thank God for William B. . . .

"I visit my folks in Albany," he said clearly.

There was a quick satisfaction in the way he had registered, for Miss Mandell stopped suddenly and rewarded him with no smile. "All right," she said after a while, her voice low and flat, indicating an even greater success than he suspected, "all right Morton, I understand"; and then the sad look struck again, and the serious eyes, and hc realized his success had been punctured; of all the looks in the world he hated serious eyes most, they always followed his most enjoyable words; and he was back to confusion. "Well well, here is my station," she said, her eyes accusing him. Unlocking her arm, she reached over and patted his shirt pocket. "Take care. You have fun now, hear?" And turning quickly, she ran down the steps, while he stood there with his arm obediently ready and his thoughts of success and pity mixing in his head. For a moment he stood still, leaning, and then straightening his arm, his body, he realized he was finally alone. WHEW. It was better than going to the bathroom after hours of tortured waiting. WHEW. He uncoiled all the tautness in him up to the sky, his outdoor ceiling, realizing all that the aloneness could mean: Now, right this barely very minute, all loose and content he could take off through the evening lights, he and baby kangaroo, and without complications spot all the friendship landmarks and feel the familiar ideas. This night stretching before him (and all the others) would be his to twist and shape any old way, alone, because the sad eyes of Miss Mandell, he knew from experience, guaranteed an end to interference. Watering all the way through his Arrid, turning up Annette Funicello and running hard for West 88th Street in time to make his first evening show, Morty felt every bit of his old control telling him he was free, *free*.

A good supper, a *great* supper from the golden rich products of the Campbell Kitchen. A fast, efficient wash-up with new Mar*vel*ous Vel and a few relaxing minutes with his not too strong not too light Viceroy's got the taste that's right Friday night treat, and he was ready. With his room and himself in order, he went out to the hall and climbed the ladder to the roof, where he could begin his weekend, as always, with El Amor. Up there he was definitely in charge, he and old El and for their quota of one hour together they ran things from their shared platform above the city. But then at eight o'clock, at the beep, delicately, precisely and with the buzzing white membrane next to his ear, Morty split the static between El and Herb Oscar and drew in the strange, exotic voice of Boston, far at the top of the square of his world, far up north. With a grin of delight he lay back on his blanket and let Boston, speaking a common language, pour over him. Alone together. In the dark, with the lights springing up all around. He soaked himself in thoughts of Boston until Johnny Johns, the jock with the sock, said this the three-oh mark y'all and Julie smoked her last Marlboro, and then reluctantly, but firmly, for he had a schedule to meet, he got up and went down to his room. Humming filter flavor flip-top box, he propped Baby beside the sink and Gleemed his teeth and gargled with ice blue Micrin. He even allowed himself a peek in the mirror and was less disappointed than usual. Then he kneeled and said the prayer that mama had taught him and made him promise to say to avoid destruction, and placing the warm, black and white voice in its quilted cigar box, he dived into his bed and melted into oneness with the mattress and the blankets, his reward for a completed week. He took a last look at the world of light and reached over and clicked off the switch and then stared up at his new world. He waited. At just barely after midnight, when the world should all be sleepin and a melody comes creepin, he turned to the Milkman's Matinee and blended Milk into the life above him. He played with streaks of white and colored lights for a while, then slowly became aware of a memory from the day looming behind the screen. He stared hard and struggled for it, reaching, then falling away from a certain well-known face, a form, finding it hard, tough work to recapture the outside. But . . . yes, unmistakably, Miss Mandell, the eyes, the no-nose, the hip that led its own life. Yes, sad eyes. He shivered into his blanket, grateful that he was here, she was there, and another form rose beside Miss Mandell, bigger, tighter, bulgier. Disgustingly familiar. That chest, the belly stretching the creased dress to the breaking point. Miss Ugh! Tomack. Shivers down the line, to his big toe, ripple shivers. What had she said, the smart belly? . . . I bet he *sleeps* with that thing . . . Yes, she had a mouth, that one, bigger than horrible Betsy Frieberg, *bigger* than Kick em in the balls Tilda Tatzi . . . Relax buddy boy, he whispered, and just in time, for he was getting plenty annoyed with Miss Tomack, sweet little Patti's voice came rustling up to him and he kicked his dirty night thoughts in the can. As if a giant eraser had done its job, the ceiling above him stretched clean and pure and white. He smiled up at the pureness . . . "I wanna be loved by you by you and nobody else but you," whispered the voice beside him, "I wanna be kissed by you . . ." He squirmed and reached over and picked up Patti's voice and cradled it against his lips. Saturday. Sun in the window. Mrs. Melchas flushing the john. Mr. Ayub vacuuming. Late it would start; he would roll over and flick on Jack Lacy, roll back and stare at the ceiling and enjoy. Under his sleep, through his dreaming, he knew how it would happen, and Saturday, sun, Mrs. Melchas, the john, Mr. Ayub, the vacuum, they never missed; nor did Morty ever disappoint Morty. At Listen to Lacy Time exactly, he blinked, listened, grinned, rolled, flicked, returned, stared, enjoyed. Zing, boom, pow. A half hour he had in which to absorb the top ten and the pick hit of the week; at the pick's last drum beat he flung back his blanket and packed with energy, he leaped up. Stroking Baby to full throttle so he could hear friendly Dick DeFreitas and the news through his shower, he ran down the hall and sloshed all over with hexachlorophene and glowed as the weisenheimer bacteria folded up and plopped off him like dead flies. He shaved closely with Gillette Foamy, feeling the impervious armor of K34 guard his face from infectious nicks and scrapes. He ate his Breakfast of Champions, staring at the excitement of the back panel, and then he carefully dressed and groomed. Thom McAn, Robert Hall, Arrow, Vitalis, Griffin Scuffyshine. Saturday cigarette, Imperial York. When he stepped out into Saturday, he and his friends were ready.

Bright, wide open, a lot of time and space to mark off and handle. He walked his carefully allotted paces to Central Park West and turned toward his itchy hand; with Jack Lacy chatting away, he hurried from 88th to Times Square, recognizing it from all the other Saturdays, and feeling the crest of the right moment, walked quickly downstairs. Taking a deep breath, he pulled a token from his collection and stuffed it into the slot and pushed his way inside, where it was long and dark and deliciously threatening. Now the most delicious part . . . For a long time he would stand and sweat, until the train with the familiar letters roared in. He would swell up with another breath, say so long city and step on . . . Get ready . . . the train . . . *roar* . . . NOW. He was inside, breathing hard, leaning against the door, hurtling through the cellar of the city, and suddenly Baby was silent and he had entered the worst and the best part, all thrills and fear and doubt. Would he make it? Would he not? Oh boy! . . . Sure he

would (like always), but . . . always the *but*. Boy. Now
came another screw of fear as the silence in his pocket
grew real. Of course she didn't like it down here and he
understood, who could blame her? But it was rough . . .
He bit his cheek and grabbed a steel strap and hung on as
they swayed crazily through flickers of dark and light.
Another sickening zoom and his ears were popping; oh
boy, up there was the river with a million pounds of water
waiting for one little leak! Swallow, Bubby, he cautioned,
and he worked up some spit and jammed it down; the ears
unpopped. PHEW. OK. Now, Bubby, look up. There, all
around him, taking over from the noise and fear, his old,
dear friends. Miss Rheingold, Kent and L&M and Viceroy
and Milky Way and Piel's and Gleem and One-A-Day and
Serutan. The jelly hardened in him and he sat down. He
crossed his legs. He folded his arms. They were all smiling
on him, flashing tans and beautiful smelling teeth, reassuring him that friendship does not flicker out under the
river, no matter what. He flashed back on them their own
friendly selves, ah there Miss Rheingold, next month Pru
Pishney, and Harmon Killebrew, deodorizing with Brake,
it is wonderful to see you in a tight spot. The question of
escape was settled and he knew he was through the danger; *they* were through, and the river could crash or not
as it pleased (till he returned). He leaned back and
flicked off stations on each hand. Ten fingers went by and
he jumped up, smiled at the friendship circle and charged
out. Down the length of the station he pounded and raced
up the stairs into the gorgeous sunlight. Hey, Baby's eager
voice was climbing all over him, tickling like Mrs.
Melchas' puppy, telling him that once again he had pulled
through. *Alive.* Soaked (but sweet smelling) through his
Arrid, he walked down the middle of the street, savoring

his achievement, smiling at everything in this strange Saturday land. The low, flat buildings, the closed down sky, the thin noise evaporating into the clean air, all on a floating dock that he had reached after a week of pulling and pushing. Well now, he honestly felt he had earned his weekly reward, so straight for the suddenly recalled drug store he headed, planning each word ahead of time and tasting the result. When the friendly guy came over, Morty leaned against the counter and casually gave his order: "Say, gimme a Alka Seltzer . . ."

The boardwalk was practically empty. A little kid with a knish, one with an Eskimo Pie. Three people on the beach. In the water one woman dunking. Long, wide, endless. Morty leaned over the rail and stared at the emptiness and the black-capped dunker puncturing it. Up and down, down and up, like mama used to bounce. In the cool, wet air Dick Partridge was coming in loud and clear beneath his chin, talking over the wind and waves and providing a link with the city, warming the great space that arched over him. Out there beyond the space and the smashing, folding water and the dunker lay the mysteries of Boston, of dateline Berlin, the King of England, or maybe . . . *nothing.* Ahhhh his big, inside secret. Nothing. All his, figured out by Morty, belonging to Morty, pulling boss Morty down here each week to check up and reconsider. Yes, nothing explained a lot; it was peace, aloneness, simplicity. Nothing meant no careful boxing, no squaring of afternoons, no chalkmarks, lines, marks in or outside his head, no one to talk bad, or talk at all. No *worry.* Only Morty on top of his Simmons mattress, floating gently up and down, far out, just he and Baby and all the great nothing. In a hundred years, when he was finished with Grossman's this is what he would do.

Dimly, but unmistakably, he could see Morty Aranow
floating around forever. And slowly, deeply he sighed for
the day of retirement.

"Oh my what a heart-rending sigh."

A familiar voice, a *very* familiar voice. Here in his
nothing. Barging in and upsetting his mattress . . . Ex-
pecting the worse, he turned . . . The Worse. Miss Mandell,
sitting on a bench with her legs crossed and her chin in her
hand, studying him like a bill. "Hello there, deep one,"
she said. Yeah, Miss Mandell all right, not just a faker.
Mad with her sad eyes for tricking him into counting on
her absence, he mumbled something close to hello and
looked longingly out to sea. "Just imagine," Miss Mandell said, "our meeting here. So you come here too. Well
well and two more holes in the ground." Around her frizz
hair flopped a green scarf, her skirt, tucked under her legs,
was escaping and whipping around the bench; she would
maybe whip away . . . ? He looked and thought and formed
his answer. "Yeah."

"Oh," she said, leaning back and smiling. "I just *adore*
Coney Island." (Nah she wouldn't whip away.) "It is so
peaceful here. A person can think, you know?"

"Yeah." Funny she should be here, she was never here
before, this one . . .

"What a coincidence," she said, getting up and sliding
over to him in front of the wind. "Do you come here
often?" She leaned over the rail the way he did, and the
clean, wet air, that a moment ago had been sprayed with
Arrid, touched his nose with a five and dime smell.
Breathing through his mouth, he said "Every Saturday,"
even as he resolved not to.

"Oh so that's what you do, you sly thing. Albany
in*deed*." In spite of the miles of boardwalk, she was very

close to him. He took a side step. *She* took. "Why do you come here, Morton?" she said.

"It's nice."

"Of course. But every week? I mean like I come to see the water . . ." She hesitated and looked around. "I'll let you in on something. I never told this to anyone, but I think you'll understand." She laughed quickly. "Well, to me, out there it is like melted rubber. Latex, you know? And that liquid rubber out there is soft and strong and it could hold me up forever. I mean in my imagination, you know? I could recline on that latex and go everyplace I wanted and leave whenever I wanted and just live a beautiful carefree existence. There. Now isn't that silly?"

"Like a mattress?" he asked suspiciously.

"Why yes, like a foam rubber mattress. That's an excellent comparison, Morton." . . . Funnny, very funnny . . . "Well," she said, "now you know *my* secret. Why do you come?"

Be careful, Buddy, he warned himself. "Oh," he said, "my mother used to take me. I never went no place else."

Her hand was all of a sudden on his arm and she grew very quiet. Then she looked at him and said "That's sweet." He twisted his head away, to avoid the funny things she always said. What kind of sweet? Mama *liked* Coney Island. She liked to dunk and hold him around as she bobbed up and down, like a big, fat beach ball. My pleasure, it's my pleasure, she would say, holding him tight against her great, soft chest, laughing, then suddenly crying and kissing. Oh my only pleasure, she would say, as under the waves he grabbed onto all the softness and they would sail up and down like one big ball. He felt mama suddenly and stopped the picture. So what sweet? It was dunking . . . He sighed.

"You're such a sigher," Miss Mandell said. "Please don't sigh so big, Morton. It breaks my heart." . . . Stroking his hand . . . She was off again. Yet, somehow, he didn't feel so bad as in Grossman's . . . "Morton," she said, "let's go walk on the sand."

"Oh I don't do that."

"Well so now you just do it. Come on, reluctant one, it's really fun." She had an Indian Lock on his wrist and was pulling him toward the steps, boy was she strong, this little Miss Twist. "Now," she said, "sit down and take off your shoes. Like so . . ." The long, spike heels were waving in the air. "And roll up your pants so they won't get dirty. Here I'll do it." No no, this he could do, he *could* . . . but her hands were touching and folding, quick and sure, and there he was looking at his bare feet, pants rolled to the knees. (A darn good thing Dick Partridge couldn't see him.) She stood up and with a good yank pulled him down the steps. He pulled back, she pulled harder, he pulled . . . The sand was soft and damp. He looked around, up at the boardwalk, figuring his journey in time—a minute ago his body was up there and he could still feel it there, now . . . Funnny . . . He reached into his pocket and Dick Partridge, who was suddenly very important, belted up to him. On the other side of Dick's voice, Miss Mandell was one big smile and the pressure of that deceptive little hand was moving him out, away from the boardwalk, steadying him as he stumbled over the peculiar sand. His hand reached again and came out with Dick Partridge and Dick was a good anchor as he dragged after Miss Mandell. She could sure make time over this stuff, twisty hip or not, and that transmission of strength told him no nonsense now, Morty. So here they were now, out in no man's land where he couldn't turn back even if he wanted to (which he didn't). She sure

knew this place, for right here she stopped and said let's
sit down now, we can be all by ourselves here. Plop.
Down she went and that steel arm yanked and he was
down. "There now, that wasn't so terrible, was it?" And
really it wasn't, he had wanted to come out here in the
middle many times, but without mama who could take
him? If only this one wasn't so funny looking and crazy
sort of. "No," he said. She made her little hissing noise
and wriggled closer and then her frizzy head was leaning
against his neck so it was a little tough to breathe.
"Ummm, you're a nice one," she said softly. Morty
stretched his neck and brought Dick Partridge up to his
ear; he was beginning to get cramps from sitting so stiff,
holding her weight against him. So then she whispered
something he couldn't hear because of Dick's voice, but
he said yeah anyway. Oh, she murmured into his neck
and said something else that sounded like I do too, and
before he could run away she was kissing him on the
mouth, Aunt Ida's kiss, wet and sloppy. And she sure
didn't use ice blue Micrin. There was nothing to do but
hold perfectly still while she kept kissing and wheezing
out of the teeny nose. Oh Morty, she said and Ah Morty
and other things he couldn't make out with Dick Partridge talking in his ear. He put up with it all, but then
she began to rub his chest and squeeze his muscle and he
began to worry; his strength bunched up all at once and
with a hard push he was free and there was sand between
them. "Why——that?" she said.

"What?"

"——do that?"

"What?"

"OH FOR GOD SAKE," she yelled, "TURN THAT THING
OFF."

That wasn't so nice, the way it was said and the thing

part, but he slid the volume down because she looked so funny. "Put it *away, please*," she said. So OK he tucked Baby into his pocket and she let out a deep breath. He sat very still with his legs crossed. She sat in her place. Finally she leaned back on her hands and cocked her head to one side and said "Morton, do you like it here?"

"Yeah. Yes."

"A lot?"

He looked at all the quiet and out to all the peaceful nothing, rocking gently like a bunch of ice blue Micrin. "Yes," he said.

"Would you like to come here in the summer and swim? And have fun?"

"Yes."

"I could take you in the water. You'd like that, wouldn't you?"

"Yes."

"And the amusement park. The loopdaloops and the carousel. I could take you there, too." Far away, over the sand, he remembered those things, things that had been asleep since mama had gone. "You *would* like that, wouldn't you?" she said.

"Yes." Oh what was her first name? . . . she smiled, all of a sudden not such a funny smile . . . "Yes, Leona."

"Well," she said, leaning way back, "if we're going together you have got to get rid of that thing."

"What thing?" Again the flip flop.

"That radio."

His forehead wrinkled up. "What?"

"That radio, Morton. I don't want it around."

"Huh?"

"It's not good for you, Morton."

What kind of silliness? "Oh I can't do that."

"You can and you must."

"Oh no."

"Yes, Morton."

"Oh no." He covered his pocket; Miss Mandell smiled and with a sudden twist leaned over and kissed him. "Can it do *that*?" she said in his ear. "Can it?" What a dumb question . . . "No." Her lips nibbled his ear like Shotzie the mouse nibbling cheese under his bed. "All right then," she whispered, "it goes." She was dumb all right, she hadn't heard a thing. "Oh no," he said. Again she leaned against him and kissed him. Hard. With her mouth open, her tongue swishing through his teeth, pushing the bacteria into his throat. He jerked away. She leaned toward him and he bounced his seat away. "Morton," she said, "don't pull away." She crawled after him; again he bounced, kept on bouncing. "Morton, don't. *Don't*." She caught up and her hand lashed out and into his pocket. She jumped up and waved her hand; high above him Baby and Dick Partridge flashed against the sky. "See, see," she said. "All right now, that's enough, we have had just about enough." Was she nuts or something, she should be in a nuthouse : . . He scrambled up and lunged for her, the way he used to jump for his hat when the kids taunted him with saloogie. She ducked and he lunged again. "Morton," she yelled, "stop it, stop it. I told you it's not good for you, Morton, I won't have it. MORTON." He leaped again and she dodged away and ran around him in circles, tying him up with an invisible rope. He was dizzy and he stopped, panting, crouching on the sand, tears blurring his eyes. Please gimme it back Louie . . . Slowly she stopped spinning and stood before him; her mouth was wide open and strings of spit linked her teeth. "So you want it, hah," she gasped. "You really want this thing, hah Morton? All right, just look, Morton. Look careful." He recalled those awful words, what they always meant and the things that always followed, and he crushed his eyes together. The white haze of sand and sky beat at his eyes and he blocked them out with his hands till the comforting blackness drove her face away. He hunched down perfectly still so maybe everything would disappear. Then he heard. Straight through Dick Partridge's voice. Bang, bang, bang, bang. It plucked his fingers apart, pushed his eyes open. He peeked out. She was smashing good old Dick's voice with her shoe, holding the little box against a rock so there was no escape. His eyes opened wide. As he stared, the box split and a piece flew against him. But the voice kept coming. "And now folks, Miss Connie Francis singing 'Come Back to Sorrento.' In Italian." And through the banging and the grunting lovely little Connie was on and singing. In Italian. Loud and clear over the sand and water. With no spit strings and no grunty breathing. But Miss Mandell only smashed harder, grunting and smashing, one piece after another flying off, until just the smallest piece was left, and *still* little Miss Connie Francis sang. Horrified, he watched the little piece that held her. SMASH. Silence, Miss Connie was gone. And Miss Mandell stood there, with the last little white piece in her hand. She looked at it with a smile and then reared back and threw it far out into the water. She brushed her hands together and walked over to Morty and Morty didn't move; he could only think how would he ever get back now, through the tunnel and under the river. "There," she said in a brand new voice, "that was all for your good." She knelt down beside him and stroked his face. "See sonny boy," she said, "I did it for you. Sweet little sonny." He looked at the black and white pieces on the sand and felt her rough hand against his face, stroking gently, and he looked up for permission, which with a smile and a nod she granted. On his hands and knees he crawled to the little pieces that now looked so strange and picked them up and stared at them. He tried to think of what they meant, knowing exactly, but unable to form them into a single picture. Then from over the sand came the voice, low and concerned. "Throw them away, Morton." That voice he knew . . . A *person* you must be, Morton, a person, you *must* . . . and the concerned looks and rotten kids and special classes and millions of people swirling around. And that hand on his face . . . and *his* hand, busy, exploring under the water. Oh . . . Desperately he tried one last time to push the picture together to form West 88th Street and aloneness at barely after midnight, and Baby and Baby's guys and dolls, but all he could feel was people and hands and the rubbery softness under water. And the little secret idea that under her awful watery dress Miss Mandell could be rubbery soft . . .

"Morton, I'm *talking* to you."

Obediently he raised his hand, now light and tingly, and flung the pieces into the water.

"That's a good boy," Miss Mandell said. She sat back with a contented look on her face. "*I'm* going to help you now," she said.

William Faulkner

Barn Burning

THE STORE IN WHICH THE JUSTICE OF THE PEACE'S court was sitting smelled of cheese. The boy, crouched on his nail keg at the back of the crowded room, knew he smelled cheese, and more: from where he sat he could see the ranked shelves close-packed with the solid, squat, dynamic shapes of tin cans whose labels his stomach read, not from the lettering which meant nothing to his mind but from the scarlet devils and the silver curve of fish— this, the cheese which he knew he smelled and the hermetic meat which his intestines believed he smelled coming in intermittent gusts momentary and brief between the other constant one, the smell and sense just a little of fear because mostly of despair and grief, the old fierce pull of blood. He could not see the table where the Justice sat and before which his father and his father's enemy (*our enemy* he thought in that despair; *ourn! mine and hisn both! He's my father!*) stood, but he could hear them, the two of them that is, because his father had said no word yet:

"But what proof have you, Mr. Harris?"

"I told you. The hog got into my corn. I caught it up and sent it back to him. He had no fence that would hold it. I told him so, warned him. The next time I put the hog in my pen. When he came to get it I gave him enough wire to patch up his pen. The next time I put the hog up and kept it. I rode down to his house and saw the wire I gave him still rolled on to the spool in his yard. I told him he could have the hog when he paid me a dollar pound fee. That evening a nigger came with the dollar and got the hog. He was a strange nigger. He said, 'He say to tell you wood and hay kin burn.' I said, 'What?' 'That whut he say to tell you,' the nigger said. 'Wood and hay kin burn.' That night my barn burned. I got the stock out but I lost the barn."

"Where is the nigger? Have you got him?"

"He was a strange nigger, I tell you. I don't know what became of him."

"But that's not proof. Don't you see that's not proof?"

"Get that boy up here. He knows." For a moment the boy thought too that the man meant his older brother until Harris said, "Not him. The little one. The boy," and, crouching, small for his age, small and wiry like his father, in patched and faded jeans even too small for him, with straight, uncombed, brown hair and eyes gray and wild as storm scud, he saw the men between himself and the table part and become a lane of grim faces, at the end of which he saw the Justice, a shabby, collarless, graying man in spectacles, beckoning him. He felt no floor under his bare feet; he seemed to walk beneath the palpable weight of the grim turning faces. His father, stiff in his black Sunday coat donned not for the trial but for the moving, did not even look at him. *He aims for me to lie*, he thought, again with that frantic grief and despair. *And I will have to do hit.*

"What's your name, boy?" the Justice said.

"Colonel Sartoris Snopes," the boy whispered.

"Hey?" the Justice said. "Talk louder. Colonel Sartoris? I reckon anybody named for Colonel Sartoris in this country can't help but tell the truth, can they?" The boy said nothing. *Enemy! Enemy!* he thought; for a moment he could not even see, could not see that the Justice's face was kindly nor discern that his voice was troubled when he spoke to the man named Harris: "Do you want me to question this boy?" But he could hear, and during those subsequent long seconds while there was absolutely no sound in the crowded little room save that of quiet and intent breathing it was as if he had swung outward at the end of a grape vine, over a ravine, and at the top of the swing had been caught in a prolonged instant of mesmerized gravity, weightless in time.

"No!" Harris said violently, explosively. "Damnation! Send him out of here!" Now time, the fluid world, rushed beneath him again, the voices coming to him again through the smell of cheese and sealed meat, the fear and despair and the old grief of blood:

"This case is closed. I can't find against you, Snopes, but I can give you advice. Leave this country and don't come back to it."

His father spoke for the first time, his voice cold and harsh, level, without emphasis: "I aim to. I don't figure to stay in a country among people who . . ." he said something unprintable and vile, addressed to no one.

"That'll do," the Justice said. "Take your wagon and get out of this country before dark. Case dismissed."

His father turned, and he followed the stiff black coat, the wiry figure walking a little stiffly from where a Confederate provost's man's musket ball had taken him in the heel on a stolen horse thirty years ago, followed the two backs now, since his older brother had appeared from somewhere in the crowd, no taller than the father but thicker, chewing tobacco steadily, between the two lines of grim-faced men and out of the store and across the worn gallery and down the sagging steps and among the dogs and half-grown boys in the mild May dust, where as he passed a voice hissed:

"Barn burner!"

Again he could not see, whirling; there was a face in a red haze, moonlike, bigger than the full moon, the owner of it half again his size, he leaping in the red haze toward the face, feeling no blow, feeling no shock when his head struck the earth, scrabbling up and leaping again, feeling no blow this time either and tasting no blood, scrabbling up to see the other boy in full flight and himself already leaping into pursuit as his father's hand jerked him back, the harsh, cold voice speaking above him: "Go get in the wagon."

It stood in a grove of locusts and mulberries across the road. His two hulking sisters in their Sunday dresses and his mother and her sister in calico and sunbonnets were already in it, sitting on and among the sorry residue of the dozen and more movings which even the boy could remember—the battered stove, the broken beds and chairs, the clock inlaid with mother-of-pearl, which would not run, stopped at some fourteen minutes past two o'clock of a dead and forgotten day and time, which had been his mother's dowry. She was crying, though when she saw him she drew her sleeve across her face and began to descend from the wagon. "Get back," the father said.

"He's hurt. I got to get some water and wash his . . ."

"Get back in the wagon," his father said. He got in too, over the tail-gate. His father mounted to the seat where the older brother already sat and struck the gaunt mules two savage blows with the peeled willow, but without heat. It was not even sadistic; it was exactly that same quality which in later years would cause his descendants to over-run the engine before putting a motor car into motion, striking and reining back in the same movement. The wagon went on, the store with its quiet crowd of grimly watching men dropped behind; a curve in the road hid it. *Forever* he thought. *Maybe he's done satisfied now, now that he has . . .* stopping himself, not to say it aloud even to himself. His mother's hand touched his shoulder.

"Does hit hurt?" she said.

"Naw," he said. "Hit don't hurt. Lemme be."

"Can't you wipe some of the blood off before hit dries?"

"I'll wash to-night," he said. "Lemme be, I tell you."

The wagon went on. He did not know where they were going. None of them ever did or ever asked, because it was always somewhere, always a house of sorts waiting for them a day or two days or even three days away. Likely his father had already arranged to make a crop on another farm before he . . . Again he had to stop himself. He (the father) always did. There was something about his wolf-like independence and even courage when the advantage was at least neutral which impressed strangers, as if they got from his latent ravening ferocity not so much a sense of dependability as a feeling that his ferocious conviction in the rightness of his own actions would be of advantage to all whose interest lay with his.

That night they camped, in a grove of oaks and beeches where a spring ran. The nights were still cool and they had a fire against it, of a rail lifted from a nearby fence and cut into lengths—a small fire, neat, niggard almost, a shrewd fire; such fires were his father's habit and custom always, even in freezing weather. Older, the boy might have remarked this and wondered why not a big one; why should not a man who had not only seen the waste and extravagance of war, but who had in his blood an inherent voracious prodigality with material not his own, have burned everything in sight? Then he might have gone a step farther and thought that that was the reason: that niggard blaze was the living fruit of nights passed during those four years in the woods hiding from all men, blue or gray, with his strings of horses (captured horses, he called them). And older still, he might have divined the true reason: that the element of fire spoke to some deep mainspring of his father's being, as the element of steel or of powder spoke to other men, as the one weapon for the preservation of integrity, else breath were not worth the breathing, and hence to be regarded with respect and used with discretion.

But he did not think this now and he had seen those same niggard blazes all his life. He merely ate his supper beside it and was already half asleep over his iron plate when his father called him, and once more he followed the stiff back, the stiff and ruthless limp, up the slope and on to the starlit road where, turning, he could see his father against the stars but without face or depth—a shape black, flat, and bloodless as though cut from tin in the iron folds of the frockcoat which had not been made for him, the voice harsh like tin and without heat like tin:

"You were fixing to tell them. You would have told him." He didn't answer. His father struck him with the flat of his hand on the side of the head, hard but without heat, exactly as he had struck the two mules at the store, exactly as he would strike either of them with any stick in order to kill a horse fly, his voice still without fear or anger: "You're getting to be a man. You got to learn. You got to learn to stick to your own blood or you ain't going to have any blood to stick to you. Do you think either of them, any man there this morning, would? Don't you know all they wanted was a chance to get at me because they knew I had them beat? Eh?" Later, twenty years later, he was to tell himself, "If I had said they wanted only truth, justice, he would have hit me again." But now he said nothing. He was not crying. He just stood there. "Answer me," his father said.

"Yes," he whispered. His father turned.

"Get on to bed. We'll be there to-morrow."

To-morrow they were there. In the early afternoon the wagon stopped before a paintless two-room house identical almost with the dozen others it had stopped before even in the boy's ten years, and again, as on the other dozen occasions, his mother and aunt got down and began to unload the wagon, although his two sisters and his father and brother had not moved.

"Likely hit ain't fitten for hawgs," one of the sisters said.

"Nevertheless, fit it will and you'll hog it and like it," his father said. "Get out of them chairs and help your Ma unload."

The two sisters got down, big, bovine, in a flutter of cheap ribbons; one of them drew from the jumbled wagon bed a battered lantern, the other a worn broom. His father handed the reins to the older son and began to climb stiffly over the wheel. "When they get unloaded, take the team to the barn and feed them." Then he said, and at first the boy thought he was still speaking to his brother: "Come with me."

"Me?" he said.

"Yes," his father said. "You."

"Abner," his mother said. His father paused and looked back—the harsh level stare beneath the shaggy, graying, irascible brows.

"I reckon I'll have a word with the man that aims to begin to-morrow owning me body and soul for the next eight months."

They went back up the road. A week ago—or before last night, that is—he would have asked where they were going, but not now. His father had struck him before last night but never before had he paused afterward to explain why; it was as if the blow and the following calm, outrageous voice still rang, repercussed, divulging nothing to him save the terrible handicap of being young, the light weight of his few years, just heavy enough to prevent his soaring free of the world as it seemed to be ordered but not heavy enough to keep him footed solid in it, to resist it and try to change the course of its events.

Presently he could see the grove of oaks and cedars and the other flowering trees and shrubs where the house would be, though not the house yet. They walked beside a fence massed with honeysuckle and Cherokee roses and came to a gate swinging open between two brick pillars, and now, beyond a sweep of drive, he saw the house for the first time and at that instant he forgot his father and the terror and despair both, and even when he remembered his father again (who had not stopped) the terror and despair did not return. Because, for all the twelve movings, they had sojourned until now in a poor country, a land of small farms and fields and houses, and he had never seen a house like this before. *Hit's big as a courthouse* he thought quietly, with a surge of peace and joy whose reason he could not have thought into words, being too young for that: *They are safe from him. People whose lives are a part of this peace and dignity are beyond his touch, he no more to them than a buzzing wasp: capable of stinging for a little moment but that's all; the spell of this peace and dignity rendering even the barns and stable and cribs which belong to it impervious to the puny flames he might contrive . . .* this, the peace and joy, ebbing for an instant as he looked again at the stiff black back, the stiff and implacable limp of the figure which was not dwarfed by the house, for the reason that it had never looked big anywhere and which now, against the serene columned backdrop, had more than ever that impervious quality of something cut ruthlessly from tin, depthless, as though, sidewise to the sun, it would cast no shadow. Watching him, the boy remarked the absolutely undeviating course which his father held and saw the stiff foot come squarely down in a pile of fresh droppings where a horse had stood in the drive and which his father could have avoided by a simple change of stride. But it ebbed only for a moment, though he could not have thought this into words either, walking on in the spell of the house, which he could even want but without envy, without sorrow, certainly never with that ravening and jealous rage which unknown to him walked in the ironlike black coat before him: *Maybe he will feel it too. Maybe it will even change him now from what maybe he couldn't help but be.*

They crossed the portico. Now he could hear his father's stiff foot as it came down on the boards with clocklike finality, a sound out of all proportion to the displacement of the body it bore and which was not dwarfed either by the white door before it, as though it had attained to a sort of vicious and ravening minimum not to be dwarfed by anything—the flat, wide, black hat, the formal coat of broadcloth which had once been black but which had now that friction-glazed greenish cast of the bodies of old house flies, the lifted sleeve which was too large, the lifted hand like a curled claw. The door opened so promptly that the boy knew the Negro must have been watching them all the time, an old man with neat grizzled hair, in a linen jacket, who stood barring the door with his body, saying, "Wipe yo foots, white man, fo you come in here. Major ain't home nohow."

"Get out of my way, nigger," his father said, without

heat too, flinging the door back and the Negro also and entering, his hat still on his head. And now the boy saw the prints of the stiff foot on the doorjamb and saw them appear on the pale rug behind the machinelike deliberation of the foot which seemed to bear (or transmit) twice the weight which the body compassed. The Negro was shouting "Miss Lula! Miss Lula!" somewhere behind them, then the boy, deluged as though by a warm wave by a suave turn of carpeted stair and a pendant glitter of chandeliers and a mute gleam of gold frames, heard the swift feet and saw her too, a lady—perhaps he had never seen her like before either—in a gray, smooth gown with lace at the throat and an apron tied at the waist and the sleeves turned back, wiping cake or biscuit dough from her hands with a towel as she came up the hall, looking not at his father at all but at the tracks on the blond rug with an expression of incredulous amazement.

"I tried," the Negro cried. "I tole him to . . ."

"Will you please go away?" she said in a shaking voice. "Major de Spain is not at home. Will you please go away?"

His father had not spoken again. He did not speak again. He did not even look at her. He just stood stiff in the center of the rug, in his hat, the shaggy iron-gray brows twitching slightly above the pebble-colored eyes as he appeared to examine the house with brief deliberation. Then with the same deliberation he turned; the boy watched him pivot on the good leg and saw the stiff foot drag round the arc of the turning, leaving a final long and fading smear. His father never looked at it, he never once looked down at the rug. The Negro held the door. It closed behind them, upon the hysteric and indistinguishable woman-wail. His father stopped at the top of the steps and scraped his boot clean on the edge of it. At the gate he stopped again. He stood for a moment, planted stiffly on the stiff foot, looking back at the house. "Pretty and white, ain't it?" he said. "That's sweat. Nigger sweat. Maybe it ain't white enough yet to suit him. Maybe he wants to mix some white sweat with it."

Two hours later the boy was chopping wood behind the house within which his mother and aunt and the two sisters (the mother and aunt, not the two girls, he knew that; even at this distance and muffled by walls the flat loud voices of the two girls emanated an incorrigible idle inertia) were setting up the stove to prepare a meal, when he heard the hooves and saw the linen-clad man on a fine sorrel mare, whom he recognized even before he saw the rolled rug in front of the Negro youth following on a fat bay carriage horse—a suffused, angry face vanishing, still at full gallop, beyond the corner of the house where his father and brother were sitting in the two tilted chairs; and a moment later, almost before he could have put the axe down, he heard the hooves again and watched the sorrel mare go back out of the yard, already galloping again. Then his father began to shout one of the sisters' names, who presently emerged backward from the kitchen door dragging the rolled rug along the ground by one end while the other sister walked behind it.

"If you ain't going to tote, go on and set up the wash pot," the first said.

"You, Sarty!" the second shouted. "Set up the wash pot!" His father appeared at the door, framed against that shabbiness, as he had been against that other bland perfection, impervious to either, the mother's anxious face at his shoulder.

"Go on," the father said. "Pick it up." The two sisters stooped, broad, lethargic; stooping, they presented an incredible expanse of pale cloth and a flutter of tawdry ribbons.

"If I thought enough of a rug to have to git hit all the way from France I wouldn't keep hit where folks coming in would have to tromp on hit," the first said. They raised the rug.

"Abner," the mother said. "Let me do it."

"You go back and git dinner," his father said. "I'll tend to this."

From the woodpile through the rest of the afternoon the boy watched them, the rug spread flat in the dust beside the bubbling wash-pot, the two sisters stooping over it with that profound and lethargic reluctance, while the father stood over them in turn, implacable and grim, driving them though never raising his voice again. He could smell the harsh homemade lye they were using; he saw his mother come to the door once and look toward them with an expression not anxious now but very like despair; he saw his father turn, and he fell to with the axe and saw from the corner of his eye his father raise from the ground a flattish fragment of field stone and examine it and return to the pot, and this time his mother actually spoke: "Abner. Abner. Please don't. Please, Abner."

Then he was done too. It was dusk; the whippoorwills had already begun. He could smell coffee from the room where they would presently eat the cold food remaining from the mid-afternoon meal, though when he entered the house he realized they were having coffee again probably because there was a fire on the hearth, before which the rug now lay spread over the backs of the two chairs. The tracks of his father's foot were gone. Where they had been were now long, water-cloudy scoriations resembling the sporadic course of a Lilliputian mowing machine.

It still hung there while they ate the cold food and then went to bed, scattered without order or claim up and down the two rooms, his mother in one bed, where his father would later lie, the older brother in the other, himself, the aunt, and the two sisters on pallets on the floor. But his father was not in bed yet. The last thing the boy remembered was the depthless, harsh silhouette of the hat and coat bending over the rug and it seemed to him that he had not even closed his eyes when the silhouette was standing over him, the fire almost dead behind it, the stiff foot prodding him awake. "Catch up the mule," his father said.

When he returned with the mule his father was standing in the black door, the rolled rug over his shoulder. "Ain't you going to ride?" he said.

"No. Give me your foot."

He bent his knee into his father's hand, the wiry, surprising power flowed smoothly, rising, he rising with it, on to the mule's bare back (they had owned a saddle once; the boy could remember it though not when or where) and with the same effortlessness his father swung the rug up in front of him. Now in the starlight they retraced the afternoon's path, up the dusty road rife with honeysuckle, through the gate and up the black tunnel of the drive to the lightless house, where he sat on the mule and felt the rough warp of the rug drag across his thighs and vanish.

"Don't you want me to help?" he whispered. His father did not answer and now he heard again that stiff foot striking the hollow portico with that wooden and clocklike deliberation, that outrageous overstatement of the weight it carried. The rug, hunched, not flung (the boy could tell that even in the darkness) from his father's shoulder struck the angle of wall and floor with a sound unbelievably loud, thunderous, then the foot again, unhurried and enormous; a light came on in the house and the boy sat, tense, breathing steadily and quietly and just a little fast, though the foot itself did not increase its beat at all, descending the steps now; now the boy could see him.

"Don't you want to ride now?" he whispered. "We kin both ride now," the light within the house altering now, flaring up and sinking. *He's coming down the stairs now,* he thought. He had already ridden the mule up beside the horse block; presently his father was up behind him and he doubled the reins over and slashed the mule across the neck, but before the animal could begin to trot the hard, thin arm came round him, the hard, knotted hand jerking the mule back to a walk.

In the first red rays of the sun they were in the lot, putting plow gear on the mules. This time the sorrel mare was in the lot before he heard it at all, the rider collarless and even bareheaded, trembling, speaking in a shaking voice as the woman in the house had done, his father merely looking up once before stooping again to the hame he was buckling, so that the man on the mare spoke to his stooping back:

"You must realize you have ruined that rug. Wasn't there anybody here, any of your women . . ." he ceased, shaking, the boy watching him, the older brother leaning now in the stable door, chewing, blinking slowly and steadily at nothing apparently. "It cost a hundred dollars. But you never had a hundred dollars. You never will. So I'm going to charge you twenty bushels of corn against your crop. I'll add it in your contract and when you come to the commissary you can sign it. That won't keep Mrs. de Spain quiet but maybe it will teach you to wipe your feet off before you enter her house again."

Then he was gone. The boy looked at his father, who still had not spoken or even looked up again, who was now adjusting the logger-head in the hame.

"Pap," he said. His father looked at him—the inscrutable face, the shaggy brows beneath which the gray eyes glinted coldly. Suddenly the boy went toward him, fast, stopping as suddenly. "You done the best you could!" he cried. "If he wanted hit done different why didn't he wait and tell you how? He won't git no twenty bushels! He won't get none! We'll gether hit and hide hit! I kin watch . . ."

"Did you put the cutter back in that straight stock like I told you?"

"No, sir," he said.

"Then go do it."

That was Wednesday. During the rest of that week he worked steadily, at what was within his scope and some which was beyond it, with an industry that did not need to be driven nor even commanded twice; he had this from his mother, with the difference that some at least of what he did he liked to do, such as splitting wood with the half-size axe which his mother and aunt had earned, or saved money somehow, to present him with at Christmas. In company with the two older women (and on one afternoon, even one of the sisters), he built pens for the shoat and the cow which were a part of his father's contract with the landlord, and one afternoon, his father being absent, gone somewhere on one of the mules, he went to the field.

They were running a middle buster now, his brother holding the plow straight while he handled the reins, and walking beside the straining mule, the rich black soil shearing cool and damp against his bare ankles, he thought *Maybe this is the end of it. Maybe even that twenty bushels that seems hard to have to pay for just a rug will be a cheap price for him to stop forever and always from being what he used to be;* thinking, dreaming now so that his brother had to speak sharply to him to mind the mule:

Maybe he even won't collect the twenty bushels. Maybe it will all add up and balance and vanish—corn, rug, fire; the terror and grief, the being pulled two ways like between two teams of horses—gone, done with for ever and ever.

Then it was Saturday; he looked up from beneath the mule he was harnessing and saw his father in the black coat and hat. "Not that," his father said. "The wagon gear." And then, two hours later, sitting in the wagon bed behind his father and brother on the seat, the wagon accomplished a final curve, and he saw the weathered paintless store with its tattered tobacco- and patent-medicine posters and the tethered wagons and saddle animals below the gallery. He mounted the gnawed steps behind his father and brother, and there again was the lane of quiet, watching faces for the three of them to walk through. He saw the man in spectacles sitting at the plank table and he did not need to be told this was a Justice of the Peace; he sent one glare of fierce, exultant, partisan defiance at the man in collar and cravat now, whom he had seen but twice before in his life, and that on a galloping horse, who now wore on his face an expression not of rage but of amazed unbelief which the boy could not have known was at the incredible circumstance of being sued by one of his own tenants, and came and stood against his father and cried at the Justice: "He ain't done it! He ain't burnt . . ."

"Go back to the wagon," his father said.

"Burnt?" the Justice said. "Do I understand this rug was burned too?"

"Does anybody here claim it was?" his father said. "Go back to the wagon." But he did not, he merely retreated to the rear of the room, crowded as that other had been, but not to sit down this time, instead, to stand pressing among the motionless bodies, listening to the voices:

"And you claim twenty bushels of corn is too high for the damage you did to the rug?"

"He brought the rug to me and said he wanted the tracks washed out of it. I washed the tracks out and took the rug back to him."

"But you didn't carry the rug back to him in the same condition it was in before you made the tracks on it."

His father did not answer, and now for perhaps half a minute there was no sound at all save that of breathing, the faint, steady suspiration of complete and intent listening.

"You decline to answer that, Mr. Snopes?" Again his father did not answer. "I'm going to find against you, Mr. Snopes. I'm going to find that you were responsible for the injury to Major de Spain's rug and hold you liable for it. But twenty bushels of corn seems a little high for a man in your circumstances to have to pay. Major de Spain claims it cost a hundred dollars. October corn will be worth about fifty cents. I figure that if Major de Spain can stand a ninety-five dollar loss on something he paid cash for, you can stand a five-dollar loss you haven't earned yet. I hold you in damages to Major de Spain to the amount of ten bushels of corn over and above your contract with him, to be paid to him out of your crop at gathering time. Court adjourned."

It had taken no time hardly, the morning was but half begun. He thought they would return home and perhaps back to the field, since they were late, far behind all other farmers. But instead his father passed on behind the wagon, merely indicating with his hand for the older brother to follow with it, and crossed the road toward the blacksmith shop opposite, pressing on after his father, overtaking him, speaking, whispering up at the harsh, calm face beneath the weathered hat: "He won't git no ten bushels neither. He won't git one. We'll . . ." until his father glanced for an instant down at him, the face absolutely calm, the grizzled eyebrows tangled above the cold eyes, the voice almost pleasant, almost gentle:

"You think so? Well, we'll wait till October anyway."

The matter of the wagon—the setting of a spoke or two and the tightening of the tires—did not take long either, the business of the tires accomplished by driving the wagon into the spring branch behind the shop and letting it stand there, the mules nuzzling into the water from time to time, and the boy on the seat with the idle reins, looking up the slope and through the sooty tunnel of the shed where the slow hammer rang and where his father sat on an up-ended cypress bolt, easily, either talking or listening, still sitting there when the boy brought the dripping wagon up out of the branch and halted it before the door.

"Take them on to the shade and hitch," his father said. He did so and returned. His father and the smith and a third man squatting on his heels inside the door were talking, about crops and animals; the boy, squatting too in the ammoniac dust and hoof-parings and scales of rust, heard his father tell a long and unhurried story out of the time before the birth of the older brother even when he had been a professional horsetrader. And then his father came up beside him where he stood before a tattered last year's circus poster on the other side of the store, gazing rapt and quiet at the scarlet horses, the incredible poisings and convolutions of tulle and tights and the painted leers of comedians, and said, "It's time to eat."

But not at home. Squatting beside his brother against the front wall, he watched his father emerge from the store and produce from a paper sack a segment of cheese and divide it carefully and deliberately into three with his pocket knife and produce crackers from the same sack.

They all three squatted on the gallery and ate, slowly, without talking; then in the store again, they drank from a tin dipper tepid water smelling of the cedar bucket and of living beech trees. And still they did not go home. It was a horse lot this time, a tall rail fence upon and along which men stood and sat and out of which one by one horses were led, to be walked and trotted and then cantered back and forth along the road while the slow swapping and buying went on and the sun began to slant westward, they—the three of them—watching and listening, the older brother with his muddy eyes and his steady, inevitable tobacco, the father commenting now and then on certain of the animals, to no one in particular.

It was after sundown when they reached home. They ate supper by lamplight, then, sitting on the doorstep, the boy watched the night fully accomplish, listening to the whippoorwills and the frogs, when he heard his mother's voice: "Abner! No! No! Oh, God. Oh, God. Abner!" and he rose, whirled, and saw the altered light through the door where a candle stub now burned in a bottle neck on the table and his father, still in the hat and coat, at once formal and burlesque as though dressed carefully for some shabby and ceremonial violence, emptying the reservoir of the lamp back into the five-gallon kerosene can from which it had been filled, while the mother tugged at his arm until he shifted the lamp to the other hand and flung her back, not savagely or viciously, just hard, into the wall, her hands flung out against the wall for balance, her mouth open and in her face the same quality of hopeless despair as had been in her voice. Then his father saw him standing in the door.

"Go to the barn and get that can of oil we were oiling the wagon with," he said. The boy did not move. Then he could speak.

"What . . ." he cried. "What are you . . ."

"Go get that oil," his father said. "Go."

Then he was moving, running, outside the house, toward the stable: this the old habit, the old blood which he had not been permitted to choose for himself, which had been bequeathed him willy nilly and which had run for so long (and who knew where, battening on what of outrage and savagery and lust) before it came to him. *I could keep on,* he thought. *I could run on and on and never look back, never need to see his face again. Only I can't. I can't,* the rusted can in his hand now, the liquid sploshing in it as he ran back to the house and into it, into the sound of his mother's weeping in the next room, and handed the can to his father.

"Ain't you going to even send a nigger?" he cried. "At least you sent a nigger before!"

This time his father didn't strike him. The hand came even faster than the blow had, the same hand which had set the can on the table with almost excruciating care flashing from the can toward him too quick for him to follow it, gripping him by the back of his shirt and on to tiptoe before he had seen it quit the can, the face stooping at him in breathless and frozen ferocity, the cold, dead voice speaking over him to the older brother who leaned against the table, chewing with that steady, curious, sidewise motion of cows:

"Empty the can into the big one and go on. I'll catch up with you."

"Better tie him up to the bedpost," the brother said.

"Do like I told you," the father said. Then the boy was moving, his bunched shirt and the hard, bony hand between his shoulder-blades, his toes just touching the floor, across the room and into the other one, past the sisters sitting with spread heavy thighs in the two chairs over the cold hearth, and to where his mother and aunt sat side by side on the bed, the aunt's arms about his mother's shoulders.

"Hold him," the father said. The aunt made a startled movement. "Not you," the father said. "Lennie. Take hold of him. I want to see you do it." His mother took him by the wrist. "You'll hold him better than that. If he gets loose don't you know what he is going to do? He will go up yonder." He jerked his head toward the road. "Maybe I'd better tie him."

"I'll hold him," his mother whispered.

"See you do then." Then his father was gone, the stiff foot heavy and measured upon the boards, ceasing at last. Then he began to struggle. His mother caught him in both arms, he jerking and wrenching at them. He would be stronger in the end, he knew that. But he had no time to wait for it. "Lemme go!" he cried. "I don't want to have to hit you!"

"Let him go!" the aunt said. "If he don't go, before God, I am going up there myself!"

"Don't you see I can't?" his mother cried. "Sarty! Sarty! No! No! Help me, Lizzie!"

Then he was free. His aunt grasped at him but it was too late. He whirled, running, his mother stumbled forward on to her knees behind him, crying to the nearer sister: "Catch him, Net! Catch him!" But that was too late too, the sister (the sisters were twins, born at the same time, yet either of them now gave the impression of being, encompassing as much living meat and volume and weight as any other two of the family) not yet having begun to rise from the chair, her head, face, alone merely turned, presenting to him in the flying instant an astonishing expanse of young female features untroubled by any surprise even, wearing only an expression of bovine interest.

Then he was out of the room, out of the house, in the mild dust of the starlit road and the heavy rifeness of honeysuckle, the pale ribbon unspooling with terrific slowness under his running feet, reaching the gate at last and turning in, running, his heart and lungs drumming, on up the drive toward the lighted house, the lighted door. He did not knock, he burst in, sobbing for breath, incapable for the moment of speech; he saw the astonished face of the Negro in the linen jacket without knowing when the Negro had appeared.

"De Spain!" he cried, panted. "Where's . . ." then he saw the white man too emerging from a white door down the hall. "Barn!" he cried. "Barn!"

"What?" the white man said. "Barn?"

"Yes!" the boy cried. "Barn!"

"Catch him!" the white man shouted.

But it was too late this time too. The Negro grasped his shirt, but the entire sleeve, rotten with washing, carried away, and he was out that door too and in the drive again, and had actually never ceased to run even while he was screaming into the white man's face.

Behind him the white man was shouting, "My horse! Fetch my horse!" and he thought for an instant of cutting across the park and climbing the fence into the road, but he did not know the park nor how high the vine-massed fence might be and he dared not risk it. So he ran on down the drive, blood and breath roaring; presently he was in the road again though he could not see it. He could not hear either: the galloping mare was almost upon him before he heard her, and even then he held his course, as if the very urgency of his wild grief and need must in a moment more find him wings, waiting until the ultimate instant to hurl himself aside and into the weed-choked roadside ditch as the horse thundered past and on, for an instant in furious silhouette against the stars, the tranquil early summer night sky which, even before the shape of the horse and rider vanished, stained abruptly and violently upward: a long, swirling roar incredible and soundless, blotting the stars, and he springing up and into the road again, running again, knowing it was too late yet still running even after he heard the shot and, an instant later, two shots, pausing now without knowing he had ceased to run, crying "Pap! Pap!", running again before he knew he had begun to run, stumbling, tripping over something and scrabbling up again without ceasing to run, looking backward over his shoulder at the glare as he got up, running on among the invisible trees, panting, sobbing, "Father! Father!"

At midnight he was sitting on the crest of a hill. He did not know it was midnight and he did not know how far he had come. But there was no glare behind him now and he sat now, his back toward what he had called home for four days anyhow, his face toward the dark woods which he would enter when breath was strong again, small, shaking steadily in the chill darkness, hugging himself into the remainder of his thin, rotten shirt, the grief and despair now no longer terror and fear but just grief and despair. *Father. My father*, he thought. "He was brave!" he cried suddenly, aloud but not loud, no more than a whisper: "He was! He was in the war! He was in Colonel Sartoris' cav'ry!" not knowing that his father had gone to that war a private in the fine old European sense, wearing no uniform, admitting the authority of and giving fidelity to no man or army or flag, going to war as Malbrouck himself did: for booty—it meant nothing and less than nothing to him if it were enemy booty or his own.

The slow constellations wheeled on. It would be dawn

and then sun-up after a while and he would be hungry. But that would be to-morrow and now he was only cold, and walking would cure that. His breathing was easier now and he decided to get up and go on, and then he found that he had been asleep because he knew it was almost dawn, the night almost over. He could tell that from the whippoorwills. They were everywhere now among the dark trees below him, constant and inflectioned and ceaseless, so that, as the instant for giving over to the day birds drew nearer and nearer, there was no interval at all between them. He got up. He was a little stiff, but walking would cure that too as it would the cold, and soon there would be the sun. He went on down the hill, toward the dark woods within which the liquid silver voices of the birds called unceasing—the rapid and urgent beating of the urgent and quiring heart of the late spring night. He did not look back.

Alan Sillitoe

The Loneliness of the Long-Distance Runner

As soon as I got to Borstal they made me a long-distance cross-country runner. I suppose they thought I was just the build for it because I was long and skinny for my age (and still am) and in any case I didn't mind it much, to tell you the truth, because running had always been made much of in our family, especially running away from the police. I've always been a good runner, quick and with a big stride as well, the only trouble being that no matter how fast I run, and I did a very fair lick even though I do say so myself, it didn't stop me getting caught by the cops after that bakery job.

You might think it a bit rare, having long-distance cross-country runners in Borstal, thinking that the first thing a long-distance runner would do when they set him loose at them fields and woods would be to run as far away from the place as he could get on a bellyful of Borstal slumgullion—but you're wrong, and I'll tell you why. The first thing is that them bastards over us aren't as daft as they most of the time look, and for another thing I am not so daft as I would look if I tried to make a break for it on my long-distance running, because to abscond and then get caught is nothing but a mug's game, and I'm not falling for it. Cunning is what counts in this life, and even that you've got to use in the slyest way you can; I'm telling you straight: they're cunning, and I'm cunning. If only "them" and "us" had the same ideas we'd get on like a house on fire, but they don't see eye to eye with us and we don't see eye to eye with them, so that's how it stands and how it will always stand. The one fact is that all of us are cunning, and because of this there's no love lost between us. So the thing is that they know I won't try to get away from them: they sit there like spiders in that crumbly manor house, perched like jumped-up jackdaws on the roof, watching out over the drives and fields like German generals from the tops of tanks. And even when I jog-trot on behind a wood and they can't see me anymore they know my sweeping-brush head will bob along that hedge-top in an hour's time and that I'll report to the bloke on the gate. Because when on a raw and frosty morning I get up at five o'clock and stand shivering my belly off on the stone floor and all the rest still have another hour to snooze before the bells go, I slink downstairs through all the corridors to the big out-side door with a permit running-card in my fist, I feel like the first and last man on the world, both at once, if you can believe what I'm trying to say. I feel like the first man because I've hardly got a stitch on and am sent against the frozen fields in a shimmy and shorts—even the first poor bastard dropped on to the earth in midwinter knew how to make a suit of leaves, or how to skin a pterodactyl for a topcoat. But there I am, frozen stiff, with nothing to get me warm except a couple of hours' long-dis-tance running before breakfast, not even a slice of bread-and-sheepdip. They're training me up fine for the big sports day when all the pig-faced snotty-nosed dukes and ladies—who can't add two and two together and would mess them-selves like loonies if they didn't have slavies to beck-and-call—come and make speeches to us about sports being just the thing to get us leading an honest life and keep our itching finger-ends off them shop locks and safe handles and hairgrips to open gas meters. They give us a bit of blue ribbon and a cup for a prize after we've shagged ourselves out running or jumping, like race horses, only we don't get so well looked-after as race horses, that's the only thing.

So there I am, standing in the doorway in shimmy and shorts, not even a dry crust in my guts, looking out at frosty flowers on the ground. I suppose you think this is enough to make me cry? Not likely. Just because I feel like the first bloke in the world wouldn't make me bawl. It makes me feel fifty times better than when I'm cooped up in that dormitory with three hundred others. No, it's sometimes when I stand there feeling like the *last* man in the world that I don't feel so good. I feel like the last man in the world because I think that all those three hundred sleepers behind me are dead. They sleep so well I think that every scruffy head's kicked the bucket in the night and I'm the only one left, and when I look out into the bushes and frozen ponds I have the feeling that it's going to get colder and colder until everything I can see, meaning my red arms as well, is going to be covered with a thousand miles of ice, all the earth, right up to the sky and over every bit of land and sea. So I try to kick this feeling out and act like I'm the first man on earth. And that makes me feel good, so as soon as I'm steamed up enough to get this feeling in me, I take a flying leap out of the doorway, and off I trot.

I'm in Essex. It's supposed to be a good Borstal, at least that's what the governor said to me when I got here from Nottingham. "We want to trust you while you are in this establishment," he said, smoothing out his newspaper with lily-white workless hands, while I read the big words upside down: *Daily Telegraph.* "If you play ball with us, we'll play ball with you." (Honest to God, you'd have thought it was going to be one long tennis match.) "We want hard honest work and we want good athletics," he said as well. "And if you give us both these things you can be sure we'll do right by you and send you back into the world an honest man." Well, I could have died laughing, especially when straight after this I hear the barking sergeant-major's voice calling me and two others to attention and marching us off like we was Grenadier Guards. And when the governor kept saying how "we" wanted you to do this, and "we" wanted you to do that, I kept looking round for the other blokes, wondering how many of them there was. Of course, I knew there were thousands of them, but as far as I knew only one was in the room. And there *are* thousands of them, all over the poxeaten country, in shops, offices, railway stations, cars, houses, pubs—In-law blokes like you and them, all on the watch for Out-law blokes like me and us—and waiting to 'phone for the coppers as soon as we make a false move. And it'll always be there, I'll tell you that now, because I haven't finished making all my false moves yet, and I dare say I won't until I kick the bucket. If the In-laws are hoping to stop me making false moves they're wasting their time. They might as well stand me up against a wall and let fly with a dozen rifles. That's the only way they'll stop me, and a few million others. Because I've been doing a lot of thinking since coming here. They can spy on us all day to see if we're pulling our puddings and if we're working good or doing our "athletics" but they can't make an X-ray of our guts to find out what we're telling ourselves. I've been asking myself all sorts of questions, and thinking about my life up to now. And I like doing all this. It's a treat. It

passes the time away and don't make Borstal seem half
so bad as the boys in our street used to say it was. And
this long-distance running lark is the best of all, because
it makes me think so good that I learn things even better
than when I'm on my bed at night. And apart from that,
what with thinking so much while I'm running I'm getting
to be one of the best runners in the Borstal. I can go my
five miles round better than anybody else I know.

So as soon as I tell myself I'm the first man ever to be
dropped into the world, and as soon as I take that first
flying leap out into the frosty grass of an early morning
when even birds haven't the heart to whistle, I get to thinking, and that's what I like. I go my rounds in a dream,
turning at lane or footpath corners without knowing I'm
turning, leaping brooks without knowing they're there,
and shouting good morning to the early cow-milker
without seeing him. It's a treat, being a long-distance runner, out in the world by yourself with not a soul to make
you bad-tempered or tell you what to do or that there's a
shop to break and enter a bit back from the next street.
Sometimes I think that I've never been so free as during
that couple of hours when I'm trotting up the path out of
the gates and turning by that bare-faced, big-bellied oak
tree at the lane end. Everything's dead, but good, because
it's dead before coming alive, not dead after being alive.
That's how I look at it. Mind you, I often feel frozen stiff
at first. I can't feel my hands or feet or flesh at all, like I'm
a ghost who wouldn't know the earth was under him if he
didn't see it now and again through the mist. But even
though some people would call this frost-pain suffering if
they wrote about it to their mams in a letter, I don't, because I know that in half an hour I'm going to be warm,
that by the time I get to the main road and am turning on

to the wheat-field footpath by the bus stop I'm going to feel as hot as a potbellied stove and as happy as a dog with a tin tail.

It's a good life, I'm saying to myself, if you don't give in to coppers and Borstal-bosses and the rest of them bastard-faced In-laws. Trot-trot-trot. Puff-puff-puff. Slap-slap-slap go my feet on the hard soil. Swish-swish-swish as my arms and side catch the bare branches of a bush. For I'm seventeen now, and when they let me out of this— if I don't make a break and see that things turn out other-wise—they'll try to get me in the army, and what's the difference between the army and this place I'm in now? They can't kid me, the bastards. I've seen the barracks near where I live, and if there weren't swaddies on guard outside with rifles you wouldn't know the difference be-tween their high walls and the place I'm in now. Even though the swaddies come out at odd times a week for a pint of ale, so what? Don't I come out three mornings a week on my long-distance running, which is fifty times better than boozing. When they first said that I was to do my long-distance running without a guard pedalling beside me on a bike I couldn't believe it; but they called it a progressive and modern place, though they can't kid me because I know it's just like any other Borstal, going by the stories I've heard, except that they let me trot about like this. Borstal's Borstal no matter what they do; but anyway I moaned about it being a bit thick sending me out so early to run five miles on an empty stomach, until they talked me round to thinking it wasn't so bad—which I knew all the time—until they called me a good sport and patted me on the back when I said I'd do it and that I'd try to win them the Borstal Blue Ribbon Prize Cup For Long-Distance Cross-Country Running (All England). And now the governor talks to me when he comes on his rounds, almost as he'd talk to his prize race horse, if he had one.

"All right, Smith?" he asks.

"Yes, sir," I answer.

He flicks his grey moustache: "How's the running coming along?"

"I've set myself to trot round the grounds after dinner just to keep my hand in, sir," I tell him.

The potbellied pop-eyed bastard gets pleased at this: "Good show. I know you'll get us that cup," he says.

And I swear under my breath: "Like boggery, I will." No, I won't get them that cup, even though the stupid tash-twitching bastard has all his hopes in me. Because what does his barmy hope mean? I ask myself. Trot-trot-trot, slap-slap-slap, over the stream and into the wood where it's almost dark and frosty-dew twigs sting my legs. It don't mean a bloody thing to me, only to him, and it means as much to him as it would mean to me if I picked up the racing paper and put my bet on a hoss I didn't know, had never seen, and didn't care a sod if I ever did see. That's what it means to him. And I'll lose that race, because I'm not a race horse at all, and I'll let him know it when I'm about to get out—if I don't sling my hook even before the race. By Christ I will. I'm a human being and I've got thoughts and secrets and bloody life inside me that he doesn't know is there, and he'll never know what's there because he's stupid. I suppose you'll laugh at this, me saying the governor's a stupid bastard when I know hardly how to write and he can read and write and add-up like a professor. But what I say is true right enough. He's stupid, and I'm not, because I can see further into the likes of him than he can see into the likes of me. Admitted, we're both cunning, but I'm more cunning and I'll win in the end even if I die in gaol at eighty-two, because I'll have more fun and fire out of my life than he'll ever get out of his. He's read a thousand books I suppose, and for all I know he might even have written a few, but I know for a dead cert, as sure as I'm sitting here, that what I'm scribbling down is worth a million to what he could ever scribble down. I don't care what any-body says, but that's the truth and can't be denied. I know when he talks to me and I look into his army mug that I'm alive and he's dead. He's as dead as a doornail. If he ran ten yards he'd drop dead. If he got ten yards into what goes on in my guts he'd drop dead as well—with sur-prise. At the moment it's dead blokes like him as have the whip-hand over blokes like me, and I'm almost dead sure it'll always be like that, but even so, by Christ, I'd rather be like I am—always on the run and breaking into shops for a packet of fags and a jar of jam—than have the whip-hand over somebody else and be dead from the toenails up. Maybe as soon as you get the whip-hand over some-body you do go dead. By God, to say that last sentence has needed a few hundred miles of long-distance running. I could no more have said that at first than I could have took a million-pound note from my back pocket. But it's true, you know, now I think of it again, and has always been true, and always will be true, and I'm surer of it every time I see the governor open that door and say Good-morning lads.

As I run and see my smoky breath going out into the air as if I had ten cigars stuck in different parts of my body I think more on the little speech the governor made when I first came. Honesty. Be honest. I laughed so much one morning I went ten minutes down in my timing because I had to stop and get rid of the stitch in my side. The governor was so worried when I got back late that he sent me to the doctor's for an X-ray and heart check. Be honest. It's like saying: Be dead, like me, and then you'll have no more pain of leaving your nice slummy house for Borstal or prison. Be honest and settle down in a cosy six pounds a week job. Well, even with all this long-distance running I haven't yet been able to decide what he means by this, although I'm just about beginning to—and I don't like what it means. Because after all my thinking I found that it adds up to something that can't be true about me, being born and brought up as I was. Because another thing people like the governor will never understand is that I *am* honest, that I've never been anything else but honest, and that I'll always be honest. Sounds funny. But it's true because I know what honest means according to me and he only knows what it means according to him. I think my honesty is the only sort in the world, and he thinks his is the only sort in the world as well. That's why this dirty great walled-up and fenced-up manor house in the middle of nowhere has been used to coop-up blokes like me. And if I had the whip-hand I wouldn't even bother to build a place like this to put all the cops, governors, posh whores, penpushers, army officers, Members of Parliament in; no, I'd stick them up against a wall and let them have it, like they'd have done with blokes like us years ago, that is, if they'd ever known what it means to be honest, which they don't and never will so help me God Almighty.

I was nearly eighteen months in Borstal before I thought about getting out. I can't tell you much about what it was like there because I haven't got the hang of describing buildings or saying how many crumby chairs and slatted windows make a room. Neither can I do much complaining, because to tell you the truth I didn't suffer in Borstal at all. I gave the same answer a pal of mine gave when someone asked him how much he hated it in the army. "I didn't hate it," he said. "They fed me, gave me a suit, and pocket-money, which was a bloody sight more than I ever got before, unless I worked myself to death for it, and most of the time they wouldn't let me work but sent me to the dole office twice a week." Well, that's more or less what I say. Borstal didn't hurt me in that respect, so since I've got no complaints I don't have to describe what they gave us to eat, what the dorms were like, or how they treated us. But in another way Borstal does something to me. No, it doesn't get my back up, because it's always been up, right from when I was born. What it does do is show me what they've been trying to frighten me with. They've got other things as well, like prison and, in the end, the rope. It's like me rushing up to thump a man and snatch the coat off his back when, suddenly, I pull up because he whips out a knife and lifts it to stick me like a pig if I come too close. That knife is Borstal, clink, the rope. But once you've seen the knife you learn a bit of unarmed combat. You have to, because you'll never get that sort of knife in your own hands, and this unarmed combat doesn't amount to much. Still, there it is, and you keep on rushing up to this man, knife or not, hoping to get one of your hands on his wrist and the other on his elbow both at the same time, and press back until he drops the knife.

You see, by sending me to Borstal they've shown me the knife, and from now on I know something I didn't know before: that it's war between me and them. I always knew this, naturally, because I was in Remand Homes as well and the boys there told me a lot about their brothers in Borstal, but it was only touch and go then, like kittens, like boxing-gloves, like dobbie. But now that they've shown me the knife, whether I ever pinch another thing in my life again or not, I know who my enemies are and what war is. They can drop all the atom bombs they like for all I care: I'll never call it war and wear a soldier's uniform, because I'm in a different sort of war, that they think is child's play. The war they think is war is suicide, and those that go and get killed in war should be put in clink for attempted suicide because that's the feeling in blokes' minds when they rush to join up or let themselves be called up. I know, because I've thought how good it would be sometimes to do myself in and the easiest way to do it, it occurred to me, was to hope for a big war so's I could join up and get killed. But I got past that when I knew I already was in a war of my own, that I was born into one, that I grew up hearing the sound of 'old soldiers' who'd been over the top at Dartmoor, half-killed at Lincoln, trapped in no-man's-land at Borstal, that sounded louder than any Jerry bombs. Government wars aren't my wars; they've got nowt to do with me, because my own war's all that I'll ever be bothered about. I remember when I was fourteen and I went out into the country with three of my cousins, all about the same age, who later went to different Borstals, and then to different regiments, from which they soon deserted, and then to different gaols where they still are as far as I know. But anyway, we were all kids then, and wanted to go out to the woods for a change, to get away from the roads of stinking hot tar one summer. We climbed over fences and went through fields, scrumping a few sour apples on our way, until we saw the wood about a mile off. Up Colliers' Pad we heard another lot of kids talking in high-school voices behind a hedge. We crept up on them and peeped through the brambles, and saw they were eating a picnic, a real posh spread out of baskets and flasks and towels. There must have been about seven of them, lads and girls sent out by their mams and dads for the afternoon. So we went on our bellies through the hedge like crocodiles and surrounded them, and then dashed into the middle, scattering the fire and batting their tabs and snatching up all there was to eat, then running off over Cherry Orchard fields into the wood, with a man chasing us who'd come up while we were ransacking their picnic. We got away all right, and had a good feed into the bargain, because we'd been clambed to death and couldn't wait long enough to get our chops ripping into them thin lettuce and ham sandwiches and creamy cakes.

Well, I'll always feel during every bit of my life like those daft kids should have felt before we broke them up. But they never dreamed that what happened was going to happen, just like the governor of this Borstal who spouts to us about honesty and all that wappy stuff don't know a bloody thing, while I know every minute of my life that a big boot is always likely to smash any nice picnic I might be barmy and dishonest enough to make for myself. I admit that there've been times when I've thought of telling the governor all this so as to put him on his guard, but when I've got as close as seeing him I've changed my mind, thinking to let him either find out for himself or go through the same mill as I've gone through. I'm not hard-hearted (in fact I've helped a few blokes in my time with the odd quid, lie, fag, or shelter from the rain when they've been on the run) but I'm boggered if I'm going to risk being put in the cells just for trying to give the governor a bit of advice he don't deserve. If my heart's soft I know the sort of people I'm going to save it for. And any advice I'd give the governor wouldn't do him the least bit of good; it'd only trip him up sooner than if he wasn't told at all, which I suppose is what I want to happen. But for the time being I'll let things go on as they are, which is something else I've learned in the last year or two. (It's a good job I can only think of these things as fast as I can write with this stub of pencil that's clutched in my paw, otherwise I'd have dropped the whole thing weeks ago.)

By the time I'm half-way through my morning course, when after a frost-bitten dawn I can see a phlegmy bit of sunlight hanging from the bare twigs of beech and sycamore, and when I've measured my half-way mark by the short-cut scrimmage down the steep bush-covered bank and into the sunken lane, when still there's not a soul in sight and not a sound except the neighing of a piebald foal in a cottage stable that I can't see, I get to thinking the deepest and daftest of all. The governor would have a fit if he could see me sliding down the bank because I could break my neck or ankle, but I can't not do it because it's the only risk I take and the only excitement I ever get, flying flat-out like one of them pterodactyls from the "Lost World" I once heard on the wireless, crazy like a cut-balled cockerel, scratching myself to bits and almost letting myself go but not quite. It's the most wonderful minute because there's not one thought or word or picture of anything in my head while I'm going down. I'm empty, as empty as I was before I was born, and I don't let myself go, I suppose, because whatever it is that's farthest down inside me don't want me to die or hurt myself bad. And it's daft to think deep, you know, because it gets you nowhere, though deep is what I am when I've passed this half-way mark because the long-distance run of an early morning makes me think that every run like this is a life—a little life, I know—but a life as full of misery and happiness and things happening as you can ever get really around yourself—and I remember that after a lot of these runs I thought that it didn't need much know-how to tell how a life was going to end once it had got well started. But as usual I was wrong, caught first by the cops and then by my own bad brain, I could never trust myself to fly scot-free over these traps, was always tripped up sooner or later no matter how many I got over to the good without even knowing it. Looking back I suppose them big trees put their branches to their snouts and gave each other the wink, and there I was whizzing down the bank and not seeing a bloody thing.

II

I don't say to myself: "You shouldn't have done the job and then you'd have stayed away from Borstal"; no, what I ram into my runner-brain is that my luck had no right to scram just when I was on my way to making the coppers think I hadn't done the job after all. The time was autumn and the night foggy enough to set me and my mate Mike roaming the streets when we should have been rooted in front of the telly or stuck into a plush posh seat at the pictures, but I was restless after six weeks away from any sort of work, and well you might ask me why I'd been bone-idle for so long because normally I sweated my thin guts out on a milling-machine with the rest of them, but you see, my dad died from cancer of the throat, and mam collected a cool five hundred in insurance and benefits from the factory where he'd worked, "for your bereave-ment," they said, or words like that.

Now I believe, and my mam must have thought the same, that a wad of crisp blue-back fivers ain't a sight of good to a living soul unless they're flying out of your hand into some shopkeeper's till, and the shopkeeper is passing you tip-top things in exchange over the counter, so as soon as she got the money, mam took me and my five brothers and sisters out to town and got us dolled-up in new clothes. Then she ordered a twenty-one-inch telly, a new carpet because the old one was covered with blood from dad's dying and wouldn't wash out, and took a taxi home with bags of grub and a new fur coat. And do you know—you wain't believe me when I tell you—she'd still near three hundred left in her bulging handbag the next day, so how could any of us go to work after that? Poor old dad, he didn't get a look in, and he was the one who'd done the suffering and dying for such a lot of lolly.

Night after night we sat in front of the telly with a ham sandwich in one hand, a bar of chocolate in the other, and a bottle of lemonade between our boots, while mam was with some fancy-man upstairs on the new bed she'd ordered, and I'd never known a family as happy as ours was in that couple of months when we'd got all the money we needed. And when the dough ran out I didn't think about anything much, but just roamed the streets—looking for another job, I told mam—hoping I suppose to get my hands on another five hundred nicker so's the nice life we'd got used to could go on and on for ever. Because it's surprising how quick you can get used to a different life. To begin with, the adverts on the telly had shown us how much more there was in the world to buy than we'd ever dreamed of when we'd looked into shop windows but hadn't seen all there was to see because we didn't have the money to buy it with anyway. And the telly made all these things seem twenty times better than we'd ever thought they were. Even adverts at the cinema were cool and tame, because now we were seeing them in private at home. We used to cock our noses up at things in shops that didn't move, but suddenly we saw their real value because they jumped and glittered around the screen and had some pasty-faced tart going head over heels to get her nail-polished grabbers on to them or her lipstick lips over them, not like the crumby adverts you saw on posters or in newspapers as dead as doornails; these were flickering around loose, half-open packets and tins, making you think that all you had to do was finish opening them before they were yours, like seeing an unlocked safe through a shop window with the man gone away for a cup of tea without thinking to guard his lolly. The films they showed were good as well, in that way, because we couldn't get our eyes unglued from the cops chasing the robbers who had satchel-bags crammed with cash and looked like getting away to spend it—until the last moment. I always hoped they would end up free to blow the lot, and could never stop wanting to put my hand out, smash into the screen (it only looked a bit of rag-screen like at the pictures) and get the copper in a half-nelson so's he'd stop following the bloke with the money-bags. Even when he'd knocked off a couple of bank clerks I hoped he wouldn't get nabbed. In fact then I wished more than ever he wouldn't because it meant the hot-chair if he did, and I wouldn't wish that on anybody no matter what they'd done, because I'd read in a book where the hot-chair worn't a quick death at all, but that you just sat there scorching to death until you were dead. And it was when these cops were chasing the crooks that we played some good tricks with the telly, because when one of them opened his big gob to spout about getting their man I'd turn the sound down and see his mouth move like a gold-fish or mackerel or a minnow mimicking what they were supposed to be acting—it was so funny the whole family nearly went into fits on the brand-new carpet that hadn't yet found its way to the bedroom. It was the best of all though when we did it to some Tory telling us about how good his government was going to be if we kept on voting for them—their slack chops rolling, opening and bumbling, hands lifting to twitch moustaches and touch-ing their buttonholes to make sure the flower hadn't wilted, so that you could see they didn't mean a word they said, especially with not a murmur coming out because we'd cut off the sound. When the governor of the Borstal first talked to me I was reminded of those times so much that I nearly killed myself trying not to laugh. Yes, we played so many good stunts on the box of tricks that mam used to call us the Telly Boys, we got so clever at it.

My pal Mike got let off with probation because it was his first job—anyway the first they ever knew about—and because they said he would never have done it if it hadn't been for me talking him into it. They said I was a menace to honest lads like Mike—hands in his pockets so that they looked stone-empty, head bent forward as if look-ing for half-crowns to fill 'em with, a ripped jersey on and his hair falling into his eyes so that he could go up to women and ask them for a shilling because he was hun-gry—and that I was the brains behind the job, the guid-ing light when it came to making up anybody's mind, but I swear to God I worn't owt like that because really I ain't got no more brains than a gnat after hiding the money in the place I did. And I—being cranky like I am—got sent to Borstal because to tell you the honest truth I'd been to Remand Homes before—though that's another story and I suppose if ever I tell it it'll be just as boring as this one is. I was glad though that Mike got away with it, and I only hope he always will, not like silly bastard me.

So on this foggy night we tore ourselves away from the telly and slammed the front door behind us, setting off up our wide street like slow tugs on a river that'd broken their hooters, for we didn't know where the house-fronts began what with the perishing cold mist all around. I was snatched to death without an overcoat: mam had forgotten to buy me one in the scrummage of shopping, and by the time I thought to remind her of it the dough was all gone. So we whistled "The Teddy Boys Picnic" to keep us warm, and I told myself that I'd get a coat soon if it was the last thing I did. Mike said he thought the same about himself, adding that he'd also get some brand-new glasses with gold rims, to wear instead of the wire frames they'd given him at the school clinic years ago. He didn't twig it was foggy at first and cleaned his glasses every time I pulled him back from a lamp-post or car, but when he saw the lights on Alfreton Road looking like octopus eyes he put them in his pocket and didn't wear them again until we did the job. We hadn't got two ha-pennies between us, and though we weren't hungry we wished we'd got a bob or two when we passed the fish and chip shops because the delicious sniffs of salt and vinegar and frying fat made our mouths water. I don't mind tell-ing you we walked the town from one end to the other and if our eyes worn't glued to the ground looking for lost wal-lets and watches they was swivelling around house win-dows and shop doors in case we saw something easy and worth nipping into.

Neither of us said as much as this to each other, but I know for a fact that that was what we was thinking. What I don't know—and as sure as I sit here I know I'll never know—is which of us was the first bastard to latch his peepers on to that baker's backyard. Oh yes, it's all right me telling myself it was me, but the truth is that I've never known whether it was Mike or not, because I do know that I didn't see the open window until he stabbed me in the ribs and pointed it out. "See it?" he said.

"Yes," I told him, "so let's get cracking."

"But what about the wall though?" he whispered, looking a bit closer.

"On your shoulders," I chipped in.

His eyes were already up there: "Will you be able to reach?" It was the only time he ever showed any life.

"Leave it to me," I said, ever-ready. "I can reach anywhere from your ham-hock shoulders."

Mike was a nipper compared to me, but underneath the scruffy draught-board jersey he wore were muscles as hard as iron, and you wouldn't think to see him walking down the street with glasses on and hands in pockets that he'd harm a fly, but I never liked to get on the wrong side of him in a fight because he's the sort that don't say a word for weeks on end—sits plugged in front of the telly, or reads a cowboy book, or just sleeps—when suddenly BIFF—half kills somebody for almost nothing at all, such as beating him in a race for the last Football Post on a Saturday night, pushing in before him at a bus stop, or bumping into him when he was day-dreaming about Dolly-on-the-Tub next door. I saw him set on a bloke once for no more than fixing him in a funny way with his eyes, and it turned out that the bloke was cock-eyed but nobody knew it because he'd just that day come to live in our street. At other times none of these things would matter a bit, and I suppose the only reason why I was pals with him was because I didn't say much from one month's end to another either.

He puts his hands up in the air like he was being covered with a Gatling-Gun, and moved to the wall like he was going to be mowed down, and I climbed up him like he was a stile or step-ladder, and there he stood, the palms of his upshot maulers flat and turned out so's I could step on 'em like they was the adjustable jackspanner under a car, not a sound of a breath nor the shiver of a flinch coming from him. I lost no time in any case, took my coat from between my teeth, chucked it up to the glass-topped wall (where the glass worn't too sharp because the jags had been worn down by years of accidental stones) and was sitting astraddle before I knew where I was. Then down the other side, with my legs rammed up into my throat when I hit the ground, the crack coming about as hard as when you fall after a high parachute drop, that one of my mates told me was like jumping off a twelve-foot wall, which this must have been. Then I picked up my bits and pieces and opened the gate for Mike, who was still grinning and full of life because the hardest part of the job was already done. "I came, I broke, I entered," like that clever-dick Borstal song.

I didn't think about anything at all, as usual, because I never do when I'm busy, when I'm draining pipes, looting sacks, yaling locks, lifting latches, forcing my bony hands and lanky legs into making something move, hardly feeling my lungs going in-whiff and out-whaff, not realizing whether my mouth is clamped tight or gaping, whether I'm hungry, itching from scabies, or whether my flies are open and flashing dirty words like muck and spit into the late-night final fog. And when I don't know anything about all this then how can I honest-to-God say I think of anything at such times? When I'm wondering what's the best way to get a window open or how to force a door, how can I be thinking or have anything on my mind? That's what the four-eyed white-smocked bloke with the note-book couldn't understand when he asked me questions for days and days after I got to Borstal; and I couldn't explain it to him then like I'm writing it down now; and even if I'd been able to maybe he still wouldn't have caught on because I don't know whether I can understand it myself even at this moment, though I'm do-ing my best you can bet.

So before I knew where I was I was inside the baker's office watching Mike picking up that cash box after he'd struck a match to see where it was, wearing a tailor-made fifty-shilling grin on his square crew-cut nut as his paws closed over the box like he'd squash it to nothing. "Out," he suddenly said, shaking it so's it rattled. "Let's scram."

"Maybe there's some more," I said, pulling half a dozen drawers out of a rollertop desk.

"No," he said, like he'd already been twenty years in the game, "this is the lot," patting his tin box, "this is it."

I pulled out another few drawers, full of bills, books and letters. "How do you know, you loony sod?"

He barged past me like a bull at a gate. "Because I do."

Right or wrong, we'd both got to stick together and do the same thing. I looked at an ever-loving babe of a brand-new typewriter, but knew it was too traceable, so blew it a kiss, and went out after him. "Hang on," I said, pull-ing the door to, "we're in no hurry."

"Not much we aren't," he says over his shoulder.

"We've got months to splash the lolly," I whispered as we crossed the yard, "only don't let that gate creak too much or you'll have the narks tuning-in."

"You think I'm barmy?" he said, creaking the gate so that the whole street heard.

I don't know about Mike, but now I started to think of how we'd get back safe through the streets with that money-box up my jumper. Because he'd clapped it into my hand as soon as we'd got to the main road, which might have meant that he'd started thinking as well, which only goes to show how you don't know what's in anybody else's mind unless you think about things yourself. But as far as my thinking went at that moment it wasn't up to much, only a bit of fright that wouldn't budge not even with a hot blow-lamp, about what we'd say if a copper asked us where we were off to with that hump in my guts.

"What is it?" he'd ask, and I'd say: "A growth." "What do you mean, a growth, my lad?" he'd say back, narky like. I'd cough and clutch myself like I was in the most tripe-twisting pain in the world, and screw my eyes up like I was on my way to the hospital, and Mike would take my arm like he was the best pal I'd got. "Cancer," I'd manage to say to Narker, which would make his slow punch-drunk brain suspect a thing or two. "A lad of your age?" So I'd groan again, and hope to make him feel a real bully of a bastard, which would be impossible, but anyway: "It's in the family. Dad died of it last month, and I'll die of it next month by the feel of it." "What, did he have it in the guts?" "No, in the throat. But it's got me in the stomach." Groan and cough. "Well, you shouldn't be out like this if you've got cancer, you should be in the hospital." I'd get ratty now: "That's where I'm trying to go if only you'd let me and stop asking so many questions. Aren't I, Mike?" Grunt from Mike as he unslung his cosh. Then just in time the copper would tell us to get on our way, kind and considerate all of a sudden, saying that the outpatient department of the hospital closes at twelve, so hadn't he better call us a taxi? He would if we liked, he says, and he'd pay for it as well. But we tell him not to bother, that he's a good bloke even if he is a copper, that we know a short cut anyway. Then just as we're turning a corner he gets it into his big batchy head that we're going the opposite way to the hospital, and calls us back. So we'd start to run . . . if you can call all that thinking.

Up in my room Mike rips open that money-box with a hammer and chisel, and before we know where we are we've got seventy-eight pounds fifteen and fourpence ha'penny *each* lying all over my bed like tea spread out on Christmas Day: cake and trifle, salad and sandwiches, jam tarts and bars of chocolate: all shared and shared alike between Mike and me because we believed in equal work and equal pay, just like the comrades my dad was in until he couldn't do a stroke anymore and had no breath left to argue with. I thought how good it was that blokes like that poor baker didn't stash all his cash in one of the big marble-fronted banks that take up every corner of the town, how lucky for us that he didn't trust them no matter how many millions of tons of concrete or how many iron bars and boxes they were made of, or how many coppers kept their blue pop-eyed peepers glued on to them, how smashing it was that he believed in money-boxes when so many shopkeepers thought it old-fashioned and tried to be modern by using a bank, which wouldn't give a couple of sincere, honest, hardworking, conscientious blokes like Mike and me a chance.

Now you'd think, and I'd think, and anybody with a bit of imagination would think, that we'd done as clean a job as could ever be done, that, with the baker's shop being at least a mile from where we lived, and with not a soul having seen us, and what with the fog and the fact that we weren't more than five minutes in the place, that the coppers should never have been able to trace us. But then, you'd be wrong, I'd be wrong, and everybody else would be wrong, no matter how much imagination was diced out between us.

Even so, Mike and I didn't splash the money about, because that would have made people think straightaway that we'd latched on to something that didn't belong to us. Which wouldn't do at all, because even in a street like ours there are people who love to do a good turn for the coppers, though I never know why they do. Some people are so mean-gutted that even if they've only got tuppence more than you and they think you're the sort that would take it if you have half the chance, they'd get you put inside if they saw you ripping lead out of a lavatory, even if it weren't their lavatory—just to keep their tuppence out of your reach. And so we didn't do anything to let on about how rich we were, nothing like going down town and coming back dressed in brand-new Teddy boy suits and carrying a set of skiffle-drums like another pal of ours who'd done a factory office about six months before. No, we took the odd bobs and pennies out and folded the notes into bundles and stuffed them up the drainpipe outside the door in the backyard. "Nobody'll ever think of looking for it there," I said to Mike. "We'll keep it doggo for a week or two, then take a few quid a week out till it's all gone. We might be thieving bastards, but we're not green."

Some days later a plain-clothes dick knocked at the door. And asked for me. I was still in bed, at eleven o'clock, and had to unroll myself from the comfortable black sheets when I heard mam calling me. "A man to see you," she said. "Hurry up, or he'll be gone."

I could hear her keeping him at the back door, nattering about how fine it had been but how it looked like rain since early this morning—and he didn't answer her except to snap out a snotty yes or no. I scrambled into my trousers and wondered why he'd come—knowing it was a copper because "a man to see you" always meant just that in our house—and if I'd had any idea that one had gone to Mike's house as well at the same time I'd have twigged it to be because of that hundred and fifty quid's worth of paper stuffed up the drainpipe outside the back door about ten inches away from that plain-clothed copper's boot, where mam still talked to him thinking she was doing me a favour, and I wishing to God she'd ask him in, though on second thoughts realizing that that would seem more suspicious than keeping him outside, because they know we hate their guts and smell a rat if they think we're trying to be nice to them. Mam wasn't born yesterday, I thought, thumping my way down the creaking stairs.

I'd seen him before: Borstal Bernard in nicky-hat, Remand Home Ronald in rowing-boat boots, Probation Pete in a pit-prop mackintosh, three-months clink in collar and tie (all this out of a Borstal skiffle-ballad that my new mate made up, and I'd tell you it in full but it doesn't belong in this story), a 'tec, who'd never had as much in his pockets as that drainpipe had up its jackses. He was like Hitler in the face, right down to the paintbrush tash, except that being six-foot tall made him seem worse. But I straightened my shoulders to look into his illiterate blue eyes—like I always do with any copper.

Then he started asking me questions, and my mother from behind said: "He's never left that television set for the last three months, so you've got nowt on him, mate. You might as well look for somebody else, because you're wasting the rates you get out of my rent and the income-tax that comes out of my pay-packet standing there like that"—which was a laugh because she'd never paid either to my knowledge, and never would, I hoped.

"Well, you know where Papplewick Street is, don't you?" the copper asked me, taking no notice of mam.

"Ain't it off Alfreton Road?" I asked him back, helpful and bright.

"You know there's a baker's half-way down on the left-hand side, don't you?"

"Ain't it next door to a pub, then?" I wanted to know.

He answered me sharp: "No, it bloody well ain't." Coppers always lose their tempers as quick as this, and more often than not they gain nothing by it. "Then I don't know it," I told him, saved by the bell.

He slid his big boot round and round on the doorstep. "Where were you last Friday night?" Back in the ring, but this was worse than a boxing match.

I didn't like him trying to accuse me of something he wasn't sure I'd done. "Was I at that baker's you mentioned? Or in the pub next door?"

"You'll get five years in Borstal if you don't give me a straight answer," he said, unbuttoning his mac even though it was cold where he was standing.

"I was glued to the telly, like mam says," I swore blind. But he went on and on with his loony questions: "Have you got a television?"

The things he asked wouldn't have taken in a kid of two, and what else could I say to the last one except: "Has the aerial fell down? Or would you like to come in and see it?"

He was liking me even less for saying that. "We know you weren't listening to the television set last Friday, and so do you, don't you?"

"P'raps not, but I was *looking* at it, because sometimes we turn the sound down for a bit of fun." I could hear mam laughing from the kitchen, and I hoped Mike's mam was doing the same if the cops had gone to him as well.

"We know you weren't in the house," he said, starting up again, cranking himself with the handle. They always say "We" "We," never "I" "I"—as if they feel braver and righter knowing there's a lot of them against only one.

"I've got witnesses," I said to him. "Mam for one. Her fancy-man, for two. Ain't that enough? I can get you a dozen more, or thirteen altogether, if it was a baker's that got robbed."

"I don't want no lies," he said, not catching on about the baker's dozen. Where do they scrape cops up from anyway? "All I want is to get from you where you put that money."

Don't get mad, I kept saying to myself, don't get mad —hearing mam setting out cups and saucers and putting the pan on the stove for bacon. I stood back and waved him inside like I was a butler. "Come and search the house. If you've got a warrant."

"Listen, my lad," he said, like the dirty bullying jumped-up bastard he was, "I don't want too much of your lip, because if we get you down to the Guildhall you'll get a few bruises and black-eyes for your trouble." And I knew he wasn't kidding either, because I'd heard about all them sort of tricks. I hoped one day though that him and all his pals would be the ones to get the black-eyes and kicks; you never knew. It might come sooner than anybody thinks, like in Hungary. "Tell me where the money is, and I'll get you off with probation."

"What money?" I asked him, because I'd heard that one before as well.

"You know what money."

"Do I look as though I'd know owt about money?" I said, pushing my fist through a hole in my shirt.

"The money that was pinched, that you know all about," he said. "You can't trick me, so it's no use trying."

"Was it three-and-eightpence ha'penny?" I asked.

"You thieving young bastard. We'll teach you to steal money that doesn't belong to you."

I turned my head around: "Mam," I called out, "get my lawyer on the blower, will you?"

"Clever, aren't you?" he said in a very unfriendly way, "but we won't rest until we clear all this up."

"Look," I pleaded, as if about to sob my socks off because he'd got me wrong, "it's all very well us talking like this, it's like a game almost, but I wish you'd tell me what it's all about, because honest-to-God I've just got out of bed and here you are at the door talking about me having pinched a lot of money, money that I don't know anything about."

He swung around now as if he'd trapped me, though I couldn't see why he might think so. "Who said anything about money? I didn't. What made you bring money into this little talk we're having?"

"It's you," I answered, thinking he was going barmy and about to start foaming at the chops, "you've got money on the brain, like all policemen. Baker's shops as well."

He screwed his face up. "I want an answer from you: where's that money?"

But I was getting fed-up with all this. "I'll do a deal."

Judging by his flash-bulb face he thought he was suddenly on to a good thing. "What sort of a deal?"

So I told him: "I'll give you all the money I've got, one and fourpence ha'penny, if you stop this third-degree and let me go in and get my breakfast. Honest, I'm clambed to death. I ain't had a bite since yesterday. Can't you hear my guts rollin'?"

His jaw dropped, but on he went, pumping me for another half hour. A routine check-up, as they say on the pictures. But I knew I was winning on points.

Then he left, but came back in the afternoon to search the house. He didn't find a thing, not a French farthing. He asked me questions again and I didn't tell him anything except lies, lies, lies, because I can go on doing that forever without batting an eyelid. He'd got nothing on me and we both of us knew it, otherwise I'd have been down at the Guildhall in no time, but he kept on keeping on because I'd been in a Remand Home for a high-wall job before; and Mike was put through the same mill because all the local cops knew he was my best pal.

When it got dark me and Mike were in our parlour with a low light on and the telly off, Mike taking it easy in the rocking chair and me slouched out on the settee, both of us puffing a packet of Woods. With the door bolted and curtains drawn we talked about the dough we'd crammed up the drainpipe. Mike thought we should take it out and both of us do a bunk to Skegness or Cleethorpes for a good time in the arcades, living like lords in a boarding house near the pier, then at least we'd both have had a big beano before getting sent down.

"Listen, you daft bleeder," I said, "we aren't going to get caught at all, *and* we'll have a good time, later." We were so clever we didn't even go out to the pictures, though we wanted to.

In the morning old Hitler-face questioned me again, with one of his pals this time, and the next day they came, trying as hard as they could to get something out of me, but I didn't budge an inch. I know I'm showing off when I say this, but in me he'd met his match, and I'd never give in to questions no matter how long it was kept up. They searched the house a couple of times as well, which made me think they thought they really had something to go by, but I know now that they hadn't, and that it was all buck-shee speculation. They turned the house upside down and inside out like an old sock, went from top to bottom and front to back but naturally didn't find a thing. The copper even poked his face up the front-room chimney (that hadn't been used or swept for years) and came down looking like Al Jolson so that he had to swill himself clean at the scullery sink. They kept tapping and pottering around the big aspidistra plant that grandma had left to mam, lifting it up from the table to look under the cloth, putting it aside so's they could move the table and get at the boards under the rug—but the big headed stupid ignorant bastards never once thought of emptying the soil out of the plant pot, where they'd have found the crumpled-up money-box that we'd buried the night we did the job. I suppose it's still there, now I think about it, and I suppose mam wonders now and again why the plant don't prosper like it used to—as if it could with a fistful of thick black tin lapped around its guts.

The last time he knocked at our door was one wet morning at five minutes to nine and I was sleep-logged in my crumby bed as usual. Mam had gone to work that day so I shouted for him to hold on a bit, and then went down to see who it was. There he stood, six-feet tall and sopping wet, and for the first time in my life I did a spiteful thing I'll never forgive myself for: I didn't ask him to come in out of the rain, because I wanted him to get double pneumonia and die. I suppose he could have pushed by me and come in if he'd wanted, but maybe he'd got used to asking questions on the doorstep and didn't want to be put off by changing his ground even though it was raining. Not that I don't like being spiteful because of any barmy principle I've got, but this bit of spite, as it turned out, did me no good at all. I should have treated him as a brother I hadn't seen for twenty years and dragged him in for a cup of tea and a fag, told him about the picture I hadn't seen the night before, asked him how his wife was after her operation and whether they'd shaved her moustache off to make it, and then sent him happy and satisfied out by the front door. But no, I thought, let's see what he's got to say for himself now.

He stood a little to one side of the door, either because it was less wet there, or because he wanted to see me from a different angle, perhaps having found it monotonous to watch a bloke's face always telling lies from the same side. "You've been identified," he said, twitching raindrops from his tash. "A woman saw you and your mate yesterday and she swears blind you are the same chaps she saw going into that bakery."

I was dead sure he was still bluffing, because Mike and I hadn't even seen each other the day before, but I looked worried. "She's a menace then to innocent people, whoever she is, because the only bakery I've been in lately is the one up our street to get some cut-bread on tick for mam."

He didn't bite on this. "So now I want to know where the money is"—as if I hadn't answered him at all.

"I think mam took it to work this morning to get herself some tea in the canteen." Rain was splashing down so hard I thought he'd get washed away if he didn't come inside. But I wasn't much bothered, and went on: "I remember I put it in the telly-vase last night—it was my only one-and-three and I was saving it for a packet of tips this morning—and I nearly had a jibbering black fit just now when I saw it had gone. I was reckoning on it for getting me through today because I don't think life's worth living without a fag, do you?"

I was getting into my stride and began to feel good, twigging that this would be my last pack of lies, and that if I kept it up for long enough this time I'd have the bastards beat: Mike and me would be off to the coast in a few weeks time having the fun of our lives, playing at penny football and latching on to a couple of tarts that would give us all they were good for. "And this weather's no good for picking-up fag-ends in the street," I said, "because they'd be sopping wet. Course, I know you could dry 'em out near the fire, but it don't taste the same you know, all said and done. Rainwater does summat to 'em that don't bear thinkin' about: it turns 'em back into hoss-tods without the taste though."

I began to wonder, at the back of my brainless eyes, why old copper-lugs didn't pull me up sharp and say he hadn't got time to listen to all this, but he wasn't looking at me anymore, and all my thoughts about Skegness went bursting to smithereens in my sludgy loaf. I could have dropped into the earth when I saw what he'd fixed his eyes on.

He was looking at *it,* an ever-loving fiver, and I could only jabber: "The one thing is to have some real fags be-

cause new hoss-tods is always better than stuff that's
been rained on and dried, and I know how you feel
about not being able to find money because one-and-
three's one-and-three in anybody's pocket, and naturally
if I see it knocking around I'll get you on the blower to-
morrow straightaway and tell you where you can find it."

I thought I'd go down in a fit: three green-backs
as well had been washed down by the water, and more
were following, lying flat at first after their fall, then
getting tilted at the corners by wind and rainspots as if
they were alive and wanted to get back into the dry snug
drain pipe out of the terrible weather, and you can't imagine how I wished they'd be able to. Old Hitler-face didn't
know what to make of it but just kept staring down and
down, and I thought I'd better keep on talking, though
I knew it wasn't much good now.

"It's a fact, I know, that money's hard to come by and
half-crowns don't get found on bus seats or in dustbins,
and I didn't see any in bed last night because I'd 'ave
known about it, wouldn't I? You can't sleep with things
like that in the bed because they're too hard, and anyway
at first they're. . ." It took Hitler-boy a long time to
catch on; they were beginning to spread over the yard a
bit, reinforced by the third colour of a ten-bob note, before his hand clamped itself on to my shoulder.

III

The pop-eyed potbellied governor said to a pop-eyed
potbellied Member of Parliament who sat next to his
pop-eyed potbellied whore of a wife that I was his only
hope for getting the Borstal Blue Ribbon Prize Cup
For Long-Distance Cross-Country Running (all England),

which I was, and it set me laughing to myself inside,
and I didn't say a word to any potbellied pop-eyed bastard that might give them real hope, though I knew the
governor anyway took my quietness to mean he'd got that
cup already stuck on the bookshelf in his office among the
few other mildewed trophies.

"He might take up running in a sort of professional
way when he gets out," and it wasn't until he'd said this
and I'd heard it with my own flap-tabs that I realized it
might be possible to do such a thing, run for money, trot
for wages on piece work at a bob a puff rising bit by bit
to a guinca a gasp and retiring through old age at thirty-
two because of lace-curtain lungs, a football heart, and
legs like varicose beanstalks. But I'd have a wife and
car and get my grinning long-distance clock in the papers
and have a smashing secretary to answer piles of letters
sent by tarts who'd mob me when they saw who I was as
I pushed my way into Woolworth's for a packet of razor
blades and a cup of tea. It was something to think about all
right, and sure enough the governor knew he'd got me
when he said, turning to me as if I would at any rate have
to be consulted about it all: "How does this matter strike
you, then, Smith, my lad?"

A line of potbellied pop-eyes gleamed at me and a
row of goldfish mouths opened and wiggled gold teeth
at me, so I gave them the answer they wanted because I'd
hold my trump card until later. "It'd suit me fine, sir,"
I said.

"Good lad. Good show. Right spirit. Splendid."

"Well," the governor said, "get that cup for us today
and I'll do all I can for you. I'll get you trained so that
you whack every man in the Free World." And I
had a picture in my brain of me running and beating

everybody in the world, leaving them all behind until
only I was trot-trotting across a big wide moor alone, doing a marvellous speed as I ripped between boulders
and reed-clumps, when suddenly: CRACK! CRACK!
—bullets that can go faster than any man running, coming
from a copper's rifle planted in a tree, winged me and
split my gizzard in spite of my perfect running, and down
I fell.

The potbellies expected me to say something else.
"Thank you, sir," I said.

Told to go, I trotted down the pavilion steps, out on to
the field because the big cross-country was about to begin and the two entries from Gunthorpe had fixed
themselves early at the starting line and were ready to
move off like white kangaroos. The sports ground looked
a treat: with big tea-tents all round and flags flying
and seats for families—empty because no mam or dad
had known what opening day meant—and boys still
running heats for the hundred yards, and lords and ladies
walking from stall to stall, and the Borstal Boys Brass
Band in blue uniforms; and up on the stands the brown
jackets of Hucknall as well as our own grey blazers, and
then the Gunthorpe lot with shirt sleeves rolled. The blue
sky was full of sunshine and it couldn't have been a better day, and all of the big show was like something out of
Ivanhoe that we'd seen on the pictures a few days before.

"Come on, Smith," Roach the sports master called
to me, "we don't want you to be late for the big race, eh?
Although I dare say you'd catch them up if you were."
The others cat-called and grunted at this, but I took no
notice and placed myself between Gunthorpe and one of
the Aylesham trusties, dropped on my knees and plucked
a few grass blades to suck on the way round. So the big

race it was, for them, watching from the grandstand under a fluttering Union Jack, a race for the governor, that he had been waiting for, and I hoped he and all the rest of his pop-eyed gang were busy placing big bets on me, hundred to one to win, all the money they had in their pockets, all the wages they were going to get for the next five years, and the more they placed the happier I'd be. Because here was a dead cert going to die on the big name they'd built for him, going to go down dying with laughter whether it choked him or not. My knees felt the cool soil pressing into them, and out of my eye's corner I saw Roach lift his hand. The Gunthorpe boy twitched before the signal was given; somebody cheered too soon; Medway bent forward; then the gun went, and I was away.

We went once around the field and then along a half-mile drive of elms, being cheered all the way, and I seemed to feel I was in the lead as we went out by the gate and into the lane, though I wasn't interested enough to find out. The five-mile course was marked by splashes of whitewash gleaming on gateposts and trunks and stiles and stones, and a boy with a waterbottle and bandage-box stood every half-mile waiting for those that dropped out or fainted. Over the first stile, without trying, I was still nearly in the lead but one; and if any of you want tips about running, never be in a hurry, and never let any of the other runners know you are in a hurry even if you are. You can always overtake on long-distance running without letting the others smell the hurry in you; and when you've used your craft like this to reach the two or three up front then you can do a big dash later that puts everybody else's hurry in the shade because you've not had to make haste up till then. I ran to a steady jog-trot rhythm,

and soon it was so smooth that I forgot I was running, and
I was hardly able to know that my legs were lifting and
falling and my arms going in and out, and my lungs didn't
seem to be working at all, and my heart stopped that wicked
thumping I always get at the beginning of a run. Because you see I never race at all; I just run, and somehow I
know that if I forget I'm racing and only jog-trot along
until I don't know I'm running I always win the race.
For when my eyes recognize that I'm getting near the end
of the course—by seeing a stile or cottage corner—I put on
a spurt, and such a fast big spurt it is because I feel that up
till then I haven't been running and that I've used up no
energy at all. And I've been able to do this because I've been
thinking; and I wonder if I'm the only one in the running
business with this system of forgetting that I'm running because I'm too busy thinking; and I wonder if any of the
other lads are on to the same lark, though I know for a fact
that they aren't. Off like the wind along the cobbled footpath and rutted lane, smoother than the flat grass track on
the field and better for thinking because it's not too smooth,
and I was in my element that afternoon knowing that nobody
could beat me at running but intending to beat myself before the day was over. For when the governor talked to me of
being honest when I first came in he didn't know what
the word meant or he wouldn't have had me here in this
race, trotting along in shimmy and shorts and sunshine.
He'd have had me where I'd have had him if I'd been in
his place: in a quarry breaking rocks until he broke his
back. At least old Hitler-face the plain-clothes dick was
honester than the governor, because he at any rate had had
it in for me and I for him, and when my case was coming up in court a copper knocked at our front door at
four o'clock in the morning and got my mother out of bed

when she was paralytic tired, reminding her she had to be in court at dead on half past nine. It was the finest bit of spite I've ever heard of, but I would call it honest, the same as my mam's words were honest when she really told that copper what she thought of him and called him all the dirty names she'd ever heard of, which took her half an hour and woke the terrace up.

I trotted on along the edge of a field bordered by the sunken lane, smelling green grass and honeysuckle, and I felt as though I came from a long line of whippets trained to run on two legs, only I couldn't see a toy rabbit in front and there wasn't a collier's cosh behind to make me keep up the pace. I passed the Gunthorpe runner whose shimmy was already black with sweat and I could just see the corner of the fenced-up copse in front where the only man I had to pass to win the race was going all out to gain the half-way mark. Then he turned into a tongue of trees and bushes where I couldn't see him anymore, and I couldn't see anybody, and I knew what the loneliness of the long-distance runner running across country felt like, realizing that as far as I was concerned this feeling was the only honesty and realness there was in the world and I knowing it would be no different ever, no matter what I felt at odd times, and no matter what anybody else tried to tell me. The runner behind me must have been a long way off because it was so quiet, and there was even less noise and movement than there had been at five o'clock of a frosty winter morning. It was hard to understand, and all I knew was that you had to run, run, run, without knowing why you were running, but on you went through fields you didn't understand and into woods that made you afraid, over hills without knowing you'd been up and down, and shooting across streams that would have cut the heart out of you had you fallen into them. And the winning post was no end to it, even though crowds might be cheering you in, because on you had to go before you got your breath back, and the only time you stopped really was when you tripped over a tree trunk and broke your neck or fell into a disused well and stayed dead in the darkness forever. So I thought: they aren't going to get me on this racing lark, this running and trying to win, this jog-trotting for a bit of blue ribbon, because it's not the way to go on at all, though they swear blind that it is. You should think about nobody and go your own way, not on a course marked out for you by people holding mugs of water and bottles of iodine in case you fall and cut yourself so that they can pick you up—even if you want to stay where you are—and get you moving again.

On I went, out of the wood, passing the man leading without knowing I was going to do so. Flip-flap, flip-flap, jog-trot, jog-trot, crunchslap-crunchslap, across the middle of a broad field again, rhythmically running in my greyhound effortless fashion, knowing I had won the race though it wasn't half over, won it if I wanted it, could go on for ten or fifteen or twenty miles if I had to and drop dead at the finish of it, which would be the same, in the end, as living an honest life like the governor wanted me to. It amounted to: win the race and be honest, and on trot-trotting I went, having the time of my life, loving my progress because it did me good and set me thinking which by now I liked to do, but not caring at all when I remembered that I had to win this race as well as run it. One of the two, I had to win the race or run it, and I knew I could do both because my legs had carried me well in front—now coming to the short cut down the bramble bank and over the sunken road—and would carry me further because they seemed made of electric cable and easily alive to keep on slapping at those ruts and roots, but I'm not going to win because the only way I'd see I came in first would be if winning meant that I was going to escape the coppers after doing the biggest bank job of my life, but winning means the exact opposite, no matter how they try to kill or kid me, means running right into their white-gloved wall-barred hands and grinning mugs and staying there for the rest of my natural long life of stone-breaking anyway, but stone-breaking in the way I want to do it and not in the way they tell me.

Another honest thought that comes is that I could swing left at the next hedge of the field, and under its cover beat my slow retreat away from the sports ground winning post. I could do three or six or a dozen miles across the turf like this and cut a few main roads behind me so's they'd never know which one I'd taken; and maybe on the last one when it got dark I could thumb a lorry-lift and get a free ride north with somebody who might not give me away. But no, I said I wasn't daft didn't I? I won't pull out with only six months left, and besides there's nothing I want to dodge and run away from; I only want a bit of my own back on the In-laws and Potbellies by letting them sit up there on their big posh seats and watch me lose this race, though as sure as God made me I know that when I do lose I'll get the dirtiest crap and kitchen jobs in the months to go before my time is up. I won't be worth a threpp'ny-bit to anybody here, which will be all the thanks I get for being honest in the only way I know. For when the governor told me to be honest it was meant to be in his way not mine, and if I kept on being honest in the way he wanted and won my race for him he'd see I got the cushiest six months still left to run; but in my own way, well, it's not allowed, and if I find a way of doing it such as I've got now then I'll get what-for in every mean trick he can set his mind to. And if you look at it in my way, who can blame him? For this is war—and ain't I said so?—and when I hit him in the only place he knows he'll be sure to get his own back on me for not collaring that cup when his heart's been set for ages on seeing himself standing up at the end of the afternoon to clap me on the back as I take the cup from Lord Earwig or some such chinless wonder with a name like that. And so I'll hit him where it hurts a lot, and he'll do all he can to get his own back, tit for tat, though I'll enjoy it most because I'm hitting first, and because I planned it longer. I don't know why I think these thoughts are better than any I've ever had, but I do, and I don't care why. I suppose it took me a long time to get going on all this because I've had no time and peace in all my bandit life, and now my thoughts are coming pat and the only trouble is I often can't stop, even when my brain feels as if it's got cramp, frostbite and creeping paralysis all rolled into one and I have to give it a rest by slap-dashing down through the brambles of the sunken lane. And all this is another uppercut I'm getting in first at people like the governor, to show how—if I can—his races are never won even though some bloke always comes unknowingly in first, how in the end the governor is going to be doomed while blokes like me will take the pickings of his roasted bones and dance like maniacs around his Borstal's ruins. And so this story's like the race and once again I won't bring off a winner to suit the governor; no, I'm being honest like he told me to, without him knowing what he means, though I don't suppose he'll ever come in with a story of his own, even if he reads this one of mine and knows who I'm talking about.

I've just come up out of the sunken lane, kneed and elbowed, thumped and bramble-scratched, and the race is two-thirds over, and a voice is going like a wireless in my mind saying that when you've had enough of feeling good like the first man on earth of a frosty morning, and you've known how it is to be taken bad like the last man on earth on a summer's afternoon, then you get at last to being like the only man on earth and don't give a bogger about either good or bad, but just trot on with your slippers slapping the good dry soil that at least would never do you a bad turn. Now the words are like coming from a crystal-set that's broken down, and something's happening inside the shell-case of my guts that bothers me and I don't know why or what to blame it on, a grinding near my ticker as though a bag of rusty screws is loose inside me and I shake them up every time I trot forward. Now and again I break my rhythm to feel my left shoulder-blade by swinging a right hand across my chest as if to rub the knife away that has somehow got stuck there. But I know it's nothing to bother about, that more likely it's caused by too much thinking that now and again I take for worry. For sometimes I'm the greatest worrier in the world I think (as you twigged I'll bet from me having got this story out) which is funny anyway because my mam don't know the meaning of the word so I don't take after her; though dad had a hard time of worry all his life up to when he filled his bedroom with hot blood and kicked the bucket that morning when nobody was in the house. I'll never forget it, straight I won't, because I was the one that found him and I often wished I hadn't. Back from a session on the fruit-machines at the fish-and-chip shop, jingling my three-lemon loot to a nail-dead house, as soon as I got in I knew something was wrong, stood leaning my head against the cold mirror above the mantelpiece trying not to open my eyes and see my stone-cold clock—because I knew I'd gone as white as a piece of chalk since coming in as if I'd been got at by a Dracula-vampire and even my penny-pocket winnings kept quiet on purpose.

Gunthorpe nearly caught me up. Birds were singing from the briar hedge, and a couple of thrushies flew like lightning into some thorny bushes. Corn had grown high in the next field and would be cut down soon with scythes and mowers; but I never wanted to notice much while running in case it put me off my stroke, so by the haystack I decided to leave it all behind and put on such a spurt, in spite of nails in my guts, that before long I'd left both Gunthorpe and the birds a good way off; I wasn't far now from going into that last mile and a half like a knife through margarine, but the quietness I suddenly trotted into between two pickets was like opening my eyes underwater and looking at the pebbles on a stream bottom, reminding me again of going back that morning to the house in which my old man had croaked, which is funny because I hadn't thought about it at all since it happened and even then I didn't brood much on it. I wonder why? I suppose that since I started to think on these long-distance runs I'm liable to have anything crop up and pester at my tripes and innards, and now that I see my bloody dad behind each grass-blade in my barmy runner-brain I'm not so sure I like to think and that it's such a good thing after all. I choke my phlegm and keep on running anyway and curse the Borstal-builders and their athletics—flappity-flap, slop-slop, crunchslap-crunchslap-crunchslap—who've maybe got their own back on me from the bright beginning by sliding magic-lantern slides into my head that never stood a chance before. Only if I take whatever comes like this in my runner's stride can I keep on keeping on like my old self and beat them back; and now I've thought on this far I know I'll win, in the crunchslap end. So anyway after a bit I went upstairs one step at a time not thinking anything about how I should find dad and what I'd do when I did. But now I'm making up for it by going over the rotten life mam led him ever since I can remember, knocking-on with different men even when he was alive and fit and she not caring whether he knew it or not, and most of the time he wasn't so blind as she thought and cursed and roared and threatened to punch her tab, and I had to stand up to stop him even though I knew she deserved it. What a life for all of us. Well, I'm not grumbling, because if I did I might just as well win this bleeding race, which I'm not going to do, though if I don't lose speed I'll win it before I know where I am, and then where would I be?

Now I can hear the sportsground noise and music as I head back for the flags and the lead-in drive, the fresh new feel of underfoot gravel going against the iron muscles of my legs. I'm nowhere near puffed despite that bag of nails that rattles as much as ever, and I can still give a big last leap like gale-force wind if I want to, but everything is under control and I know now that there ain't another long-distance cross-country running runner in England to touch my speed and style. Our doddering bastard of a governor, our half-dead gangrened gaffer is hollow like an empty petrol drum, and he wants me and my running life to give him glory, to put in him blood and throbbing veins he never had, wants his potbellied pals to be his witnesses as I gasp and stagger up to his winning post so's he can say: "My Borstal gets that cup, you see. I win my bet, because it pays to be honest and try to gain the prizes I offer to my lads, and they know it, have known it all along. They'll always be honest now, because I made them so." And his pals will think: "He trains his lads to live right, after all; he deserves a medal but we'll get him made a Sir"—and at this very moment as the birds come back to whistling I can tell myself I'll never care a sod what any of the chinless spineless In-laws think or say. They've seen me and they're cheering now and loudspeakers set around the field like elephant's ears are spreading out the big news that I'm well in the lead, and can't do anything else but stay there. But I'm still thinking of the Out-law death my dad died, telling the doctors to scat from the house when they wanted him to finish up in hospital (like a bleeding guinea-pig, he raved at them). He got up in bed to throw them out and even followed them down the stairs in his shirt though he was no more than skin and stick. They tried to tell him he'd want some drugs but he didn't fall for it, and only took the pain-killer that mam and I got from a herb-seller in the next street. It's not till now that I know what guts he had, and when I went into the room that morning he was lying on his stomach with the clothes thrown back, looking like a skinned rabbit, his grey head resting just on the edge of the bed, and on the floor must have been all the blood he'd had in his body, right from his toenails up, for nearly all of the lino and carpet was covered in it, thin and pink.

And down the drive I went, carrying a heart blocked up like Boulder Dam across my arteries, the nail-bag clamped down tighter and tighter as though in a woodwork vice, yet with my feet like birdwings and arms like talons ready to fly across the field except that I didn't want to give anybody that much of a show, or win the race by accident. I smell the hot dry day now as I run towards the end, passing a mountain-heap of grass emptied from cans hooked on to the fronts of lawnmowers pushed by my pals; I rip a piece of tree-bark with my fingers and stuff it in my mouth, chewing wood and dust and maybe maggots as I run until I'm nearly sick, yet swallowing what I can of it just the same because a little birdie whistled to me that I've got to go on living for at least a bloody sight longer yet but that for six months I'm not going to smell that grass or taste that dusty bark or trot this lovely path. I hate to have to say this but something bloody-well made me cry, and crying is a thing I haven't bloody-well done since I was a kid of two or three. Because I'm slowing down now for Gunthorpe to catch me up, and I'm doing it in a place just where the drive turns in to the sportsfield—where they can see what I'm doing, especially the governor and his gang from the grandstand, and I'm going so slow I'm almost marking time. Those on the nearest seats haven't caught on yet to what's happening and are still cheering like mad ready for when I make that mark, and I keep on wondering when the bleeding hell Gunthorpe behind me is going to nip by on to the field because I can't hold this up all day, and I think Oh Christ it's just my rotten luck that Gunthorpe's dropped out and that I'll be here for half an hour before the next bloke comes up, but even so, I say, I won't budge, I won't go for that last hundred yards if I have to sit down cross-legged on the grass and have the governor and his chinless wonders pick me up and carry me there, which is against their rules so you can bet they'd never do it because they're not clever enough to break the rules— like I would be in their place—even though they are their own. No, I'll show him what honesty means if it's the last thing I do, though I'm sure he'll never understand because if he and all them like him did it'd mean they'd be on my side which is impossible. By God I'll stick this out like my dad stuck out his pain and kicked them doctors down the stairs: if he had guts for that then I've got guts for this and here I stay waiting for Gunthorpe or Aylesham to bash that turf and go right slap-up against that bit of clothes-line stretched across the winning post. As for me, the only time I'll hit that clothes-line will be when I'm dead and a comfortable coffin's been got ready on the other side. Until then I'm a long-distance runner, crossing country all on my own no matter how bad it feels.

The Essex boys were shouting themselves blue in the face telling me to get a move on, waving their arms, standing up and making as if to run at that rope themselves because they were only a few yards to the side of it. You cranky lot, I thought, stuck at that winning post, and yet I knew they didn't mean what they were shouting, were really on my side and always would be, not able to keep their maulers to themselves, in and out of copshops and clink. And there they were now having the time of their lives letting themselves go in cheering me which made the governor think they were heart and soul on his side when he wouldn't have thought any such thing if he'd had a grain of sense. And I could hear the lords and ladies now from the grandstand, and could see them standing up to wave me in: "Run!" they were shouting in their posh voices. "Run!" But I was deaf, daft and blind, and stood where I was, still tasting the bark in my mouth and still blubbing like a baby, blubbing now out of gladness that I'd got them beat at last.

Because I heard a roar and saw the Gunthorpe gang

throwing their coats up in the air and I felt the pat-pat of feet on the drive behind me getting closer and closer and suddenly a smell of sweat and a pair of lungs on their last gasp passed me by and went swinging on towards that rope, all shagged out and rocking from side to side, grunting like a Zulu that didn't know any better, like the ghost of me at ninety when I'm heading for that fat upholstered coffin. I could have cheered him myself: "Go on, go on, get cracking. Knot yourself up on that piece of tape." But he was already there, and so I went on, trot-trotting after him until I got to the rope, and collapsed, with a murderous sounding roar going up through my ears while I was still on the wrong side of it.

It's about time to stop; though don't think I'm not still running, because I am, one way or another. The governor at Borstal proved me right; he didn't respect my honesty at all; not that I expected him to, or tried to explain it to him, but if he's supposed to be educated then he should have more or less twigged it. He got his own back right enough, or thought he did, because he had me carting dustbins about every morning from the big full-working kitchen to the garden-bottoms where I had to empty them; and in the afternoon I spread out slops over spuds and carrots growing in the allotments. In the evenings I scrubbed floors, miles and miles of them. But it wasn't a bad life for six months, which was another thing he could never understand and would have made it grimmer if he could, and it was worth it when I look back on it, considering all the thinking I did, and the fact that the boys caught on to me losing the race on purpose and never had enough good words to say about me, or curses to throw out (to themselves) at the governor.

The work didn't break me; if anything it made me

stronger in many ways, and the governor knew, when I left, that his spite had got him nowhere. For since leaving Borstal they tried to get me in the army, but I didn't pass the medical and I'll tell you why. No sooner was I out, after that final run and six-months hard, than I went down with pleurisy, which means as far as I am concerned that I lost the governor's race all right, and won my own twice over, because I know for certain that if I hadn't raced my race I wouldn't have got this pleurisy, which keeps me out of khaki but doesn't stop me doing the sort of work my itchy fingers want to do.

I'm out now and the heat's switched on again, but the rats haven't got me for the last big thing I pulled. I counted six hundred and twenty-eight pounds and am still living off it because I did the job all on my own, and after it I had the peace to write all this, and it'll be money enough to keep me going until I finish my plans for doing an even bigger snatch, something up my sleeve I wouldn't tell to a living soul. I worked out my systems and hiding-places while pushing scrubbing-brushes around them Borstal floors, planned my outward life of innocence and honest work, yet at the same time grew perfect in the razor-edges of my craft for what I knew I had to do once free; and what I'll do again if netted by the poaching coppers.

In the meantime (as they say in one or two books I've read since, useless though because all of them ended on a winning post and didn't teach me a thing) I'm going to give this story to a pal of mine and tell him that if I do get captured again by the coppers he can try and get it put into a book or something, because I'd like to see the governor's face when he reads it, if he does, which I don't suppose he will; even if he did read it though I don't think he'd know what it was all about. And if I don't get caught the bloke I give this story to will never give me away; he's lived in our terrace for as long as I can remember, and he's my pal. That I do know.

James Baldwin

Sonny's Blues

I READ ABOUT IT IN THE PAPER, IN THE SUBWAY, ON MY way to work. I read it, and I couldn't believe it, and I read it again. Then perhaps I just stared at it, at the newsprint spelling out his name, spelling out the story. I stared at it in the swinging lights of the subway car, and in the faces and bodies of the people, and in my own face, trapped in the darkness which roared outside.

It was not to be believed and I kept telling myself that, as I walked from the subway station to the high school. And at the same time I couldn't doubt it. I was scared, scared for Sonny. He became real to me again. A great block of ice got settled in my belly and kept melting there slowly all day long, while I taught my classes algebra. It was a special kind of ice. It kept melting, sending trickles of ice water all up and down my veins, but it never got less. Sometimes it hardened and seemed to expand until I felt my guts were going to come spilling out or that I was going to choke or scream. This would always be at a moment when I was remembering some specific thing Sonny had once said or done.

When he was about as old as the boys in my classes his face had been bright and open, there was a lot of copper in it; and he'd had wonderfully direct brown eyes, and great gentleness and privacy. I wondered what he looked like now. He had been picked up, the evening before, in a raid on an apartment downtown, for peddling and using heroin.

I couldn't believe it: but what I mean by that is that I couldn't find any room for it anywhere inside me. I had kept it outside me for a long time. I hadn't wanted to know. I had had suspicions, but I didn't name them, I kept putting them away. I told myself that Sonny was wild, but he wasn't crazy. And he'd always been a good boy, he hadn't ever turned hard or evil or disrespectful, the way kids can, so quick, so quick, especially in Harlem. I didn't want to believe that I'd ever see my brother going down, coming to nothing, all that light in his face gone out, in the condition I'd already seen so many others. Yet it happened and here I was, talking about algebra to a lot of boys who might, every one of them for all I knew, be popping off needles every time they went to the head. Maybe it did more for them than algebra could.

I was sure that the first time Sonny had ever had horse, he couldn't have been much older than these boys were now. These boys, now, were living as we'd been living then, they were growing up with a rush and their heads bumped abruptly against the low ceiling of their actual possibilities. They were filled with rage. All they really knew were two darknesses, the darkness of their lives, which was now closing in on them, and the darkness of the movies, which had blinded them to that other darkness, and in which they now, vindictively, dreamed, at once more together than they were at any other time, and more alone.

When the last bell rang, the last class ended, I let out my breath. It seemed I'd been holding it for all that time. My clothes were wet—I may have looked as though I'd been sitting in a steam bath, all dressed up, all afternoon. I sat alone in the classroom a long time. I listened to the boys outside, downstairs, shouting and cursing and laugh-ing. Their laughter struck me for perhaps the first time. It was not the joyous laughter which—God knows why—one associates with children. It was mocking and insular, its intent to denigrate. It was disenchanted, and in this, also, lay the authority of their curses. Perhaps I was listen-ing to them because I was thinking about my brother and in them I heard my brother. And myself.

One boy was whistling a tune, at once very complicated and very simple, it seemed to be pouring out of him as though he were a bird, and it sounded very cool and moving through all that harsh, bright air, only just hold-ing its own through all those other sounds.

I stood up and walked over to the window and looked down into the courtyard. It was the beginning of the spring and the sap was rising in the boys. A teacher passed through them every now and again, quickly, as though he or she couldn't wait to get out of that courtyard, to get those boys out of their sight and off their minds. I started collecting my stuff. I thought I'd better get home and talk to Isabel.

The courtyard was almost deserted by the time I got downstairs. I saw this boy standing in the shadow of a doorway, looking just like Sonny. I almost called his name. Then I saw that it wasn't Sonny, but somebody we used to know, a boy from around our block. He'd been Sonny's friend. He'd never been mine, having been too young for me, and, anyway, I'd never liked him. And now, even though he was a grown-up man, he still hung around that block, still spent hours on the street corners, was always high and raggy. I used to run into him from time to time and he'd often work around to asking me for a quarter or fifty cents. He always had some real good excuse, too, and I always gave it to him, I don't know why.

But now, abruptly, I hated him. I couldn't stand the way he looked at me, partly like a dog, partly like a cunning child. I wanted to ask him what the hell he was doing in the school courtyard.

He sort of shuffled over to me, and he said, "I see you got the papers. So you already know about it."

"You mean about Sonny? Yes, I already know about it. How come they didn't get you?"

He grinned. It made him repulsive and it also brought to mind what he'd looked like as a kid. "I wasn't there; I stay away from them people."

"Good for you." I offered him a cigarette and I watched him through the smoke. "You come all the way down here just to tell me about Sonny?"

"That's right." He was sort of shaking his head and his eyes looked strange, as though they were about to cross. The bright sun deadened his damp dark brown skin and it made his eyes look yellow and showed up the dirt in his kinked hair. He smelled funky. I moved a little away from him and I said, "Well, thanks. But I already know about it and I got to get home."

"I'll walk you a little ways," he said. We started walking. There were a couple of kids still loitering in the courtyard and one of them said goodnight to me and looked strangely at the boy beside me.

"What're you going to do?" he asked me. "I mean, about Sonny?"

"Look. I haven't seen Sonny for over a year, I'm not sure I'm going to do anything. Anyway, what the hell *can* I do?"

"That's right," he said quickly, "ain't nothing you can do. Can't much help old Sonny no more, I guess."

It was what I was thinking and so it seemed to me he had no right to say it.

"I'm surprised at Sonny, though," he went on—he had a funny way of talking, he looked straight ahead as though he were talking to himself—"I thought Sonny was a smart boy, I thought he was too smart to get hung."

"I guess he thought so too," I said sharply, "and that's how he got hung. And how about you? You're pretty goddamn smart, I bet."

Then he looked directly at me, just for a minute. "I ain't smart," he said. "If I was smart, I'd have reached for a pistol a long time ago."

"Look. Don't tell *me* your sad story, if it was up to me, I'd give you one." Then I felt guilty—guilty, probably, for never having supposed that the poor bastard *had* a story of his own, much less a sad one, and I asked, quickly, "What's going to happen to him now?"

He didn't answer this. He was off by himself some place. "Funny thing," he said, and from his tone we might have been discussing the quickest way to get to Brooklyn, "when I saw the papers this morning, the first thing I asked myself was if I had anything to do with it. I felt sort of responsible."

I began to listen more carefully. The subway station was on the corner, just before us, and I stopped. He stopped, too. We were in front of a bar and he ducked slightly, peering in, but whoever he was looking for didn't seem to be there. The juke box was blasting away with something black and bouncy and I half watched the barmaid as she danced her way from the juke box to her place behind the bar. And I watched her face as she laughingly responded to something someone said to her, still keeping time to the music. When she smiled one saw the little girl, one sensed the doomed, still-struggling woman beneath the battered face of the semi-whore.

"I never *give* Sonny nothing," the boy said finally, "but a long time ago I come to school high and Sonny asked me how it felt." He paused, I couldn't bear to watch him, I watched the barmaid, and I listened to the music which seemed to be causing the pavement to shake. "I told him it felt great." The music stopped, the barmaid paused and watched the juke box until the music began again. "It did."

All this was carrying me some place I didn't want to go. I certainly didn't want to know how it felt. It filled everything, the people, the houses, the music, the dark, quicksilver barmaid, with menace; and this menace was their reality.

"What's going to happen to him now?" I asked again.

"They'll send him away some place and they'll try to cure him." He shook his head. "Maybe he'll even think he's kicked the habit. Then they'll let him loose"—he gestured, throwing his cigarette into the gutter. "That's all."

"What do you mean, that's *all*?"

But I knew what he meant.

"I *mean*, that's *all*." He turned his head and looked at me, pulling down the corners of his mouth. "Don't you know what I mean?" he asked, softly.

"How the hell *would* I know what you mean?" I almost whispered it, I don't know why.

"That's right," he said to the air, "how would *he* know what I mean?" He turned toward me again, patient and calm, and yet I somehow felt him shaking, shaking as though he were going to fall apart. I felt that ice in my guts again, the dread I'd felt all afternoon; and again I watched the barmaid, moving about the bar, washing glasses, and singing. "Listen. They'll let him out and then it'll just start all over again. That's what I mean."

"You mean—they'll let him out. And then he'll just start working his way back in again. You mean he'll never kick the habit. Is that what you mean?"

"That's right," he said, cheerfully. "*You* see what I mean."

"Tell me," I said at last, "why does he want to die? He must want to die, he's killing himself, why does he want to die?"

He looked at me in surprise. He licked his lips. "He don't want to die. He wants to live. Don't nobody want to die, ever."

Then I wanted to ask him—too many things. He could not have answered, or if he had, I could not have borne the answers. I started walking. "Well, I guess it's none of my business."

"It's going to be rough on old Sonny," he said. We reached the subway station. "This is your station?" he asked. I nodded. I took one step down. "Damn!" he said, suddenly. I looked up at him. He grinned again. "Damn it if I didn't leave all my money home. You ain't got a dollar on you, have you? Just for a couple of days, is all."

All at once something inside gave and threatened to come pouring out of me. I didn't hate him any more. I felt that in another moment I'd start crying like a child.

"Sure," I said. "Don't sweat." I looked in my wallet and didn't have a dollar, I only had a five. "Here," I said. "That hold you?"

He didn't look at it—he didn't want to look at it. A terrible closed look came over his face, as though he were keeping the number on the bill a secret from him and me. "Thanks," he said, and now he was dying to see me go. "Don't worry about Sonny. Maybe I'll write him or something."

"Sure," I said. "You do that. So long."

"Be seeing you," he said. I went on down the steps.

And I didn't write Sonny or send him anything for a long time. When I finally did, it was just after my little girl died, he wrote me back a letter which made me feel like a bastard.

Here's what he said:

Dear brother,

You don't know how much I needed to hear from you. I wanted to write you many a time but I dug how much I must have hurt you and so I didn't write. But now I feel like a man who's been trying to climb up out of some deep, real deep and funky hole and just saw the sun up there, outside. I got to get outside.

I can't tell you much about how I got here. I mean I don't know how to tell you. I guess I was afraid of something or I was trying to escape from something and you know I have never been very strong in the head (smile). I'm glad Mama and Daddy are dead and can't see what's happened to their son and I swear if I'd known what I was doing I would never have hurt you so, you and a lot of other fine people who were nice to me and who believed in me.

I don't want you to think it had anything to do with me being a musician. It's more than that. Or maybe less than that. I can't get anything straight in my head down here and I try not to think about what's going to happen to me when I get outside again. Sometime I think I'm going to flip and *never* get outside and sometime I think I'll come straight back. I tell you one thing, though, I'd rather blow my brains out than go through this again. But that's what they all say, so they tell me. If I tell you when I'm coming to New York and if you could meet me, I sure would appreciate it. Give my love to Isabel and the kids and I was sure sorry to hear about little Gracie. I wish I could be like Mama and say the Lord's will be done, but I don't know it seems to me that trouble is the one thing that never does get stopped and I don't know what good it does to blame it on the Lord. But maybe it does some good if you believe it.

Your brother,
Sonny

Then I kept in constant touch with him and I sent him whatever I could and I went to meet him when he came back to New York. When I saw him many things I thought I had forgotten came flooding back to me. This was because I had begun, finally, to wonder about Sonny, about the life that Sonny lived inside. This life, whatever it was, had made him older and thinner and it had deepened the distant stillness in which he had always moved. He looked very unlike my baby brother. Yet, when he smiled, when we shook hands, the baby brother I'd never known looked out from the depths of his private life, like an animal waiting to be coaxed into the light.

"How you been keeping?" he asked me.

"All right. And you?"

"Just fine." He was smiling all over his face. "It's good to see you again."

"It's good to see you."

The seven years' difference in our ages lay between us like a chasm: I wondered if these years would ever operate between us as a bridge. I was remembering, and it made it hard to catch my breath, that I had been there when he was born; and I had heard the first words he had ever spoken. When he started to walk, he walked from our mother straight to me. I caught him just before he fell when he took the first steps he ever took in this world.

"How's Isabel?"

"Just fine. She's dying to see you."

"And the boys?"

"They're fine, too. They're anxious to see their uncle."

"Oh, come on. You know they don't remember me."

"Are you kidding? Of course they remember you."

He grinned again. We got into a taxi. We had a lot to say to each other, far too much to know how to begin.

As the taxi began to move, I asked, "You still want to go to India?"

He laughed. "You still remember that. Hell, no. This place is Indian enough for me."

"It used to belong to them," I said.

And he laughed again. "They damn sure knew what they were doing when they got rid of it."

Years ago, when he was around fourteen, he'd been all hipped on the idea of going to India. He read books about people sitting on rocks, naked, in all kinds of weather, but mostly bad, naturally, and walking barefoot through hot coals and arriving at wisdom. I used to say that it sounded to me as though they were getting away from wisdom as fast as they could. I think he sort of looked down on me for that.

"Do you mind," he asked, "if we have the driver drive alongside the park? On the west side—I haven't seen the city in so long."

"Of course not," I said. I was afraid that I might sound as though I were humoring him, but I hoped he wouldn't take it that way.

So we drove along, between the green of the park and the stony, lifeless elegance of hotels and apartment buildings, toward the vivid, killing streets of our childhood. These streets hadn't changed, though housing projects jutted up out of them now like rocks in the middle of a boiling sea. Most of the houses in which we had grown up had vanished, as had the stores from which we had stolen, the basements in which we had first tried sex, the rooftops from which we had hurled tin cans and bricks. But houses exactly like the houses of our past yet dominated the landscape, boys exactly like the boys we once had been found themselves smothering in these houses, came down into the streets for light and air and found themselves encircled by disaster. Some escaped the trap, most didn't. Those who got out always left something of themselves behind, as some animals amputate a leg and leave it in the trap. It might be said, perhaps, that I had escaped, after all, I was a school teacher; or that Sonny had, he hadn't lived in Harlem for years. Yet, as the cab moved uptown through streets which seemed, with a rush, to darken with dark people, and as I covertly studied Sonny's face, it came to me that what we both were seeking through our separate cab windows was that part of ourselves which had been left behind. It's always at the hour of trouble and confrontation that the missing member aches.

We hit 110th Street and started rolling up Lenox Avenue. And I'd known this avenue all my life, but it seemed to me again, as it had seemed on the day I'd first heard about Sonny's trouble, filled with a hidden menace which was its very breath of life.

"We almost there," said Sonny.

"Almost." We were both too nervous to say anything more.

We live in a housing project. It hasn't been up long. A few days after it was up it seemed uninhabitably new, now, of course, it's already rundown. It looks like a parody of the good, clean, faceless life—God knows the people who live in it do their best to make it a parody. The beat-looking grass lying around isn't enough to make their lives green, the hedges will never hold out the streets, and they know it. The big windows fool no one, they aren't big enough to make space out of no space. They don't bother with the windows, they watch the TV screen instead. The playground is most popular with the children who don't play at jacks, or skip rope, or roller skate, or swing, and they can be found in it after dark. We moved in partly because it's not too far from where I teach, and partly for the kids; but it's really just like the houses in which Sonny and I grew up. The same things happen, they'll have the same things to remember. The moment Sonny and I started into the house I had the feeling that I was simply bringing him back into the danger he had almost died trying to escape.

Sonny has never been talkative. So I don't know why I was sure he'd be dying to talk to me when supper was over the first night. Everything went fine, the oldest boy remembered him, and the youngest boy liked him, and Sonny had remembered to bring something for each of them; and Isabel, who is really much nicer than I am, more open and giving, had gone to a lot of trouble about dinner and was genuinely glad to see him. And she's always been able to tease Sonny in a way that I haven't. It was nice to see her face so vivid again and to hear her laugh and watch her make Sonny laugh. She wasn't, or, anyway, she didn't seem to be, at all uneasy or embarrassed. She chatted as though there were no subject which had to be avoided and she got Sonny past his first, faint stiffness. And thank God she was there, for I was filled with that icy dread again. Everything I did seemed awkward to me, and everything I said sounded freighted with hidden meaning. I was trying to remember everything I'd heard about dope addiction and I couldn't help watching Sonny for signs. I wasn't doing it out of malice. I was trying to find out something about my brother. I was dying to hear him tell me he was safe.

"Safe!" my father grunted, whenever Mama suggested trying to move to a neighborhood which might be safer for children. "Safe, hell! Ain't no place safe for kids, nor nobody."

He always went on like this, but he wasn't, ever, really as bad as he sounded, not even on weekends, when he got drunk. As a matter of fact, he was always on the lookout for "something a little better," but he died before he found it. He died suddenly, during a drunken weekend in the middle of the war, when Sonny was fifteen. He and Sonny hadn't ever got on too well. And this was partly because Sonny was the apple of his father's eye. It was because he loved Sonny so much and was frightened for him, that he was always fighting with him. It doesn't do any good to fight with Sonny. Sonny just moves back, inside himself, where he can't be reached. But the principal reason that they never hit it off is that they were so much alike. Daddy was big and rough and loud-talking, just the opposite of Sonny, but they both had—that same privacy.

Mama tried to tell me something about this, just after Daddy died. I was home on leave from the army.

This was the last time I ever saw my mother alive. Just the same, this picture gets all mixed up in my mind with pictures I had of her when she was younger. The way I always see her is the way she used to be on a Sunday afternoon, say, when the old folks were talking after the big Sunday dinner. I always see her wearing pale blue. She'd be sitting on the sofa. And my father would be sitting in the easy chair, not far from her. And the living room would be full of church folks and relatives. There they sit, in chairs all around the living room, and the night is creeping up outside, but nobody knows it yet. You can see the darkness growing against the windowpanes and you hear the street noises every now and again, or maybe the jangling beat of a tambourine from one of the churches close by, but it's real quiet in the room. For a moment nobody's talking, but every face looks darkening, like the sky outside. And my mother rocks a little from the waist, and my father's eyes are closed. Everyone is looking at something a child can't see. For a minute they've forgotten the children. Maybe a kid is lying on the rug, half asleep. Maybe somebody's got a kid in his lap and is absent-mindedly stroking the kid's head. Maybe there's a kid, quiet and big-eyed, curled up in a big chair in the corner. The silence, the darkness coming, and the darkness in the faces frightens the child obscurely. He hopes that the hand which strokes his forehead will never stop—will never die. He hopes that there will never come a time when the old folks won't be sitting around the living room, talking about where they've come from, and what they've seen, and what's happened to them and their kinfolk.

But something deep and watchful in the child knows that this is bound to end, is already ending. In a moment someone will get up and turn on the light. Then the old folks will remember the children and they won't talk any more that day. And when light fills the room, the child is filled with darkness. He knows that everytime this happens he's moved just a little closer to that darkness outside. The darkness outside is what the old folks have been talking about. It's what they've come from. It's what they endure. The child knows that they won't talk any more because if he knows too much about what's happened to *them*, he'll know too much too soon, about what's going to happen to *him*.

The last time I talked to my mother, I remember I was restless. I wanted to get out and see Isabel. We weren't married then and we had a lot to straighten out between us.

There Mama sat, in black, by the window. She was humming an old church song, *Lord, you brought me from a long ways off*. Sonny was out somewhere. Mama kept watching the streets.

"I don't know," she said, "if I'll ever see you again, after you go off from here. But I hope you'll remember the things I tried to teach you."

"Don't talk like that," I said, and smiled. "You'll be here a long time yet."

She smiled, too, but she said nothing. She was quiet for a long time. And I said, "Mama, don't you worry about nothing. I'll be writing all the time, and you be getting the checks. . . ."

"I want to talk to you about your brother," she said, suddenly. "If anything happens to me he ain't going to have nobody to look out for him."

"Mama," I said, "ain't nothing going to happen to you *or* Sonny. Sonny's all right. He's a good boy and he's got good sense."

"It ain't a question of his being a good boy," Mama said, "nor of his having good sense. It ain't only the bad ones, nor yet the dumb ones that gets sucked under." She stopped, looking at me. "Your Daddy once had a brother," she said, and she smiled in a way that made me feel she was in pain. "You didn't never know that, did you?"

"No," I said, "I never knew that," and I watched her face.

"Oh, yes," she said, "your Daddy had a brother." She looked out of the window again. "I know you never saw your Daddy cry. But *I* did—many a time, through all these years."

I asked her, "What happened to his brother? How come nobody's ever talked about him?"

This was the first time I ever saw my mother look old.

"His brother got killed," she said, "when he was just a little younger than you are now. I knew him. He was a fine boy. He was maybe a little full of the devil, but he didn't mean nobody no harm."

Then she stopped and the room was silent, exactly as it had sometimes been on those Sunday afternoons. Mama kept looking out into the streets.

"He used to have a job in the mill," she said, "and, like all young folks, he just liked to perform on Saturday nights. Saturday nights, him and your father would drift around to different places, go to dances and things like that, or just sit around with people they knew, and your father's brother would sing, he had a fine voice, and play along with himself on his guitar. Well, this particular Saturday night, him and your father was coming home from some place, and they were both a little drunk and there was a moon that night, it was bright like day. Your father's brother was feeling kind of good, and he was whistling to himself, and he had his guitar slung over his shoulder. They were coming down a hill and beneath them was a road that turned off from the highway. Well, your father's brother, being always kind of frisky, decided to run down this hill, and he did, with that guitar banging and clanging behind him, and he ran across the road, and he was making water behind a tree. And your father was sort of amused at him and he was still coming down the hill, kind of slow. Then he heard a car motor and that same minute his brother stepped from behind the tree, into the road, in the moonlight. And he started to cross the road. And your father started to run down the hill, he says he don't know why. This car was full of white men. They was all drunk, and when they seen your father's brother they let out a great whoop and holler and they aimed the car straight at him. They was having fun, they just wanted to scare him, the way they do sometimes, you know. But they was drunk. And I guess the boy, being drunk, too, and scared, kind of lost his head. By the time he jumped it was too late. Your father says he heard his brother scream when the car rolled over him, and he heard the wood of that guitar when it give, and he heard them strings go flying, and he heard them white men shouting, and the car kept on a-going and it ain't stopped till this day. And, time your father got down the hill, his brother weren't nothing but blood and pulp."

Tears were gleaming on my mother's face. There wasn't anything I could say.

"He never mentioned it," she said, "because I never let him mention it before you children. Your Daddy was like a crazy man that night and for many a night thereafter. He says he never in his life seen anything as dark as that road after the lights of that car had gone away. Weren't nothing, weren't nobody on that road, just your Daddy and his brother and that busted guitar. Oh, yes. Your Daddy never did really get right again. Till the day he died he weren't sure but that every white man he saw was the man that killed his brother."

She stopped and took out her handkerchief and dried her eyes and looked at me.

"I ain't telling you all this," she said, "to make you scared or bitter or to make you hate nobody. I'm telling you this because you got a brother. And the world ain't changed."

I guess I didn't want to believe this. I guess she saw this in my face. She turned away from me, toward the window again, searching those streets.

"But I praise my Redeemer," she said at last, "that He called your Daddy home before me. I ain't saying it to throw no flowers at myself, but, I declare, it keeps me from feeling too cast down to know I helped your father get safely through this world. Your father always acted like he was the roughest, strongest man on earth. And everybody took him to be like that. But if he hadn't had *me* there—to see his tears!"

She was crying again. Still, I couldn't move. I said, "Lord, Lord, Mama, I didn't know it was like that."

"Oh, honey," she said, "there's a lot that you don't know. But you are going to find it out." She stood up from the window and came over to me. "You got to hold on to your brother," she said, "and don't let him fall, no matter what it looks like is happening to him and no matter how evil you gets with him. You going to be evil with him many a time. But don't you forget what I told you, you hear?"

"I won't forget," I said. "Don't you worry, I won't forget. I won't let nothing happen to Sonny."

My mother smiled as though she were amused at something she saw in my face. Then, "You may not be able to stop nothing from happening. But you got to let him know you's *there*."

Two days later I was married, and then I was gone. And I had a lot of things on my mind and I pretty well forgot my promise to Mama until I got shipped home on a special furlough for her funeral.

And, after the funeral, with just Sonny and me alone in the empty kitchen, I tried to find out something about him.

"What do you want to do?" I asked him.

"I'm going to be a musician," he said.

For he had graduated, in the time I had been away, from dancing to the juke box to finding out who was playing what, and what they were doing with it, and he had bought himself a set of drums.

"You mean, you want to be a drummer?" I somehow had the feeling that being a drummer might be all right for other people but not for my brother Sonny.

"I don't think," he said, looking at me very gravely, "that I'll ever be a good drummer. But I think I can play a piano."

I frowned. I'd never played the role of the older brother quite so seriously before, had scarcely ever, in fact, *asked* Sonny a damn thing. I sensed myself in the presence of something I didn't really know how to handle, didn't understand. So I made my frown a little deeper as I asked: "What kind of musician do you want to be?"

He grinned. "How many kinds do you think there are?"

"Be *serious*," I said.

He laughed, throwing his head back, and then looked at me, "I *am* serious."

"Well, then, for Christ's sake, stop kidding around and answer a serious question. I mean, do you want to be a concert pianist, you want to play classical music and all that, or—or what?" Long before I finished he was laughing again. "For Christ's *sake*, Sonny!"

He sobered, but with difficulty. "I'm sorry. But you sound so—*scared!*" and he was off again.

"Well, you may think it's funny now, baby, but it's not going to be so funny when you have to make your living at it, let me tell you *that*." I was furious because I knew he was laughing at me and I didn't know why.

"No," he said, very sober now, and afraid, perhaps, that he'd hurt me, "I don't want to be a classical pianist. That isn't what interests me. I mean"—he paused, looking hard at me, as though his eyes would help me to understand, and then gestured helplessly, as though perhaps his hand would help—"I mean, I'll have a lot of studying to do, and I'll have to study *everything*, but, I mean, I want to play *with*—jazz musicians." He stopped. "I want to play jazz," he said.

Well, the word had never before sounded as heavy, as real, as it sounded that afternoon in Sonny's mouth. I just looked at him and I was probably frowning a real frown by this time. I simply couldn't see why on earth he'd want to spend his time hanging around nightclubs, clowning around on bandstands, while people pushed each other around a dance floor. It seemed—beneath him, somehow. I had never thought about it before, had never been forced to, but I suppose I had always put jazz musicians in a class with what Daddy called "good-time people."

"Are you *serious*?"

"Hell, *yes*, I'm serious."

He looked more helpless than ever, and annoyed, and deeply hurt.

I suggested, helpfully: "You mean—like Louis Armstrong?"

His face closed as though I'd struck him. "No. I'm not talking about none of that old-time, down home crap."

"Well, look, Sonny, I'm sorry, don't get mad. I just don't altogether get it, that's all. Name somebody—you know, a jazz musician you admire."

"Bird."

"Who?"

"Bird! Charlie Parker! Don't they teach you nothing in the goddamn army?"

I lit a cigarette. I was surprised and then a little amused to discover that I was trembling. "I've been out of touch," I said. "You'll have to be patient with me. Now. Who's this Parker character?"

"He's just one of the greatest jazz musicians alive," said Sonny, sullenly, his hands in his pockets, his back to me. "Maybe *the* greatest," he added, bitterly, "that's probably why *you* never heard of him."

"All right," I said, "I'm ignorant. I'm sorry. I'll go out and buy all the cat's records right away, all right?"

"It don't," said Sonny, with dignity, "make any difference to me. I don't care what you listen to. Don't do me no favors."

I was beginning to realize that I'd never seen him so upset before. With another part of my mind I was thinking that this would probably turn out to be one of those things kids go through and that I shouldn't make it seem important by pushing it too hard. Still, I didn't think it would do any harm to ask: "Doesn't all this take a lot of time? Can you make a living at it?"

He turned back to me and half leaned, half sat, on the kitchen table. "Everything takes time," he said, "and—well, yes, sure, I can make a living at it. But what I don't seem to be able to make you understand is that it's the only thing I want to do."

"Well, Sonny," I said, gently, "you know people can't always do exactly what they *want* to do—"

"*No*, I don't know that," said Sonny, surprising me. "I think people *ought* to do what they want to do, what else are they alive for?"

"You getting to be a big boy," I said desperately, "it's time you started thinking about your future."

"I'm thinking about my future," said Sonny, grimly. "I think about it all the time."

I gave up. I decided, if he didn't change his mind, that we could always talk about it later. "In the meantime," I said, "you got to finish school." We had already decided that he'd have to move in with Isabel and her folks. I knew this wasn't the ideal arrangement because Isabel's folks are inclined to be dicty and they hadn't especially wanted Isabel to marry me. But I didn't know what else to do. "And we have to get you fixed up at Isabel's."

There was a long silence. He moved from the kitchen table to the window. "That's a terrible idea. You know it yourself."

"Do you have a *better* idea?"

He just walked up and down the kitchen for a minute. He was as tall as I was. He had started to shave. I suddenly had the feeling that I didn't know him at all.

He stopped at the kitchen table and picked up my cigarettes. Looking at me with a kind of mocking, amused defiance, he put one between his lips. "You mind?"

"You smoking already?"

He lit the cigarette and nodded, watching me through the smoke. "I just wanted to see if I'd have the courage to smoke in front of you." He grinned and blew a great cloud of smoke to the ceiling. "It was easy." He looked at my face. "Come on, now. I bet you was smoking at my age, tell the truth."

I didn't say anything but the truth was on my face, and he laughed. But now there was something very strained in his laugh. "Sure. And I bet that ain't all you was doing."

He was frightening me a little. "Cut the crap," I said. "We already decided that you was going to go and live at Isabel's. Now what's got into you all of a sudden?"

"*You* decided it," he pointed out. "*I* didn't decide nothing." He stopped in front of me, leaning against the stove, arms loosely folded. "Look, brother. I don't want to stay in Harlem no more, I really don't." He was very earnest. He looked at me, then over toward the kitchen window. There was something in his eyes I'd never seen before, some thoughtfulness, some worry all his own. He rubbed the muscle of one arm. "It's time I was getting out of here."

"Where do you want to *go*, Sonny?"

"I want to join the army. Or the navy, I don't care. If I say I'm old enough, they'll believe me."

Then I got mad. It was because I was so scared. "You must be crazy. You goddamn fool, what the hell do you want to go and join the *army* for?"

"I just told you. To get out of Harlem."

"Sonny, you haven't even finished *school*. And if you really want to be a musician, how do you expect to study if you're in the *army*?"

He looked at me, trapped, and in anguish. "There's

ways. I might be able to work out some kind of deal. Anyway I'll have the G.I. Bill when I come out."

"*If* you come out." We stared at each other. "Sonny, please. Be reasonable. I know the setup is far from perfect. But we got to do the best we can."

"I ain't learning nothing in school," he said. "Even when I go." He turned away from me and opened the window and threw his cigarette out into the narrow alley. I watched his back. "At least, I ain't learning nothing you'd want me to learn." He slammed the window so hard I thought the glass would fly out, and turned back to me. "And I'm sick of the stink of these garbage cans!"

"Sonny," I said, "I know how you feel. But if you don't finish school now, you're going to be sorry later that you didn't." I grabbed him by the shoulders. "And you only got another year. It ain't so bad. And I'll come back and I swear I'll help you do *whatever* you want to do. Just try to put up with it till I come back. Will you please do that? For me?"

He didn't answer and he wouldn't look at me.

"Sonny. You hear me?"

He pulled away. "I hear you. But you never hear anything *I* say."

I didn't know what to say to that. He looked out of the window and then back at me. "OK," he said, and sighed. "I'll try."

Then I said, trying to cheer him up a little, "They got a piano at Isabel's. You can practice on it."

And as a matter of fact, it did cheer him up for a minute. "That's right," he said to himself. "I forgot that." His face relaxed a little. But the worry, the thoughtfulness, played on it still, the way shadows play on a face which is staring into the fire.

But I thought I'd never hear the end of that piano. At first, Isabel would write me, saying how nice it was that Sonny was so serious about his music and how, as soon as he came in from school, or wherever he had been when he was supposed to be at school, he went straight to that piano and stayed there until suppertime. And, after supper, he went back to that piano and stayed there until everybody went to bed. He was at the piano all day Saturday and all day Sunday. Then he bought a record player and started playing records. He'd play one record over and over again, all day long sometimes, and he'd improvise along with it on the piano. Or he'd play one section of the record, one chord, one change, one progression, then he'd do it on the piano. Then back to the record. Then back to the piano.

Well, I really don't know how they stood it. Isabel finally confessed that it wasn't like living with a person at all, it was like living with sound. And the sound didn't make any sense to her, didn't make any sense to any of them—naturally. They began, in a way, to be afflicted by this presence that was living in their home. It was as though Sonny were some sort of god, or monster. He moved in an atmosphere which wasn't like theirs at all. They fed him and he ate, he washed himself, he walked in and out of their door; he certainly wasn't nasty or unpleasant or rude, Sonny isn't any of those things; but it was as though he were all wrapped up in some cloud, some fire, some vision all his own; and there wasn't any way to reach him.

At the same time, he wasn't really a man yet, he was still a child, and they had to watch out for him in all kinds of ways. They certainly couldn't throw him out. Neither did they dare to make a great scene about that piano because even they dimly sensed, as I sensed, from so many thousands of miles away, that Sonny was at that piano playing for his life.

But he hadn't been going to school. One day a letter came from the school board and Isabel's mother got it— there had, apparently, been other letters but Sonny had torn them up. This day, when Sonny came in, Isabel's mother showed him the letter and asked where he'd been spending his time. And she finally got it out of him that he'd been down in Greenwich Village, with musicians and other characters, in a white girl's apartment. And this scared her and she started to scream at him and what came up, once she began—though she denies it to this day—was what sacrifices they were making to give Sonny a decent home and how little he appreciated it.

Sonny didn't play the piano that day. By evening, Isabel's mother had calmed down but then there was the old man to deal with, and Isabel herself. Isabel says she did her best to be calm but she broke down and started crying. She says she just watched Sonny's face. She could tell, by watching him, what was happening with him. And what was happening was that they penetrated his cloud, they had reached him. Even if their fingers had been a thousand times more gentle than human fingers ever are, he could hardly help feeling that they had stripped him naked and were spitting on that nakedness. For he also had to see that his presence, that music, which was life or death to him, had been torture for them and that they had endured it, not at all for his sake, but only for mine. And Sonny couldn't take that. He can take it a little better today than he could then but he's still not very good at it and, frankly, I don't know anybody who is.

The silence of the next few days must have been louder

than the sound of all the music ever played since time began. One morning, before she went to work, Isabel was in his room for something and she suddenly realized that all of his records were gone. And she knew for certain that he was gone. And he was. He went as far as the navy would carry him. He finally sent me a postcard from some place in Greece and that was the first I knew that Sonny was still alive. I didn't see him any more until we were both back in New York and the war had long been over.

He was a man by then, of course, but I wasn't willing to see it. He came by the house from time to time, but we fought almost every time we met. I didn't like the way he carried himself, loose and dreamlike all the time, and I didn't like his friends, and his music seemed to be merely an excuse for the life he led. It sounded just that weird and disordered.

Then we had a fight, a pretty awful fight, and I didn't see him for months. By and by I looked him up, where he was living, in a furnished room in the Village, and I tried to make it up. But there were lots of people in the room and Sonny just lay on his bed, and he wouldn't come downstairs with me, and he treated these other people as though they were his family and I weren't. So I got mad and then he got mad, and then I told him that he might just as well be dead as live the way he was living. Then he stood up and he told me not to worry about him any more in life, that he *was* dead as far as I was concerned. Then he pushed me to the door and the other people looked on as though nothing were happening, and he slammed the door behind me. I stood in the hallway, staring at the door. I heard somebody laugh in the room and then the tears came to my eyes. I started down the steps, whistling to keep from crying, I kept whistling to myself, *You going to need me, baby, one of these cold, rainy days.*

I read about Sonny's trouble in the spring. Little Grace died in the fall. She was a beautiful little girl. But she only lived a little over two years. She died of polio and she suffered. She had a slight fever for a couple of days, but it didn't seem like anything and we just kept her in bed. And we would certainly have called the doctor, but the fever dropped, she seemed to be all right. So we thought it had just been a cold. Then, one day, she was up, playing, Isabel was in the kitchen fixing lunch for the two boys when they'd come in from school, and she heard Grace fall down in the living room. When you have a lot of children you don't always start running when one of them falls, unless they start screaming or something. And, this time, Grace was quiet. Yet, Isabel says that when she heard that *thump* and then that silence, something happened in her to make her afraid. And she ran to the living room and there was little Grace on the floor, all twisted up, and the reason she hadn't screamed was that she couldn't get her breath. And when she did scream, it was the worst sound, Isabel says, that she'd ever heard in all her life, and she still hears it sometimes in her dreams. Isabel will sometimes wake me up with a low, moaning, strangled sound and I have to be quick to awaken her and hold her to me and where Isabel is weeping against me seems a mortal wound.

I think I may have written Sonny the very day that little Grace was buried. I was sitting in the living room in the dark, by myself, and I suddenly thought of Sonny. My trouble made his real.

One Saturday afternoon, when Sonny had been living with us, or, anyway, been in our house, for nearly two weeks, I found myself wandering aimlessly about the living room, drinking from a can of beer, and trying to work up the courage to search Sonny's room. He was out, he was usually out whenever I was home, and Isabel had taken the children to see their grandparents. Suddenly I was standing still in front of the living room window, watching Seventh Avenue. The idea of searching Sonny's room made me still. I scarcely dared to admit to myself what I'd be searching for. I didn't know what I'd do if I found it. Or if I didn't.

On the sidewalk across from me, near the entrance to a barbecue joint, some people were holding an old-fashioned revival meeting. The barbecue cook, wearing a dirty white apron, his conked hair reddish and metallic in the pale sun, and a cigarette between his lips, stood in the doorway, watching them. Kids and older people paused in their errands and stood there, along with some older men and a couple of very tough-looking women who watched everything that happened on the avenue, as though they owned it, or were maybe owned by it. Well, they were watching this, too. The revival was being carried on by three sisters in black, and a brother. All they had were their voices and their Bibles and a tambourine. The brother was testifying and while he testified two of the sisters stood together, seeming to say, amen, and the third sister walked around with the tambourine outstretched and a couple of people dropped coins into it. Then the brother's testimony ended and the sister who had been taking up the collection dumped the coins into her palm and transferred them to the pocket of her long black robe. Then she raised both hands, striking the tambourine against the air, and then against one hand, and she started to sing. And the two other sisters and the brother joined in.

It was strange, suddenly, to watch, though I had been seeing these street meetings all my life. So, of course, had everybody else down there. Yet, they paused and watched and listened and I stood still at the window. *"Tis the old ship of Zion,"* they sang, and the sister with the tambourine kept a steady, jangling beat, *"it has rescued many a thousand!"* Not a soul under the sound of their voices was hearing this song for the first time, not one of them had been rescued. Nor had they seen much in the way of rescue work being done around them. Neither did they especially believe in the holiness of the three sisters and the brother, they knew too much about them, knew where they lived, and how. The woman with the tambourine, whose voice dominated the air, whose face was bright with joy, was divided by very little from the woman who stood watching her, a cigarette between her heavy, chapped lips, her hair a cuckoo's nest, her face scarred and swollen from many beatings, and her black eyes glittering like coal. Perhaps they both knew this, which was why, when, as rarely, as they addressed each other, they addressed each other as Sister. As the singing filled the air the watching, listening faces underwent a change, the eyes focusing on something within; the music seemed to soothe a poison out of them; and time seemed, nearly, to fall away from the sullen, belligerent, battered faces, as though they were fleeing back to their first condition, while dreaming of their last. The barbecue cook half shook his head and smiled, and dropped his cigarette and disappeared into his joint. A man fumbled in his pockets for change and stood holding it in his hand impatiently, as though he had just remembered a pressing appointment further up the avenue. He looked furious. Then I saw Sonny, standing on the edge of the crowd. He was carrying a wide, flat notebook with a green cover, and it made him look, from where I was standing, almost like a schoolboy. The coppery sun brought out the copper in his skin, he was very faintly smiling, standing very still. Then the singing stopped, the tambourine turned into a collection plate again. The furious man dropped in his coins and vanished, so did a couple of the women, and Sonny dropped some change in the plate, looking directly at the woman with a little smile. He started across the avenue, toward the house. He has a slow, loping walk, something like the way Harlem hipsters walk, only he's imposed on this his own half-beat. I had never really noticed it before.

I stayed at the window, both relieved and apprehensive. As Sonny disappeared from my sight, they began singing again. And they were still singing when his key turned in the lock.

"Hey," he said.

"Hey, yourself. You want some beer?"

"No. Well, maybe." But he came up to the window and stood beside me, looking out. "What a warm voice," he said.

They were singing *If I could only hear my mother pray again*!

"Yes," I said, "and she can sure beat that tambourine."

"But what a terrible song," he said, and laughed. He dropped his notebook on the sofa and disappeared into the kitchen. "Where's Isabel and the kids?"

"I think they went to see their grandparents. You hungry?"

"No." He came back into the living room with his can of beer. "You want to come some place with me tonight?"

I sensed, I don't know how, that I couldn't possibly say no. "Sure. Where?"

He sat down on the sofa and picked up his notebook and started leafing through it. "I'm going to sit in with some fellows in a joint in the Village."

"You mean, you're going to play, tonight?"

"That's right." He took a swallow of his beer and moved back to the window. He gave me a sidelong look. "If you can stand it."

"I'll try," I said.

He smiled to himself and we both watched as the meeting across the way broke up. The three sisters and the brother, heads bowed, were singing *God be with you till we meet again*. The faces around them were very quiet. Then the song ended. The small crowd dispersed. We watched the three women and the lone man walk slowly up the avenue.

"When she was singing before," said Sonny, abruptly, "her voice reminded me for a minute of what heroin feels like sometimes—when it's in your veins. It makes you feel sort of warm and cool at the same time. And distant. And—and sure." He sipped his beer, very deliberately not looking at me. I watched his face. "It makes you feel—in control. Sometimes you've got to have that feeling."

"Do you?" I sat down slowly in the easy chair.

"Sometimes." He went to the sofa and picked up his notebook again. "Some people do."

"In order," I asked, "to play?" And my voice was very ugly, full of contempt and anger.

"Well"—he looked at me with great, troubled eyes, as though, in fact, he hoped his eyes would tell me things he could never otherwise say—"they *think* so. And *if* they think so—!"

"And what do *you* think?" I asked.

He sat on the sofa and put his can of beer on the floor. "I don't know," he said, and I couldn't be sure if he were answering my question or pursuing his thoughts. His face didn't tell me. "It's not so much to *play*. It's to *stand* it, to be able to make it at all. On any level." He frowned and smiled: "In order to keep from shaking to pieces."

"But these friends of yours," I said, "they seem to shake themselves to pieces pretty goddamn fast."

"Maybe." He played with the notebook. And something told me that I should curb my tongue, that Sonny was doing his best to talk, that I should listen. "But of course you only know the ones that've gone to pieces. Some don't—or at least they haven't *yet* and that's just about all *any* of us can say." He paused. "And then there are some who just live, really, in hell, and they know it and they see what's happening and they go right on. I don't know." He sighed, dropped the notebook, folded his arms. "Some guys, you can tell from the way they play, they on something *all* the time. And you can see that, well, it makes something real for them. But of course," he picked up his beer from the floor and sipped it and put the can down again, "they *want* to, too, you've got to see that. Even some of them that say they don't—*some*, not all."

"And what about you?" I asked—I couldn't help it. "What about you? Do *you* want to?"

He stood up and walked to the window and remained silent for a long time. Then he sighed. "Me," he said. Then: "While I was downstairs before, on my way here, listening to that woman sing, it struck me all of a sudden how much suffering she must have had to go through—to sing like that. It's *repulsive* to think you have to suffer that much."

I said: "But there's no way not to suffer—is there, Sonny?"

"I believe not," he said and smiled, "but that's never stopped anyone from trying." He looked at me. "Has it?" I realized, with this mocking look, that there stood between us, forever, beyond the power of time or forgiveness, the fact that I had held silence—so long!—when he had needed human speech to help him. He turned back to the window. "No, there's no way not to suffer. But you try all kinds of ways to keep from drowning in it, to keep on top of it, and to make it seem—well, like *you*. Like you did something, all right, and now you're suffering for it. You know?" I said nothing. "Well you know," he said, impatiently, "why *do* people suffer? Maybe it's better to do something to give it a reason, *any* reason."

"But we just agreed," I said, "that there's no way not to suffer. Isn't it better, then, just to—take it?"

"But nobody just takes it," Sonny cried, "that's what I'm telling you! *Everybody* tries not to. You're just hung up on the *way* some people try—it's not *your* way!"

The hair on my face began to itch, my face felt wet. "That's not true," I said, "that's not true. I don't give a damn what other people do, I don't even care how they suffer. I just care how *you* suffer." And he looked at me. "Please believe me," I said, "I don't want to see you—die —trying not to suffer."

"I won't," he said, flatly, "die trying not to suffer. At least, not any faster than anybody else."

"But there's no need," I said, trying to laugh, "is there? in killing yourself."

I wanted to say more, but I couldn't. I wanted to talk about will power and how life could be—well, beautiful. I wanted to say that it was all within; but was it? or, rather, wasn't that exactly the trouble? And I wanted to promise that I would never fail him again. But it would all have sounded—empty words and lies.

So I made the promise to myself and prayed that I would keep it.

"It's terrible sometimes, inside," he said, "that's what's the trouble. You walk these streets, black and funky and cold, and there's not really a living ass to talk to, and there's nothing shaking, and there's no way of getting it out—that storm inside. You can't talk it and you can't make love with it, and when you finally try to get with it and play it, you realize *nobody's* listening. So *you've* got to listen. You got to find a way to listen."

And then he walked away from the window and sat on the sofa again, as though all the wind had suddenly been knocked out of him. "Sometimes you'll do *anything* to play, even cut your mother's throat." He laughed and looked at me. "Or your brother's." Then he sobered. "Or your own." Then: "Don't worry. I'm all right now and I think I'll *be* all right. But I can't forget—where I've been. I don't mean just the physical place I've been, I mean where I've *been*. And *what* I've been."

"What have you been, Sonny?" I asked.

He smiled—but sat sideways on the sofa, his elbow resting on the back, his fingers playing with his mouth and chin, not looking at me. "I've been something I didn't recognize, didn't know I could be. Didn't know anybody could be." He stopped, looking inward, looking helplessly young, looking old. "I'm not talking about it now because I feel *guilty* or anything like that—maybe it would be better if I did, I don't know. Anyway, I can't really talk about it. Not to you, not to anybody," and now he turned and faced me. "Sometimes, you know, and it was actually when I was most *out* of the world, I felt that I was in it, that I was *with* it, really, and I could play or I didn't really have to *play*, it just came out of me, it was there. And I don't know how I played, thinking about it now, but I know I did awful things, those times, sometimes, to people. Or it wasn't that I *did* anything to them—it was that they weren't real." He picked up the beer can; it was empty; he rolled it between his palms: "And other times —well, I needed a fix, I needed to find a place to lean, I needed to clear a space to *listen*—and I couldn't find it, and I—went crazy, I did terrible things to *me*, I was terrible *for* me." He began pressing the beer can between his hands, I watched the metal begin to give. It glittered, as he played with it, like a knife, and I was afraid he would cut himself, but I said nothing. "Oh well. I can never tell you. I was all by myself at the bottom of something, stinking and sweating and crying and shaking, and I smelled it, you know? *my* stink, and I thought I'd die if I couldn't get away from it and yet, all the same, I knew that everything I was doing was just locking me in with it. And I didn't know," he paused, still flattening the beer can, "I didn't know, I still *don't* know, something kept telling me that maybe it was good to smell your own stink, but I didn't think that *that* was what I'd been trying to do— and—who can stand it?" and he abruptly dropped the ruined beer can, looking at me with a small, still smile, and then rose, walking to the window as though it were the lodestone rock. I watched his face, he watched the avenue. "I couldn't tell you when Mama died—but the reason I wanted to leave Harlem so bad was to get away from drugs. And then, when I ran away, that's what I was running from—really. When I came back, nothing had changed, *I* hadn't changed, I was just—older." And he stopped, drumming with his fingers on the windowpane. The sun had vanished, soon darkness would fall. I watched his face. "It can come again," he said, almost as though speaking to himself. Then he turned to me. "It can come again," he repeated. "I just want you to know that."

"All right," I said, at last. "So it can come again. All right."

He smiled, but the smile was sorrowful. "I had to try to tell you," he said.

"Yes," I said. "I understand that."

"You're my brother," he said, looking straight at me, and not smiling at all.

"Yes," I repeated, "yes. I understand that."

He turned back to the window, looking out. "All that hatred down there," he said, "all that hatred and misery and love. It's a wonder it doesn't blow the avenue apart."

We went to the only nightclub on a short, dark street, downtown. We squeezed through the narrow, chattering, jam-packed bar to the entrance of the big room, where the bandstand was. And we stood there for a moment, for the lights were very dim in this room and we couldn't see. Then, "Hello, boy," said a voice and an enormous black man, much older than Sonny or myself, erupted out of all that atmospheric lighting and put an arm around Sonny's shoulder. "I been sitting right here," he said, "waiting for you."

He had a big voice, too, and heads in the darkness turned toward us.

Sonny grinned and pulled a little away, and said, "Creole, this is my brother. I told you about him."

Creole shook my hand. "I'm glad to meet you, son," he said, and it was clear that he was glad to meet me *there*, for Sonny's sake. And he smiled, "You got a real musician in *your* family," and he took his arm from Sonny's shoulder and slapped him, lightly, affectionately, with the back of his hand.

"Well. Now I've heard it all," said a voice behind us. This was another musician, and a friend of Sonny's, a coal-black, cheerful-looking man, built close to the ground. He immediately began confiding to me, at the top of his lungs, the most terrible things about Sonny, his teeth gleaming like a lighthouse and his laugh coming up out of him like the beginning of an earthquake. And it turned out that everyone at the bar knew Sonny, or almost everyone; some were musicians, working there, or nearby, or not working, some were simply hangers-on, and some were there to hear Sonny play. I was introduced to all of them and they were all very polite to me. Yet, it was clear that, for them, I was only Sonny's brother. Here, I was in Sonny's world. Or, rather: his kingdom. Here, it was not even a question that his veins bore royal blood.

They were going to play soon and Creole installed me, by myself, at a table in a dark corner. Then I watched them, Creole, and the little black man, and Sonny, and the others, while they horsed around, standing just below the bandstand. The light from the bandstand spilled just a little short of them and, watching them laughing and gesturing and moving about, I had the feeling that they, nevertheless, were being most careful not to step into that circle of light too suddenly: that if they moved into the light too suddenly, without thinking, they would perish in flame. Then, while I watched, one of them, the small, black man, moved into the light and crossed the bandstand and started fooling around with his drums. Then— being funny and being, also, extremely ceremonious— Creole took Sonny by the arm and led him to the piano. A woman's voice called Sonny's name and a few hands started clapping. And Sonny, also being funny and being ceremonious, and so touched, I think, that he could have cried, but neither hiding it nor showing it, riding it like a man, grinned, and put both hands to his heart and bowed from the waist.

Creole then went to the bass fiddle and a lean, very bright-skinned brown man jumped up on the bandstand and picked up his horn. So there they were, and the atmosphere on the bandstand and in the room began to change and tighten. Someone stepped up to the microphone and announced them. Then there were all kinds of murmurs. Some people at the bar shushed others. The waitress ran around, frantically getting in the last orders, guys and chicks got closer to each other, and the lights on the bandstand, on the quartet, turned to a kind of indigo. Then they all looked different there. Creole looked about him for the last time, as though he were making certain that all his chickens were in the coop, and then he— jumped and struck the fiddle. And there they were.

All I know about music is that not many people ever really hear it. And even then, on the rare occasions when something opens within, the music enters, what we mainly hear, or hear corroborated, are personal, private, vanishing evocations. But the man who creates the music is hearing something else, is dealing with the roar rising from the void and imposing order on it as it hits the air. What is evoked in him, then, is of another order, more terrible because it has no words, and triumphant, too, for that same reason. And his triumph, when he triumphs, is ours. I just watched Sonny's face. His face was troubled, he was working hard, but he wasn't with it. And I had the feeling that, in a way, everyone on the bandstand was waiting for him, both waiting for him and pushing him along. But as I began to watch Creole, I realized that it was Creole who held them all back. He had them on a short rein. Up there, keeping the beat with his whole body, wailing on the fiddle, with his eyes half closed, he was listening to everything, but he was listening to Sonny. He was having a dialogue with Sonny. He wanted Sonny to leave the shoreline and strike out for the deep water. He was Sonny's witness that deep water and drowning were not the same thing—he had been there, and he knew. And he wanted Sonny to know. He was waiting for Sonny to do the things on the keys which would let Creole know that Sonny was in the water.

And, while Creole listened, Sonny moved, deep within, exactly like someone in torment. I had never before thought of how awful the relationship must be between the musician and his instrument. He has to fill it, this instrument, with the breath of life, his own. He has to make it do what he wants it to do. And a piano is just a piano. It's made out of so much wood and wires and little hammers and big ones, and ivory. While there's only so much you can do with it, the only way to find this out is to try; to try and make it do everything.

And Sonny hadn't been near a piano for over a year. And he wasn't on much better terms with his life, not the life that stretched before him now. He and the piano stammered, started one way, got scared, stopped; started another way, panicked, marked time, started again; then seemed to have found a direction, panicked again, got stuck. And the face I saw on Sonny I'd never seen before. Everything had been burned out of it, and, at the same time, things usually hidden were being burned in, by the fire and fury of the battle which was occurring in him up there.

Yet, watching Creole's face as they neared the end of the first set, I had the feeling that something had happened, something I hadn't heard. Then they finished, there was scattered applause, and then, without an instant's warning, Creole started into something else, it was almost sardonic, it was *Am I Blue*. And, as though he commanded, Sonny began to play. Something began to happen. And Creole let out the reins. The dry, low, black man said something awful on the drums, Creole answered, and the drums talked back. Then the horn insisted, sweet and high, slightly detached perhaps, and Creole listened, commenting now and then, dry, and driving, beautiful and calm and old. Then they all came together again, and Sonny was part of the family again. I could tell this from his face. He seemed to have found, right there beneath his fingers, a damn brand-new piano. It seemed that he couldn't get over it. Then, for awhile, just being happy with Sonny, they seemed to be agreeing with him that brand-new pianos certainly were a gas.

Then Creole stepped forward to remind them that what they were playing was the blues. He hit something in all of them, he hit something in me, myself, and the music tightened and deepened, apprehension began to beat the air. Creole began to tell us what the blues were all about. They were not about anything very new. He and his boys up there were keeping it new, at the risk of ruin, destruction, madness, and death, in order to find new ways to make us listen. For, while the tale of how we suffer, and how we are delighted, and how we may triumph is never new, it always must be heard. There isn't any other tale to tell, it's the only light we've got in all this darkness.

And this tale, according to that face, that body, those strong hands on those strings, has another aspect in every country, and a new depth in every generation. Listen, Creole seemed to be saying, listen. Now these are Sonny's blues. He made the little black man on the drums know it, and the bright, brown man on the horn. Creole wasn't trying any longer to get Sonny in the water. He was wishing him Godspeed. Then he stepped back, very slowly, filling the air with the immense suggestion that Sonny speak for himself.

Then they all gathered around Sonny and Sonny played. Every now and again one of them seemed to say, amen. Sonny's fingers filled the air with life, his life. But that life contained so many others. And Sonny went all the way back, he really began with the spare, flat statement of the opening phrase of the song. Then he began to make it his. It was very beautiful because it wasn't hurried and it was no longer a lament. I seemed to hear with what burning he had made it his, with what burning we had yet to make it ours, how we could cease lamenting. Freedom lurked around us and I understood, at last, that he could help us to be free if we would listen, that he would never be free until we did. Yet, there was no battle in his face now. I heard what he had gone through, and would continue to go through until he came to rest in earth. He had made it his: that long line, of which we knew only Mama and Daddy. And he was giving it back, as everything must be given back, so that, passing through death, it can live forever. I saw my mother's face again, and felt, for the first time, how the stones of the road she had walked on must have bruised her feet. I saw the moonlit road where my father's brother died. And it brought something else back to me, and carried me past it. I saw my little girl again and felt Isabel's tears again, and I felt my own tears begin to rise. And I was yet aware that this was only a moment, that the world waited outside, as hungry as a tiger, and that trouble stretched above us, longer than the sky.

Then it was over. Creole and Sonny let out their breath, both soaking wet, and grinning. There was a lot of applause and some of it was real. In the dark, the girl came by and I asked her to take drinks to the bandstand. There was a long pause, while they talked up there in the indigo light and after awhile I saw the girl put a Scotch and milk on top of the piano for Sonny. He didn't seem to notice it, but just before they started playing again, he sipped from it and looked toward me, and nodded. Then he put it back on top of the piano. For me, then, as they began to play again, it glowed and shook above my brother's head like the very cup of trembling.

Ernest Hemingway

Soldier's Home

KREBS WENT TO THE WAR FROM A METHODIST COLLEGE in Kansas. There is a picture which shows him among his fraternity brothers, all of them wearing exactly the same height and style collar. He enlisted in the Marines in 1917 and did not return to the United States until the second division returned from the Rhine in the summer of 1919.

There is a picture which shows him on the Rhine with two German girls and another corporal. Krebs and the corporal look too big for their uniforms. The German girls are not beautiful. The Rhine does not show in the picture.

By the time Krebs returned to his home town in Oklahoma the greeting of heroes was over. He came back much too late. The men from the town who had been drafted had all been welcomed elaborately on their return. There had been a great deal of hysteria. Now the reaction had set in. People seemed to think it was rather ridiculous for Krebs to be getting back so late, years after the war was over.

At first Krebs, who had been at Belleau Wood, Soissons, the Champagne, St. Mihiel and in the Argonne did not want to talk about the war at all. Later he felt the need to talk but no one wanted to hear about it. His town had heard too many atrocity stories to be thrilled by actualities. Krebs found that to be listened to at all he had to lie, and after he had done this twice he, too, had a reaction against the war and against talking about it. A distaste for everything that had happened to him in the war set in because of the lies he had told. All of the times that had been able to make him feel cool and clear inside himself when he thought of them; the times so long back when he had done the one thing, the only thing for a man to do, easily and naturally, when he might have done something else, now lost their cool, valuable quality and then were lost themselves.

His lies were quite unimportant lies and consisted in attributing to himself things other men had seen, done or heard of, and stating as facts certain apocryphal incidents familiar to all soldiers. Even his lies were not sensational at the pool room. His acquaintances, who had heard detailed accounts of German women found chained to machine guns in the Argonne forest and who could not comprehend, or were barred by their patriotism from interest in, any German machine gunners who were not chained, were not thrilled by his stories.

Krebs acquired the nausea in regard to experience that is the result of untruth or exaggeration, and when he occasionally met another man who had really been a soldier and they talked a few minutes in the dressing room at a dance he fell into the easy pose of the old soldier among other soldiers: that he had been badly, sickeningly frightened all the time. In this way he lost everything.

During this time, it was late summer, he was sleeping late in bed, getting up to walk down town to the library to get a book, eating lunch at home, reading on the front porch until he became bored and then walking down through the town to spend the hottest hours of the day in the cool dark of the pool room. He loved to play pool.

In the evening he practised on his clarinet, strolled down town, read and went to bed. He was still a hero to his two young sisters. His mother would have given him breakfast in bed if he had wanted it. She often came in when he was in bed and asked him to tell her about the war, but her attention always wandered. His father was non-committal.

Before Krebs went away to the war he had never been allowed to drive the family motor car. His father was in the real estate business and always wanted the car to be at his command when he required it to take clients out into the country to show them a piece of farm property. The car always stood outside the First National Bank building where his father had an office on the second floor. Now, after the war, it was still the same car.

Nothing was changed in the town except that the young girls had grown up. But they lived in such a complicated world of already defined alliances and shifting feuds that Krebs did not feel the energy or the courage to break into it. He liked to look at them, though. There were so many good-looking young girls. Most of them had their hair cut short. When he went away only little girls wore their hair like that or girls that were fast. They all wore sweaters and shirt waists with round Dutch collars. It was a pattern. He liked to look at them from the front porch as they walked on the other side of the street. He liked to watch them walking under the shade of the trees. He liked the round Dutch collars above their sweaters. He liked their silk stockings and flat shoes. He liked their bobbed hair and the way they walked.

When he was in town their appeal to him was not very strong. He did not like them when he saw them in the Greek's ice cream parlor. He did not want them them-

selves really. They were too complicated. There was something else. Vaguely he wanted a girl but he did not want
to have to work to get her. He would have liked to have a
girl but he did not want to have to spend a long time getting her. He did not want to get into the intrigue and the
politics. He did not want to have to do any courting. He
did not want to tell any more lies. It wasn't worth it.

He did not want any consequences. He did not want
any consequences ever again. He wanted to live along
without consequences. Besides he did not really need a
girl. The army had taught him that. It was all right to pose
as though you had to have a girl. Nearly everybody did
that. But it wasn't true. You did not need a girl. That was
the funny thing. First a fellow boasted how girls mean
nothing to him, that he never thought of them, that they
could not touch him. Then a fellow boasted that he could
not get along without girls, that he had to have them all
the time, that he could not go to sleep without them.

That was all a lie. It was all a lie both ways. You did
not need a girl unless you thought about them. He learned
that in the army. Then sooner or later you always got one.
When you were really ripe for a girl you always got one.
You did not have to think about it. Sooner or later it
would come. He had learned that in the army.

Now he would have liked a girl if she had come to him
and not wanted to talk. But here at home it was all too
complicated. He knew he could never get through it all
again. It was not worth the trouble. That was the thing
about French girls and German girls. There was not all
this talking. You couldn't talk much and you did not need
to talk. It was simple and you were friends. He thought
about France and then he began to think about Germany.
On the whole he had liked Germany better. He did not

want to leave Germany. He did not want to come home. Still, he had come home. He sat on the front porch.

He liked the girls that were walking along the other side of the street. He liked the look of them much better than the French girls or the German girls. But the world they were in was not the world he was in. He would like to have one of them. But it was not worth it. They were such a nice pattern. He liked the pattern. It was exciting. But he would not go through all the talking. He did not want one badly enough. He liked to look at them all, though. It was not worth it. Not now when things were getting good again.

He sat there on the porch reading a book on the war. It was a history and he was reading about all the engagements he had been in. It was the most interesting reading he had ever done. He wished there were more maps. He looked forward with a good feeling to reading all the really good histories when they would come out with good detail maps. Now he was really learning about the war. He had been a good soldier. That made a difference.

One morning after he had been home about a month his mother came into his bedroom and sat on the bed. She smoothed her apron.

"I had a talk with your father last night, Harold," she said, "and he is willing for you to take the car out in the evenings."

"Yeah?" said Krebs, who was not fully awake. "Take the car out? Yeah?"

"Yes. Your father has felt for some time that you should be able to take the car out in the evenings whenever you wished but we only talked it over last night."

"I'll bet you made him," Krebs said.

"No. It was your father's suggestion that we talk the matter over."

"Yeah. I'll bet you made him," Krebs sat up in bed.

"Will you come down to breakfast, Harold?" his mother said.

"As soon as I get my clothes on," Krebs said.

His mother went out of the room and he could hear her frying something downstairs while he washed, shaved and dressed to go down into the dining-room for breakfast. While he was eating breakfast his sister brought in the mail.

"Well, Hare," she said. "You old sleepy-head. What do you ever get up for?"

Krebs looked at her. He liked her. She was his best sister.

"Have you got the paper?" he asked.

She handed him *The Kansas City Star* and he shucked off its brown wrapper and opened it to the sporting page. He folded *The Star* open and propped it against the water pitcher with his cereal dish to steady it, so he could read while he ate.

"Harold," his mother stood in the kitchen doorway, "Harold, please don't muss up the paper. Your father can't read his *Star* if it's been mussed."

"I won't muss it," Krebs said.

His sister sat down at the table and watched him while he read.

"We're playing indoor over at school this afternoon," she said. "I'm going to pitch."

"Good," said Krebs. "How's the old wing?"

"I can pitch better than lots of the boys. I tell them all you taught me. The other girls aren't much good."

"Yeah?" said Krebs.

"I tell them all you're my beau. Aren't you my beau, Hare?"

"You bet."

"Couldn't your brother really be your beau just because he's your brother?"

"I don't know."

"Sure you know. Couldn't you be my beau, Hare, if I was old enough and if you wanted to?"

"Sure. You're my girl now."

"Am I really your girl?"

"Sure."

"Do you love me?"

"Uh, huh."

"Will you love me always?"

"Sure."

"Will you come over and watch me play indoor?"

"Maybe."

"Aw, Hare, you don't love me. If you loved me, you'd want to come over and watch me play indoor."

Krebs's mother came into the dining-room from the kitchen. She carried a plate with two fried eggs and some crisp bacon on it and a plate of buckwheat cakes.

"You run along, Helen," she said. "I want to talk to Harold."

She put the eggs and bacon down in front of him and brought in a jug of maple syrup for the buckwheat cakes. Then she sat down across the table from Krebs.

"I wish you'd put down the paper a minute, Harold," she said.

Krebs took down the paper and folded it.

"Have you decided what you are going to do yet, Harold?" his mother said, taking off her glasses.

"No," said Krebs.

"Don't you think it's about time?" His mother did not say this in a mean way. She seemed worried.

"I hadn't thought about it," Krebs said.

"God has some work for every one to do," his mother said. "There can be no idle hands in His Kingdom."

"I'm not in His Kingdom," Krebs said.

"We are all of us in His Kingdom."

Krebs felt embarrassed and resentful as always.

"I've worried about you so much, Harold," his mother went on. "I know the temptations you must have been exposed to. I know how weak men are. I know what your own dear grandfather, my own father, told us about the Civil War and I have prayed for you. I pray for you all day long, Harold."

Krebs looked at the bacon fat hardening on his plate.

"Your father is worried, too," his mother went on. "He thinks you have lost your ambition, that you haven't got a definite aim in life. Charley Simmons, who is just your age, has a good job and is going to be married. The boys are all settling down; they're all determined to get somewhere; you can see that boys like Charley Simmons are on their way to being really a credit to the community."

Krebs said nothing.

"Don't look that way, Harold," his mother said. "You know we love you and I want to tell you for your own good how matters stand. Your father does not want to hamper your freedom. He thinks you should be allowed to drive the car. If you want to take some of the nice girls out riding with you, we are only too pleased. We want you to enjoy yourself. But you are going to have to settle down to work, Harold. Your father doesn't care what you start in at. All work is honorable as he says. But you've got to make a start at something. He asked me to speak to you this morning and then you can stop in and see him at his office."

"Is that all?" Krebs said.

"Yes. Don't you love your mother, dear boy?"

"No," Krebs said.

His mother looked at him across the table. Her eyes were shiny. She started crying.

"I don't love anybody," Krebs said.

It wasn't any good. He couldn't tell her, he couldn't make her see it. It was silly to have said it. He had only hurt her. He went over and took hold of her arm. She was crying with her head in her hands.

"I didn't mean it," he said. "I was just angry at something. I didn't mean I didn't love you."

His mother went on crying. Krebs put his arm on her shoulder.

"Can't you believe me, mother?"

His mother shook her head.

"Please, please, mother. Please believe me."

"All right," his mother said chokily. She looked up at him. "I believe you, Harold."

Krebs kissed her hair. She put her face up to him.

"I'm your mother," she said. "I held you next to my heart when you were a tiny baby."

Krebs felt sick and vaguely nauseated.

"I know, Mummy," he said. "I'll try and be a good boy for you."

"Would you kneel and pray with me, Harold?" his mother asked.

They knelt down beside the dining-room table and Krebs's mother prayed.

"Now, you pray, Harold," she said.

"I can't," Krebs said.

"Try, Harold."

"I can't."

"Do you want me to pray for you?"

"Yes."

So his mother prayed for him and then they stood up and Krebs kissed his mother and went out of the house. He had tried so to keep his life from being complicated. Still, none of it had touched him. He had felt sorry for his mother and she had made him lie. He would go to Kansas City and get a job and she would feel all right about it. There would be one more scene maybe before he got away. He would not go down to his father's office. He would miss that one. He wanted his life to go smoothly. It had just gotten going that way. Well, that was all over now, anyway. He would go over to the schoolyard and watch Helen play indoor baseball.

Joseph Conrad

The Secret Sharer

ON MY RIGHT HAND THERE WERE LINES OF FISHING stakes resembling a mysterious system of half-submerged bamboo fences, incomprehensible in its division of the domain of tropical fishes, and crazy of aspect as if abandoned forever by some nomad tribe of fishermen now gone to the other end of the ocean; for there was no sign of human habitation as far as the eye could reach. To the left a group of barren islets, suggesting ruins of stone walls, towers, and blockhouses, had its foundations sct in a blue sea that itself looked solid, so still and stable did it lie below my feet; even the track of light from the westering sun shone smoothly, without that animated glitter which tells of an imperceptible ripple. And when I turned my head to take a parting glance at the tug which had just left us anchored outside the bar, I saw the straight line of the flat shore joined to the stable sea, edge to edge, with a perfect and unmarked closeness, in one leveled floor half brown, half blue under the enormous dome of the sky. Corresponding in their insignificance to the islets of the sea, two small clumps of trees, one on each side of the only fault in the impeccable joint, marked the mouth of the river Meinam we had just left on the first preparatory stage of our homeward journey; and, far back on the inland level, a larger and loftier mass, the grove surrounding the great Paknam pagoda, was the only thing on which the eye could rest from the vain task of exploring the mono-tonous sweep of the horizon. Here and there gleams as of a few scattered pieces of silver marked the windings of the great river; and on the nearest of them, just within the bar, the tug steaming right into the land became lost to my sight, hull and funnel and masts, as though the impassive earth had swallowed her up without an effort, without a tremor. My eye followed the light cloud of her smoke, now here, now there, above the plain, according to the devious curves of the stream, but always fainter and farther away, till I lost it at last behind the miter-shaped hill of the great pagoda. And then I was left alone with my ship, anchored at the head of the Gulf of Siam.

She floated at the starting point of a long journey, very still in an immense stillness, the shadows of her spars flung far to the eastward by the setting sun. At that moment I was alone on her decks. There was not a sound in her—and around us nothing moved, nothing lived, not a canoe on the water, not a bird in the air, not a cloud in the sky. In this breathless pause at the threshold of a long passage we seemed to be measuring our fitness for a long and arduous enterprise, the appointed task of both our existences to be carried out, far from all human eyes, with only sky and sea for spectators and for judges.

There must have been some glare in the air to interfere with one's sight, because it was only just before the sun left us that my roaming eyes made out beyond the highest ridge of the principal islet of the group something which did away with the solemnity of perfect solitude. The tide of darkness flowed on swiftly; and with tropical sudden-ness a swarm of stars came out above the shadowy earth, while I lingered yet, my hand resting lightly on my ship's rail as if on the shoulder of a trusted friend. But, with all that multitude of celestial bodies staring down at one, the comfort of quiet communion with her was gone for good. And there were also disturbing sounds by this time— voices, footsteps forward; the steward flitted along the main deck, a busily ministering spirit; a hand bell tinkled urgently under the poop deck. . . .

I found my two officers waiting for me near the supper table, in the lighted cuddy. We sat down at once, and as I helped the chief mate, I said:

"Are you aware that there is a ship anchored inside the islands? I saw her mastheads above the ridge as the sun went down."

He raised sharply his simple face, overcharged by a terrible growth of whisker, and emitted his usual ejaculations: "Bless my soul, sir! You don't say so!"

My second mate was a round-cheeked, silent young man, grave beyond his years, I thought; but as our eyes happened to meet I detected a slight quiver on his lips. I looked down at once. It was not my part to encourage sneering on board my ship. It must be said, too, that I knew very little of my officers. In consequence of certain events of no particular significance, except to myself, I had been appointed to the command only a fortnight before. Neither did I know much of the hands forward. All these people had been together for eighteen months or so, and my position was that of the only stranger on board. I mention this because it has some bearing on what is to follow. But what I felt most was my being a stranger to the ship; and if all the truth must be told, I was somewhat of a stranger to myself. The youngest man on board (barring the second mate), and untried as yet by a position of the fullest responsibility, I was willing to take the adequacy of the others for granted. They had simply to be equal to their tasks; but I wondered how far I should turn out faithful to that ideal conception of one's own personality every man sets up for himself secretly.

Meantime the chief mate, with an almost visible effect of collaboration on the part of his round eyes and frightful whiskers, was trying to evolve a theory of the anchored ship. His dominant trait was to take all things into earnest consideration. He was of a painstaking turn of mind. As he used to say, he "liked to account to himself" for practically everything that came in his way, down to a miserable scorpion he had found in his cabin a week before. The why and the wherefore of that scorpion—how it got on board and came to select his room rather than the pantry (which was a dark place and more what a scorpion would be partial to), and how on earth it managed to drown itself in the inkwell of his writing desk—had exercised him infinitely. The ship within the islands was much more easily accounted for; and just as we were about to rise from the table he made his pronouncement. She was, he doubted not, a ship from home lately arrived. Probably she drew too much water to cross the bar except at the top of spring tides. Therefore she went into that natural harbor to wait for a few days in preference to remaining in an open roadstead.

"That's so," confirmed the second mate, suddenly, in his slightly hoarse voice. "She draws over twenty feet. She's the Liverpool ship *Sephora* with a cargo of coal. Hundred and twenty-three days from Cardiff."

We looked at him in surprise.

"The tugboat skipper told me when he came on board for your letters, sir," explained the young man. "He expects to take her up the river the day after tomorrow."

After thus overwhelming us with the extent of his information he slipped out of the cabin. The mate observed regretfully that he "could not account for that young fellow's whims." What prevented him telling us all about it at once, he wanted to know.

I detained him as he was making a move. For the last two days the crew had had plenty of hard work, and the night before they had very little sleep. I felt painfully that I—a stranger—was doing something unusual when I directed him to let all hands turn in without setting an anchor watch. I proposed to keep on deck myself till one o'clock or thereabouts. I would get the second mate to relieve me at that hour.

"He will turn out the cook and the steward at four," I concluded, "and then give you a call. Of course at the slightest sign of any sort of wind we'll have the hands up and make a start at once."

He concealed his astonishment. "Very well, sir." Outside the cuddy he put his head in the second mate's door to inform him of my unheard-of caprice to take a five hours' anchor watch on myself. I heard the other raise his voice incredulously: "What? The captain himself?" Then a few more murmurs, a door closed, then another. A few moments later I went on deck.

My strangeness, which had made me sleepless, had prompted that unconventional arrangement, as if I had expected in those solitary hours of the night to get on terms with the ship of which I knew nothing, manned by men of whom I knew very little more. Fast alongside a wharf, littered like any ship in port with a tangle of unrelated things, invaded by unrelated shore people, I had hardly seen her yet properly. Now, as she lay cleared for sea, the stretch of her main deck seemed to me very fine under the stars. Very fine, very roomy for her size, and very inviting. I descended the poop and paced the waist, my mind picturing to myself the coming passage through the Malay Archipelago, down the Indian Ocean, and up the Atlantic. All its phases were familiar enough to me, every characteristic, all the alternatives which were likely to face me on the high seas—everything! . . . except the novel responsibility of command. But I took heart from the reasonable thought that the ship was like other ships, the men like other men, and that the sea was not likely to keep any special surprises expressly for my discomfiture.

Arrived at that comforting conclusion, I bethought myself of a cigar and went below to get it. All was still down there. Everybody at the after end of the ship was sleeping profoundly. I came out again on the quarterdeck, agreeably at ease in my sleeping suit on that warm breathless night, barefooted, a glowing cigar in my teeth, and, going forward, I was met by the profound silence of the fore end of the ship. Only as I passed the door of the forecastle I heard a deep, quiet, trustful sigh of some sleeper inside. And suddenly I rejoiced in the great security of the sea as compared with the unrest of the land, in my choice of that untempted life presenting no disquieting problems, invested with an elementary moral beauty by the absolute straightforwardness of its appeal and by the singleness of its purpose.

The riding light in the fore-rigging burned with a clear, untroubled, as if symbolic, flame, confident and bright in the mysterious shades of the night. Passing on my way aft along the other side of the ship, I observed that the rope side ladder, put over, no doubt, for the master of the tug when he came to fetch away our letters, had not been hauled in as it should have been. I became annoyed at this, for exactitude in small matters is the very soul of discipline. Then I reflected that I had myself peremptorily dismissed my officers from duty, and by my own act had prevented the anchor watch being formally set and things properly attended to. I asked myself whether it was wise ever to interfere with the established routine of duties even from the kindest of motives. My action might have made me appear eccentric. Goodness only knew how that absurdly whiskered mate would "account" for my conduct, and what the whole ship thought of that informality of their new captain. I was vexed with myself.

Not from compunction certainly, but, as it were mechanically, I proceeded to get the ladder in myself. Now a side ladder of that sort is a light affair and comes in easily, yet my vigorous tug, which should have brought it flying on board, merely recoiled upon my body in a totally unexpected jerk. What the devil! . . . I was so astounded by the immovableness of that ladder that I remained stock-still, trying to account for it to myself like that imbecile mate of mine. In the end, of course, I put my head over the rail.

The side of the ship made an opaque belt of shadow on the darkling glassy shimmer of the sea. But I saw at once something elongated and pale floating very close to the ladder. Before I could form a guess a faint flash of phosphorescent light, which seemed to issue suddenly from the naked body of a man, flickered in the sleeping water with the elusive, silent play of summer lightning in a night sky. With a gasp I saw revealed to my stare a pair of feet, the long legs, a broad livid back immersed right up to the neck in a greenish cadaverous glow. One hand, awash, clutched the bottom rung of the ladder. He was complete but for the head. A headless corpse! The cigar dropped out of my gaping mouth with a tiny plop and a short hiss quite audible in the absolute stillness of all things under heaven. At that I suppose he raised up his face, a dimly pale oval in the shadow of the ship's side. But even then I could only barely make out down there the shape of his black-haired head. However, it was enough for the horrid, frost-bound sensation which had gripped me about the chest to pass off. The moment of vain exclamations was past, too. I only climbed on the spare spar and leaned over the rail as far as I could, to bring my eyes nearer to that mystery floating alongside.

As he hung by the ladder, like a resting swimmer, the sea lightning played about his limbs at every stir; and he appeared in it ghastly, silvery, fishlike. He remained as mute as a fish, too. He made no motion to get out of the water, either. It was inconceivable that he should not attempt to come on board, and strangely troubling to suspect that perhaps he did not want to. And my first words were prompted by just that troubled incertitude.

"What's the matter?" I asked in my ordinary tone, speaking down to the face upturned exactly under mine.

"Cramp," it answered, no louder. Then slightly anxious, "I say, no need to call anyone."

"I was not going to," I said.

"Are you alone on deck?"

"Yes."

I had somehow the impression that he was on the point of letting go the ladder to swim away beyond my ken—mysterious as he came. But, for the moment, this being appearing as if he had risen from the bottom of the sea (it was certainly the nearest land to the ship) wanted only to know the time. I told him. And he, down there, tentatively:

"I suppose your captain's turned in?"

"I am sure he isn't," I said.

He seemed to struggle with himself, for I heard something like the low, bitter murmur of doubt. "What's the good?" His next words came out with a hestitating effort.

"Look here, my man. Could you call him out quietly?"

I thought the time had come to declare myself.

"*I* am the captain."

I heard a "By Jove!" whispered at the level of the water. The phosphorescence flashed in the swirl of the water all about his limbs, his other hand seized the ladder.

"My name's Leggatt."

The voice was calm and resolute. A good voice. The self-possession of that man had somehow induced a corresponding state in myself. It was very quietly that I remarked:

"You must be a good swimmer."

"Yes. I've been in the water practically since nine o'clock. The question for me now is whether I am to let go this ladder and go on swimming till I sink from exhaustion, or—to come on board here."

I felt this was no mere formula of desperate speech, but a real alternative in the view of a strong soul. I should have gathered from this that he was young; indeed, it is only the young who are ever confronted by such clear issues. But at the time it was pure intuition on my part. A mysterious communication was established already between us two—in the face of that silent, darkened tropical sea. I was young, too; young enough to make no comment. The man in the water began suddenly to climb up the ladder, and I hastened away from the rail to fetch some clothes.

Before entering the cabin I stood still, listening in the

lobby at the foot of the stairs. A faint snore came through the closed door of the chief mate's room. The second mate's door was on the hook, but the darkness in there was absolutely soundless. He, too, was young and could sleep like a stone. Remained the steward, but he was not likely to wake up before he was called. I got a sleeping suit out of my room and, coming back on deck, saw the naked man from the sea sitting on the main hatch, glimmering white in the darkness, his elbows on his knees and his head in his hands. In a moment he had concealed his damp body in a sleeping suit of the same gray-stripe pattern as the one I was wearing and followed me like my double on the poop. Together we moved right aft, bare-footed, silent.

"What is it?" I asked in a deadened voice, taking the lighted lamp out of the binnacle, and raising it to his face.

"An ugly business."

He had rather regular features; a good mouth; light eyes under somewhat heavy, dark eyebrows; a smooth, square forehead; no growth on his cheeks; a small, brown mustache, and a well-shaped, round chin. His expression was concentrated, meditative, under the inspecting light of the lamp I held up to his face; such as a man thinking hard in solitude might wear. My sleeping suit was just right for his size. A well-knit young fellow of twenty-five at most. He caught his lower lip with the edge of white, even teeth.

"Yes," I said, replacing the lamp in the binnacle. The warm, heavy tropical night closed upon his head again.

"There's a ship over there," he murmured.

"Yes, I know. The *Sephora*. Did you know of us?"

"Hadn't the slightest idea. I am the mate of her—" He paused and corrected himself. "I should say I *was*."

"Aha! Something wrong?"

"Yes. Very wrong indeed. I've killed a man."

"What do you mean? Just now?"

"No, on the passage. Weeks ago. Thirty-nine south. When I say a man——"

"Fit of temper," I suggested, confidently.

The shadowy, dark head, like mine, seemed to nod imperceptibly above the ghostly gray of my sleeping suit. It was, in the night, as though I had been faced by my own reflection in the depths of a somber and immense mirror.

"A pretty thing to have to own up to for a Conway boy," murmured my double, distinctly.

"You're a Conway boy?"

"I am," he said, as if startled. Then, slowly . . . "Perhaps, you too——"

It was so; but being a couple of years older I had left before he joined. After a quick interchange of dates a silence fell; and I thought suddenly of my absurd mate with his terrific whiskers and the "Bless my soul—you don't say so" type of intellect. My double gave me an inkling of his thoughts by saying:

"My father's a parson in Norfolk. Do you see me before a judge and jury on that charge? For myself I can't see the necessity. There are fellows that an angel from heaven——And I am not that. He was one of those creatures that are just simmering all the time with a silly sort of wickedness. Miserable devils that have no business to live at all. He wouldn't do his duty and wouldn't let anybody else do theirs. But what's the good of talking! You know well enough the sort of ill-conditioned snarling cur——"

He appealed to me as if our experiences had been as

identical as our clothes. And I knew well enough the pestiferous danger of such a character where there are no means of legal repression. And I knew well enough also that my double there was no homicidal ruffian. I did not think of asking him for details, and he told me the story roughly in brusque, disconnected sentences. I needed no more. I saw it all going on as though I were myself inside that other sleeping suit.

"It happened while we were setting a reefed foresail, at dusk. Reefed foresail! You understand the sort of weather. The only sail we had left to keep the ship running; so you may guess what it had been like for days. Anxious sort of job, that. He gave me some of his cursed insolence at the sheet. I tell you I was overdone with this terrific weather that seemed to have no end to it. Terrific, I tell you—and a deep ship. I believe the fellow himself was half crazed with funk. It was no time for gentlemanly reproof, so I turned round and felled him like an ox. He up and at me. We closed just as an awful sea made for the ship. All hands saw it coming and took to the rigging, but I had him by the throat, and went on shaking him like a rat, the men above us yelling, 'Look out! look out!' Then a crash as if the sky had fallen on my head. They say that for over ten minutes hardly anything was to be seen of the ship—just the three masts and a bit of the forecastle head and of the poop all awash driving along in a smother of foam. It was a miracle that they found us, jammed together behind the forebits. It's clear that I meant business, because I was holding him by the throat still when they picked us up. He was black in the face. It was too much for them. It seems they rushed us aft together, gripped as we were, screaming 'Murder!' like a lot of lunatics, and broke into the cuddy. And the ship running for her life, touch and go all the time, any minute her last in a sea fit to turn your hair gray only a-looking at it. I understand that the skipper, too, started raving like the rest of them. The man had been deprived of sleep for more than a week, and to have this sprung on him at the height of a furious gale nearly drove him out of his mind. I wonder they didn't fling me overboard after getting the carcass of their precious shipmate out of my fingers. They had rather a job to separate us, I've been told. A sufficiently fierce story to make an old judge and a respectable jury sit up a bit. The first thing I heard when I came to myself was the maddening howling of that endless gale, and on that the voice of the old man. He was hanging on to my bunk, staring into my face out of his sou'wester.

" 'Mr. Leggatt, you have killed a man. You can act no longer as chief mate of this ship.' "

His care to subdue his voice made it sound monotonous. He rested a hand on the end of the skylight to steady himself with, and all that time did not stir a limb, so far as I could see. "Nice little tale for a quiet tea party," he concluded in the same tone.

One of my hands, too, rested on the end of the skylight; neither did I stir a limb, so far as I knew. We stood less than a foot from each other. It occurred to me that if old "Bless my soul—you don't say so" were to put his head up the companion and catch sight of us, he would think he was seeing double, or imagine himself come upon a scene of weird witchcraft; the strange captain having a quiet confabulation by the wheel with his own gray ghost. I became very much concerned to prevent anything of the sort. I heard the other's soothing undertone.

"My father's a parson in Norfolk," it said. Evidently he had forgotten he had told me this important fact before.

Truly a nice little tale.

"You had better slip down into my stateroom now," I said, moving off steathily. My double followed my movements; our bare feet made no sound; I let him in, closed the door with care, and, after giving a call to the second mate, returned on deck for my relief.

"Not much sign of any wind yet," I remarked when he approached.

"No, sir. Not much," he assented, sleepily, in his hoarse voice, with just enough deference, no more, and barely suppressing a yawn.

"Well, that's all you have to look out for. You have got your orders."

"Yes, sir."

I paced a turn or two on the poop and saw him take up his position face forward with his elbow in the ratlines of the mizzen-rigging before I went below. The mate's faint snoring was still going on peacefully. The cuddy lamp was burning over the table on which stood a vase with flowers, a polite attention from the ships' provision merchant—the last flowers we should see for the next three months at the very least. Two bunches of bananas hung from the beam symmetrically, one on each side of the rudder casing. Everything was as before in the ship—except that two of her captain's sleeping suits were simultaneously in use, one motionless in the cuddy, the other keeping very still in the captain's stateroom.

It must be explained here that my cabin had the form of the capital letter L, the door being within the angle and opening into the short part of the letter. A couch was to the left, the bed-place to the right; my writing desk and the chronometers' table faced the door. But anyone opening it, unless he stepped right inside, had no view of what

I call the long (or vertical) part of the letter. It contained some lockers surmounted by a book case; and a few clothes, a thick jacket or two, caps, oilskin coat, and such like, hung on hooks. There was at the bottom of that part a door opening into my bathroom, which could be entered also directly from the saloon. But that way was never used.

The mysterious arrival had discovered the advantage of this particular shape. Entering my room, lighted strongly by a big bulkhead lamp swung on gimbals above my writing desk, I did not see him anywhere till he stepped out quietly from behind the coats hung in the recessed part.

"I heard somebody moving about, and went in there at once," he whispered.

I, too, spoke under my breath.

"Nobody is likely to come in here without knocking and getting permission."

He nodded. His face was thin and the sunburn faded, as though he had been ill. And no wonder. He had been, I heard presently, kept under arrest in his cabin for nearly seven weeks. But there was nothing sickly in his eyes or in his expression. He was not a bit like me, really; yet as we stood leaning over my bed-place, whispering side by side, with our dark heads together and our backs to the door, anybody bold enough to open it stealthily would have been treated to the uncanny sight of a double captain busy talking in whispers with his other self.

"But all this doesn't tell me how you came to hang on to our side ladder," I inquired, in the hardly audible murmurs we used, after he had told me something more of the proceedings on board the *Sephora* once the bad weather was over.

"When we sighted Java Head I had had time to think all those matters out several times over. I had six weeks of doing nothing else, and with only an hour or so every evening for a tramp on the quarter-deck."

He whispered, his arms folded on the side of my bed-place, staring through the open port. And I could imagine perfectly the manner of this thinking out—a stubborn if not a steadfast operation; something of which I should have been perfectly incapable.

"I reckoned it would be dark before we closed with the land," he continued, so low that I had to strain my hearing, near as we were to each other, shoulder touching shoulder almost. "So I asked to speak to the old man. He always seemed very sick when he came to see me—as if he could not look me in the face. You know, that foresail saved the ship. She was too deep to have run long under bare poles. And it was I that managed to set it for him. Anyway, he came. When I had him in my cabin—he stood by the door looking at me as if I had the halter around my neck already—I asked him right away to leave my cabin door unlocked at night while the ship was going through Sunda Straits. There would be the Java coast within two or three miles, off Angier Point. I wanted nothing more. I've had a prize for swimming my second year in the Conway."

"I can believe it," I breathed out.

"God only knows why they locked me in every night. To see some of their faces you'd have thought they were afraid I'd go about at night strangling people. Am I a murdering brute? Do I look it? By Jove! if I had been he wouldn't have trusted himself like that into my room. You'll say I might have chucked him aside and bolted out, there and then—it was dark already. Well, no. And for the same reason I wouldn't think of trying to smash the door. There would have been a rush to stop me at the noise, and I did not mean to get into a confounded scrimmage. Somebody else might have got killed—for I would not have broken out only to get chucked back, and I did not want any more of that work. He refused, looking more sick than ever. He was afraid of the men, and also of that old second mate of his who had been sailing with him for years—a gray-headed old humbug; and his steward, too, had been with him devil knows how long—seventeen years or more—a dogmatic sort of loafer who hated me like poison, just because I was the chief mate. No chief mate ever made more than one voyage in the *Sephora*, you know. Those two old chaps ran the ship. Devil only knows what the skipper wasn't afraid of (all his nerve went to pieces altogether in that hellish spell of bad weather we had)—of what the law would do to him—of his wife, perhaps. Oh, yes! she's on board. Though I don't think she would have meddled. She would have been only too glad to have me out of the ship in any way. The 'brand of Cain' business, don't you see. That's all right. I was ready enough to go off wandering on the face of the earth—and that was price enough to pay for an Abel of that sort. Anyhow, he wouldn't listen to me. 'This thing must take its course. I represent the law here.' He was shaking like a leaf. 'So you won't?' 'No!' 'Then I hope you will be able to sleep on that,' I said, and turned my back on him. 'I wonder that *you* can,' cries he, and locks the door.

"Well, after that, I couldn't. Not very well. That was three weeks ago. We have had a slow passage through the Java Sea; drifted about Carimata for ten days. When we anchored here they thought, I suppose, it was all right. The nearest land (and that's five miles) is the ship's destination; the consul would soon set about catching me;

and there would have been no object in bolting to these islets there. I don't suppose there's a drop of water on them. I don't know how it was, but tonight that steward, after bringing me my supper, went out to let me eat it, and left the door unlocked. And I ate it—all there was, too. After I had finished I strolled out on the quarter-deck. I don't know that I meant to do anything. A breath of fresh air was all I wanted, I believe. Then a sudden temptation came over me. I kicked off my slippers and was in the water before I had made up my mind fairly. Somebody heard the splash and they raised an awful hullabaloo. 'He's gone! Lower the boats! He's committed suicide! No, he's swimming.' Certainly I was swimming. It's not so easy for a swimmer like me to commit suicide by drowning. I landed on the nearest islet before the boat left the ship's side. I heard them pulling about in the dark, hailing, and so on, but after a bit they gave up. Everything quieted down and the anchorage became as still as death. I sat down on a stone and began to think. I felt certain they would start searching for me at daylight. There was no place to hide on those stony things—and if there had been, what would have been the good? But now I was clear of that ship, I was not going back. So after a while I took off all my clothes, tied them up in a bundle with a stone inside, and dropped them in the deep water on the outer side of that islet. That was suicide enough for me. Let them think what they liked, but I didn't mean to drown myself. I meant to swim till I sank—but that's not the same thing. I struck out for another of these little islands, and it was from that one that I first saw your riding light. Something to swim for. I went on easily, and on the way I came upon a flat rock a foot or two above water. In the daytime, I dare say, you might make it out with a glass from your poop. I scrambled up on it and rested myself for a bit. Then I made another start. That last spell must have been over a mile."

His whisper was getting fainter and fainter, and all the time he stared straight out through the porthole, in which there was not even a star to be seen. I had not interrupted him. There was something that made comment impossible in his narrative, or perhaps in himself; a sort of feeling, a quality, which I can't find a name for. And when he ceased, all I found was a futile whisper: "So you swam for our light?"

"Yes—straight for it. It was something to swim for. I couldn't see any stars low down because the coast was in the way, and I couldn't see the land, either. The water was like glass. One might have been swimming in a con-founded thousand-feet deep cistern with no place for scrambling out anywhere; but what I didn't like was the notion of swimming round and round like a crazed bul-lock before I gave out; and as I didn't mean to go back . . . No. Do you see me being hauled back, stark naked, off one of these little islands by the scruff of the neck and fighting like a wild beast? Somebody would have got killed for certain, and I did not want any of that. So I went on. Then your ladder—"

"Why didn't you hail the ship?" I asked, a little louder.

He touched my shoulder lightly. Lazy footsteps came right over our heads and stopped. The second mate had crossed from the other side of the poop and might have been hanging over the rail, for all we knew.

"He couldn't hear us talking—could he?" My double breathed into my very ear, anxiously.

His anxiety was an answer, a sufficient answer, to the question I had put to him. An answer containing all the difficulty of that situation. I closed the porthole quietly, to make sure. A louder word might have been overheard.

"Who's that?" he whispered then.

"My second mate. But I don't know much more of the fellow than you do."

And I told him a little about myself. I had been appointed to take charge while I least expected anything of the sort, not quite a fortnight ago. I didn't know either the ship or the people. Hadn't had the time in port to look about me or size anybody up. And as to the crew, all they knew was that I was appointed to take the ship home. For the rest, I was almost as much of a stranger on board as himself, I said. And at the moment I felt it most acutely. I felt that it would take very little to make me a suspect person in the eyes of the ship's company.

He had turned about meantime; and we, the two strangers in the ship, faced each other in identical attitudes.

"Your ladder—" he murmured, after a silence. "Who'd have thought of finding a ladder hanging over at night in a ship anchored out here! I felt just then a very unpleasant faintness. After the life I've been leading for nine weeks, anybody would have got out of condition. I wasn't capable of swimming round as far as your rudder chains. And, lo and behold! there was a ladder to get hold of. After I gripped it I said to myself, 'What's the good?' When I saw a man's head looking over I thought I would swim away presently and leave him shouting—in whatever language it was. I didn't mind being looked at. I—I liked it. And then you speaking to me so quietly—as if you had expected me—made me hold on a little longer. It had been a confounded lonely time—I don't mean while swimming. I was glad to talk a little to somebody that didn't belong to the *Sephora*. As to asking for the captain, that was a mere impulse. It could have been no use, with all the ship knowing about me and the other people pretty certain to be round here in the morning. I don't know—I wanted to be seen, to talk with somebody, before I went on. I don't know what I would have said. . . . 'Fine night, isn't it?' or something of the sort."

"Do you think they will be round here presently?" I asked with some incredulity.

"Quite likely," he said, faintly.

He looked extremely haggard all of a sudden. His head rolled on his shoulders.

"H'm. We shall see then. Meantime get into that bed," I whispered. "Want help? There."

It was a rather high bed-place with a set of drawers underneath. This amazing swimmer really needed the lift I gave him by seizing his leg. He tumbled in, rolled over on his back, and flung one arm across his eyes. And then, with his face nearly hidden, he must have looked exactly as I used to look in that bed. I gazed upon my other self for a while before drawing across carefully the two green serge curtains which ran on a brass rod. I thought for a moment of pinning them together for greater safety, but I sat down on the couch, and once there I felt unwilling to rise and hunt for a pin. I would do it in a moment. I was extremely tired, in a peculiarly intimate way, by the strain of stealthiness, by the effort of whispering and the general secrecy of this excitement. It was three o'clock by now and I had been on my feet since nine, but I was not sleepy; I could not have gone to sleep. I sat there, fagged out, looking at the curtains, trying to clear my mind of the confused sensation of being in two places at once, and greatly bothered by an exasperating knocking in my head. It was a relief to discover suddenly that it was not in my head at all, but on the outside of the door. Before I could collect myself the words "Come in" were out of my mouth, and the steward entered with a tray, bringing in my morning coffee. I had slept, after all, and I was so frightened that I shouted, "This way! I am here, steward," as though he had been miles away. He put down the tray on the table next the couch and only then said, very quietly, "I can see you are here, sir." I felt him give me a keen look, but I dared not meet his eyes just then. He must have wondered why I had drawn the curtains of my bed before going to sleep on the couch. He went out, hooking the door open as usual.

I heard the crew washing decks above me. I knew I would have been told at once if there had been any wind. Calm, I thought, and I was doubly vexed. Indeed, I felt dual more than ever. The steward reappeared suddenly in the doorway. I jumped up from the couch so quickly that he gave a start.

"What do you want here?"

"Close your port, sir—they are washing decks."

"It is closed," I said, reddening.

"Very well, sir." But he did not move from the doorway and returned my stare in an extraordinary, equivocal manner for a time. Then his eyes wavered, all his expression changed, and in a voice unusually gentle, almost coaxingly:

"May I come in to take the empty cup away, sir?"

"Of course!" I turned my back on him while he popped in and out. Then I unhooked and closed the door and even pushed the bolt. This sort of thing could not go on very long. The cabin was as hot as an oven, too. I took a peep at my double, and discovered that he had not moved, his arm was still over his eyes; but his chest heaved; his hair was wet; his chin glistened with perspiration. I reached over him and opened the port.

"I must show myself on deck," I reflected.

Of course, theoretically, I could do what I liked, with no one to say nay to me within the whole circle of the horizon; but to lock my cabin door and take the key away I did not dare. Directly I put my head out of the companion I saw the group of my two officers, the second mate barefooted, the chief mate in long india-rubber boots, near the break of the poop, and the steward halfway down the poop ladder talking to them eagerly. He happened to catch sight of me and dived, the second ran down on the main deck shouting some order or other, and the chief mate came to meet me, touching his cap.

There was a sort of curiosity in his eye that I did not like. I don't know whether the steward had told them that I was "queer" only, or downright drunk, but I know the man meant to have a good look at me. I watched him coming with a smile which, as he got into point-blank range, took effect and froze his very whiskers. I did not give him time to open his lips.

"Square the yards by lifts and braces before the hands go to breakfast."

It was the first particular order I had given on board that ship; and I stayed on deck to see it executed, too. I had felt the need of asserting myself without loss of time. That sneering young cub got taken down a peg or two on that occasion, and I also seized the opportunity of having a good look at the face of every foremast man as they filed past me to go to the after braces. At breakfast time, eating nothing myself, I presided with such frigid dignity that the two mates were only too glad to escape from the cabin as soon as decency permitted and all the time the dual working of my mind distracted me almost to the point of insanity. I was constantly watching myself, my secret self, as dependent on my actions as my own personality, sleeping in that bed, behind that door which faced me as I sat at the head of the table. It was very much like being mad, only it was worse because one was aware of it.

I had to shake him for a solid minute, but when at last he opened his eyes it was in the full possession of his senses, with an inquiring look.

"All's well so far," I whispered. "Now you must vanish into the bathroom."

He did so, as noiseless as a ghost, and I then rang for the steward, and facing him boldly, directed him to tidy up my stateroom while I was having my bath—"and be quick about it." As my tone admitted of no excuses, he said, "Yes sir," and ran off to fetch his dustpan and brushes. I took a bath and did most of my dressing, splashing, and whistling softly for the steward's edification, while the secret sharer of my life stood drawn up bolt upright in that little space, his face looking very sunken in daylight, his eyelids lowered under the stern, dark line of his eyebrows drawn together by a slight frown.

When I left him there to go back to my room the steward was finishing dusting. I sent for the mate and engaged him in some insignificant conversation. It was, as it were, trifling with the terrific character of his whiskers; but my object was to give him an opportunity for a good look at my cabin. And then I could at last shut, with a clear conscience, the door of my stateroom and get my double back into the recessed part. There was nothing else for it. He had to sit still on a small folding stool, half smothered by the heavy coats hanging there. We listened to the steward going into the bathroom out of the saloon, filling the water bottles there, scrubbing the bath, setting things to rights, whisk, bang, clatter—out again into the saloon—turn the key—click. Such was my scheme for keeping my second self invisible. Nothing better could be contrived under the circumstances. And there we sat; I at my writing desk ready to appear busy with some papers, he behind me, out of sight of the door. It would not have been prudent to talk in daytime; and I could not have stood the excitement of that queer sense of whispering to myself. Now and then, glancing over my shoulder, I saw him far back there, sitting rigidly on the low stool, his bare feet close together, his arms folded, his head hanging on his breast—and perfectly still. Anybody would have taken him for me.

I was fascinated by it myself. Every moment I had to glance over my shoulder. I was looking at him when a voice outside the door said:

"Beg pardon, sir."

"Well!" . . . I kept my eyes on him, and so, when the voice outside the door announced, "There's a ship's boat coming our way, sir," I saw him give a start—the first movement he had made for hours. But he did not raise his bowed head.

"All right. Get the ladder over."

I hesitated. Should I whisper something to him? But what? His immobility seemed to have been never disturbed. What could I tell him he did not know already? . . . Finally I went on deck.

II

The skipper of the *Sephora* had a thin red whisker all round his face, and the sort of complexion that goes with hair of that color; also the particular, rather smeary shade of blue in the eyes. He was not exactly a showy figure; his shoulders were high, his stature but middling—one leg slightly more bandy than the other. He shook hands, looking vaguely around. A spiritless tenacity was his main characteristic, I judged. I behaved with a politeness which seemed to disconcert him. Perhaps he was shy. He mumbled to me as if he were ashamed of what he was saying; gave his name (it was something like Archbold—but at this distance of years I hardly am sure), his ship's name, and a few other particulars of that sort, in the manner of a criminal making a reluctant and doleful confession. He had had terrible weather on the passage out—terrible—terrible—wife aboard, too.

By this time we were seated in the cabin and the steward brought in a tray with a bottle and glasses. "Thanks! No." Never took liquor. Would have some water, though. He drank two tumblerfuls. Terrible thirsty work. Ever since daylight had been exploring the islands round his ship.

"What was that for—fun?" I asked, with an appearance of polite interest.

"No!" He sighed. "Painful duty."

As he persisted in his mumbling and I wanted my double to hear every word, I hit upon the notion of informing him that I regretted to say I was hard of hearing.

"Such a young man, too!" he nodded, keeping his smeary blue, unintelligent eyes fastened upon me. What was the cause of it—some disease? he inquired, without the least sympathy and as if he thought that, if so, I'd got no more than I deserved.

"Yes; disease," I admitted in a cheerful tone which seemed to shock him. But my point was gained, because he had to raise his voice to give me his tale. It is not worth while to record that version. It was just over two months since all this had happened, and he had thought so much about it that he seemed completely muddled as to its bearings, but still immensely impressed.

"What would you think of such a thing happening on board your own ship? I've had the *Sephora* for these fifteen years. I am a well-known shipmaster."

He was densely distressed—and perhaps I should have sympathized with him if I had been able to detach my mental vision from the unsuspected sharer of my cabin as though he were my second self. There he was on the other side of the bulkhead, four or five feet from us, no more, as we sat in the saloon. I looked politely at Captain Archbold (if that was his name), but it was the other I saw, in a gray sleeping suit, seated on a low stool, his bare feet close together, his arms folded, and every word said between us falling into the ears of his dark head bowed on his chest.

"I have been at sea now, man and boy, for seven-and-thirty years, and I've never heard of such a thing happening in an English ship. And that it should be my ship. Wife on board, too."

I was hardly listening to him.

"Don't you think," I said, "that the heavy sea which, you told me, came aboard just then might have killed the man? I have seen the sheer weight of a sea kill a man very neatly, by simply breaking his neck."

"Good God!" he uttered, impressively, fixing his smeary blue eyes on me. "The sea! No man killed by the sea ever looked like that." He seemed positively scandalized at my suggestion. And as I gazed at him, certainly not prepared for anything original on his part, he advanced his head close to mine and thrust his tongue out at me so suddenly that I couldn't help starting back.

After scoring over my calmness in this graphic way he

nodded wisely. If I had seen the sight, he assured me, I would never forget it as long as I lived. The weather was too bad to give the corpse a proper sea burial. So next day at dawn they took it up on the poop, covering its face with a bit of bunting; he read a short prayer, and then, just as it was, in its oilskins and long boots, they launched it amongst those mountainous seas that seemed ready every moment to swallow up the ship herself and the terrified lives on board of her.

"That reefed foresail saved you," I threw in.

"Under God—it did," he exclaimed fervently. "It was by a special mercy, I firmly believe, that it stood some of those hurricane squalls."

"It was the setting of that sail which—" I began.

"God's own hand in it," he interrupted me. "Nothing less could have done it. I don't mind telling you that I hardly dared give the order. It seemed impossible that we could touch anything without losing it, and then our last hope would have been gone."

The terror of that gale was on him yet. I let him go on for a bit, then said, casually—as if returning to a minor subject:

"You were very anxious to give up your mate to the shore people, I believe?"

He was. To the law. His obscure tenacity on that point had in it something incomprehensible and a little awful; something, as it were, mystical, quite apart from his anxiety that he should not be suspected of "countenancing any doings of that sort." Seven-and-thirty virtuous years at sea, of which over twenty of immaculate command, and the last fifteen in the *Sephora* seemed to have laid him under some pitiless obligation.

"And you know," he went on, groping shamefacedly

amongst his feelings, "I did not engage that young fellow. His people had some interest with my owners. I was in a way forced to take him on. He looked very smart, very gentlemanly, and all that. But do you know—I never liked him, somehow. I am a plain man. You see, he wasn't exactly the sort for the chief mate of a ship like the *Sephora*."

I had become so connected in thoughts and impressions with the secret sharer of my cabin that I felt as if I, personally, were being given to understand that I, too, was not the sort that would have done for the chief mate of a ship like the *Sephora*. I had no doubt of it in my mind.

"Not at all the style of man. You understand," he insisted, superfluously, looking hard at me.

I smiled urbanely. He seemed at a loss for a while.

"I suppose I must report a suicide."

"Beg pardon?"

"Sui-cide! That's what I'll have to write to my owners directly I get in."

"Unless you manage to recover him before tomorrow," I assented, dispassionately. . . . . "I mean, alive."

He mumbled something which I really did not catch, and I turned my ear to him in a puzzled manner. He fairly bawled:

"The land—I say, the mainland is at least seven miles off my anchorage."

"About that."

My lack of excitement, of curiosity, of surprise, of any sort of pronounced interest, began to arouse his distrust. But except for the felicitous pretense of deafness I had not tried to pretend anything. I had felt utterly incapable of playing the part of ignorance properly, and therefore was afraid to try. It is also certain that he had brought some ready-made suspicions with him, and that he viewed my politeness as a strange and unnatural phenomenon. And yet how else could I have received him? Not heartily! That was impossible for psychological reasons, which I need not state here. My only object was to keep off his inquiries. Surlily? Yes, but surliness might have provoked a point-blank question. From its novelty to him and from its nature, punctilious courtesy was the manner best calculated to restrain the man. But there was the danger of his breaking through my defense bluntly. I could not, I think, have met him by a direct lie, also for psychological (not moral) reasons. If he had only known how afraid I was of his putting my feeling of identity with the other to the test! But, strangely enough—(I thought of it only afterward)—I believe that he was not a little disconcerted by the reverse side of that weird situation, by something in me that reminded him of the man he was seeking— suggested a mysterious similitude to the young fellow he had distrusted and disliked from the first.

However that might have been, the silence was not very prolonged. He took another oblique step.

"I reckon I had no more than a two-mile pull to your ship. Not a bit more."

"And quite enough, too, in this awful heat," I said.

Another pause full of mistrust followed. Necessity, they say, is mother of invention, but fear, too, is not barren of ingenious suggestions. And I was afraid he would ask me point-blank for news of my other self.

"Nice little saloon, isn't it?" I remarked, as if noticing for the first time the way his eyes roamed from one closed door to the other. "And very well fitted out, too. Here, for instance," I continued, reaching over the back of my seat negligently and flinging the door open, "is my bathroom."

He made an eager movement, but hardly gave it a glance. I got up, shut the door of the bathroom, and invited him to have a look round, as if I were very proud of my accommodation. He had to rise and be shown round, but he went through the business without any raptures whatever.

"And now we'll have a look at my stateroom," I declared, in a voice as loud as I dared to make it, crossing the cabin to the starboard side with purposely heavy steps.

He followed me in and gazed around. My intelligent double had vanished. I played my part.

"Very convenient—isn't it?"

"Very nice. Very com . . ." He didn't finish, and went out brusquely as if to escape from some unrighteous wiles of mine. But it was not to be. I had been too frightened not to feel vengeful; I felt I had him on the run, and I meant to keep him on the run. My polite insistence must have had something menacing in it, because he gave in suddenly. And I did not let him off a single item; mate's room, pantry, storerooms, the very sail locker which was also under the poop—he had to look into them all. When at last I showed him out on the quarter-deck he drew a long, spiritless sigh and mumbled dismally that he must really be going back to his ship now. I desired my mate, who had joined us, to see to the captain's boat.

The man of whiskers gave a blast on the whistle which he used to wear hanging round his neck, and yelled, "*Sephoras* away!" My double down there in my cabin must have heard, and certainly could not feel more relieved than I. Four fellows came running out from somewhere forward and went over the side, while my own men, appearing on deck too, lined the rail. I escorted my visitor to the gangway ceremoniously, and nearly overdid it. He was a tenacious beast. On the very ladder he lingered, and in that unique, guiltily conscientious manner of sticking to the point:

"I say . . . you . . . you don't think that—"

I covered his voice loudly:

"Certainly not. . . . I am delighted. Good-by."

I had an idea of what he meant to say, and just saved myself by the privilege of defective hearing. He was too shaken generally to insist, but my mate, close witness of that parting, looked mystified and his face took on a thoughtful cast. As I did not want to appear as if I wished to avoid all communication with my officers, he had the opportunity to address me.

"Seems a very nice man. His boat's crew told our chaps a very extraordinary story, if what I am told by the steward is true. I suppose you had it from the captain, sir?"

"Yes. I had a story from the captain."

"A very horrible affair—isn't it, sir?"

"It is."

"Beats all these tales we hear about murders in Yankee ships."

"I don't think it beats them. I don't think it resembles them in the least."

"Bless my soul—you don't say so! But of course I've no acquaintance whatever with American ships, not I, so I couldn't go against your knowledge. It's horrible enough for me. . . . But the queerest part is that those fellows seemed to have some idea the man was hidden aboard here. They had really. Did you ever hear of such a thing?"

"Preposterous—isn't it?"

We were walking to and fro athwart the quarterdeck. No one of the crew forward could be seen (the day was Sunday), and the mate pursued:

"There was some little dispute about it. Our chaps took offense. 'As if we would harbor a thing like that,' they said. 'Wouldn't you like to look for him in our coal hole?' Quite a tiff. But they made it up in the end. I suppose he did drown himself. Don't you, sir?"

"I don't suppose anything."

"You have no doubt in the matter, sir?"

"None whatever."

I left him suddenly. I felt I was producing a bad impression, but with my double down there it was most trying to be on deck. And it was almost as trying to be below. Altogether a nerve-trying situation. But on the whole I felt less torn in two when I was with him. There was no one in the whole ship whom I dared take into my confidence. Since the hands had got to know his story, it would have been impossible to pass him off for anyone else, and an accidental discovery was to be dreaded now more than ever. . . .

The steward being engaged in laying the table for dinner, we could talk only with our eyes when I first went down. Later in the afternoon we had a cautious try at whispering. The Sunday quietness of the ship was against us; the stillness of air and water around her was against us; the elements, the men were against us—everything was against us in our secret partnership; time itself—for this could not go on forever. The very trust in Providence was, I suppose, denied to his guilt. Shall I confess that this thought cast me down very much? And as to the chapter of accidents which counts for so much in the book of success, I could only hope that it was closed. For what favorable accident could be expected?

"Did you hear everything?" were my first words as soon

as we took up our position side by side, leaning over my bed-place.

He had. And the proof of it was his earnest whisper, "The man told you he hardly dared to give the order."

I understood the reference to be to that saving foresail.

"Yes. He was afraid of it being lost in the setting."

"I assure you he never gave the order. He may think he did, but he never gave it. He stood there with me on the break of the poop after the maintopsail blew away, and whimpered about our last hope—positively whimpered about it and nothing else—and the night coming on! To hear one's skipper go on like that in such weather was enough to drive any fellow out of his mind. It worked me up into a sort of desperation. I just took it into my own hands and went away from him, boiling, and—. But what's the use telling you? *You* know! . . . Do you think that if I had not been pretty fierce with them I should have got the men to do anything? Not it! The bosun perhaps? Perhaps! It wasn't a heavy sea—it was a sea gone mad! I suppose the end of the world will be something like that; and a man may have the heart to see it coming once and be done with it—but to have to face it day after day—I don't blame anybody. I was precious little better than the rest. Only—I was an officer of that old coal-wagon, anyhow—"

"I quite understand," I conveyed that sincere assurance into his ear. He was out of breath with whispering; I could hear him pant slightly. It was all very simple. The same strung-up force which had given twenty-four men a chance, at least, for their lives, had, in a sort of recoil, crushed an unworthy mutinous existence.

But I had no leisure to weigh the merits of the matter— footsteps in the saloon, a heavy knock. "There's enough wind to get under way with, sir." Here was the call of a new claim upon my thoughts and even upon my feelings.

"Turn the hands up," I cried through the door. "I'll be on deck directly."

I was going out to make the acquaintance of my ship. Before I left the cabin our eyes met—the eyes of the only two strangers on board. I pointed to the recessed part where the little campstool awaited him and laid my finger on my lips. He made a gesture—somewhat vague—a little mysterious, accompanied by a faint smile, as if of regret.

This is not the place to enlarge upon the sensations of a man who feels for the first time a ship move under his feet to his own independent word. In my case they were not unalloyed. I was not wholly alone with my command; for there was that stranger in my cabin. Or rather, I was not completely and wholly with her. Part of me was absent. That mental feeling of being in two places at once affected me physically as if the mood of secrecy had penetrated my very soul. Before an hour had elapsed since the ship had begun to move, having occasion to ask the mate (he stood by my side) to take a compass bearing of the Pagoda, I caught myself reaching up to his ear in whispers. I say I caught myself, but enough had escaped to startle the man. I can't describe it otherwise than by saying that he shied. A grave, preoccupied manner, as though he were in possession of some perplexing intelligence, did not leave him henceforth. A little later I moved away from the rail to look at the compass with such a stealthy gait that the helmsman noticed it—and I could not help noticing the unusual roundness of his eyes. These are trifling instances, though it's to no commander's advantage to be suspected of ludicrous eccentricities. But I was also more seriously affected. There are to a seaman certain words, gestures, that should in given conditions come as naturally, as instinctively as the winking of a menaced eye. A certain order should spring on to his lips without thinking; a certain sign should get itself made, so to speak, without reflection. But all unconscious alertness had abandoned me. I had to make an effort of will to recall myself back (from the cabin) to the conditions of the moment. I felt that I was appearing an irresolute commander to those people who were watching me more or less critically.

And, besides, there were the scares. On the second day out, for instance, coming off the deck in the afternoon (I had straw slippers on my bare feet) I stopped at the open pantry door and spoke to the steward. He was doing something there with his back to me. At the sound of my voice he nearly jumped out of his skin, as the saying is, and incidentally broke a cup.

"What on earth's the matter with you?" I asked, astonished.

He was extremely confused. "Beg pardon, sir. I made sure you were in your cabin."

"You see I wasn't."

"No, sir. I could have sworn I had heard you moving in there not a moment ago. It's most extraordinary . . . very sorry, sir."

I passed on with an inward shudder. I was so identified with my secret double that I did not even mention the fact in those scanty, fearful whispers we exchanged. I suppose he had made some slight noise of some kind or other. It would have been miraculous if he hadn't at one time or another. And yet, haggard as he appeared, he looked always perfectly self-controlled, more than calm—almost invulnerable. On my suggestion he remained almost entirely in the bathroom, which, upon the whole, was the safest place. There could be really no shadow of an excuse for anyone ever wanting to go in there, once the steward had done with it. It was a very tiny place. Sometimes he reclined on the floor, his legs bent, his head sustained on one elbow. At others I would find him on the campstool, sitting in his gray sleeping suit and with his cropped dark hair like a patient, unmoved convict. At night I would smuggle him into my bed-place, and we would whisper together, with the regular footfalls of the officer of the watch passing and repassing over our heads. It was an infinitely miserable time. It was lucky that some tins of fine preserves were stowed in a locker in my stateroom; hard bread I could always get hold of; and so he lived on stewed chicken, paté de foie gras, asparagus, cooked oysters, sardines—on all sorts of abominable sham delicacies out of tins. My carly morning coffee he always drank; and it was all I dared do for him in that respect.

Every day there was the horrible maneuvering to go through so that my room and then the bathroom should be done in the usual way. I came to hate the sight of the steward, to abhor the voice of that harmless man. I felt that it was he who would bring on the disaster of discovery. It hung like a sword over our heads.

The fourth day out, I think (we were then working down the east side of the Gulf of Siam, tack for tack, in light winds and smooth water)—the fourth day, I say, of this miserable juggling with the unavoidable, as we sat at our evening meal, that man, whose slightest movement I dreaded, after putting down the dishes ran upon deck busily. This could not be dangerous. Presently he came down again; and then it appeared that he had remembered a coat of mine which I had thrown over a rail to dry after having been wetted in a shower which had passed over the ship in the afternoon. Sitting stolidly at the head of the table I became terrified at the sight of the garment on his arm. Of course he made for my door. There was no time to lose.

"Steward," I thundered. My nerves were so shaken that I could not govern my voice and conceal my agitation. This was the sort of thing that made my terrifically whiskered mate tap his forehead with his forefinger. I had detected him using that gesture while talking on deck with a confidential air to the carpenter. It was too far to hear a word, but I had no doubt that this pantomime could only refer to the strange new captain.

"Yes, sir," the pale-faced steward turned resignedly to me. It was this maddening course of being shouted at, checked without rhyme or reason, arbitrarily chased out of my cabin, suddenly called into it, sent flying out of his pantry on incomprehensible errands, that accounted for the growing wretchedness of his expression.

"Where are you going with that coat?"

"To your room, sir."

"Is there another shower coming?"

"I'm sure I don't know, sir. Shall I go up again and see, sir?"

"No! never mind."

My object was attained, as of course my other self in there would have heard everything that passed. During this interlude my two officers never raised their eyes off their respective plates; but the lip of that confounded cub, the second mate, quivered visibly.

I expected the steward to hook my coat on and come out at once. He was very slow about it; but I dominated my nervousness sufficiently not to shout after him. Suddenly I became aware (it could be heard plainly enough) that the fellow for some reason or other was opening the door of the bathroom. It was the end. The place was literally not big enough to swing a cat in. My voice died in my throat and I went stony all over. I expected to hear a yell of surprise and terror, and made a movement, but had not the strength to get on my legs. Everything remained still. Had my second self taken the poor wretch by the throat? I don't know what I would have done next moment if I had not seen the steward come out of my room, close the door, and then stand quietly by the sideboard.

Saved, I thought. But, no! Lost! Gone! He was gone!

I laid my knife and fork down and leaned back in my chair. My head swam. After a while, when sufficiently recovered to speak in a steady voice, I instructed my mate to put the ship round at eight o'clock himself.

"I won't come on deck," I went on. "I think I'll turn in, and unless the wind shifts I don't want to be disturbed before midnight. I feel a bit seedy."

"You did look middling bad a little while ago," the chief mate remarked without showing any great concern.

They both went out, and I stared at the steward clearing the table. There was nothing to be read on that wretched man's face. But why did he avoid my eyes I asked myself. Then I thought I should like to hear the sound of his voice.

"Steward!"

"Sir!" Startled as usual.

"Where did you hang up that coat?"

"In the bathroom, sir." The usual anxious tone. "It's not quite dry yet, sir."

For some time longer I sat in the cuddy. Had my double vanished as he had come? But of his coming there was an explanation, whereas his disappearance would be inexplicable. . . . I went slowly into my dark room, shut the door, lighted the lamp, and for a time dared not turn round. When at last I did I saw him standing bolt upright in the narrow recessed part. It would not be true to say I had a shock, but an irresistible doubt of his bodily existence flitted through my mind. Can it be, I asked myself, that he is not visible to other eyes than mine? It was like being haunted. Motionless, with a grave face, he raised his hands slightly at me in a gesture which meant clearly, "Heavens! what a narrow escape!" Narrow indeed. I think I had come creeping quietly as near insanity as any man who has not actually gone over the border. That gesture restrained me, so to speak.

The mate with the terrific whiskers was now putting the ship on the other tack. In the moment of profound silence which follows upon the hands going to their stations I heard on the poop his raised voice: "Hard alee!" and the distant shout of the order repeated on the maindeck. The sails, in that light breeze, made but a faint fluttering noise. It ceased. The ship was coming round slowly; I held my breath in the renewed stillness of expectation; one wouldn't have thought that there was a single living soul on her decks. A sudden brisk shout, "Mainsail haul!" broke the spell, and in the noisy cries and rush overhead of the men running away with the main brace we two, down in my cabin, came together in our usual position by the bed-place.

He did not wait for my question. "I heard him fumbling here and just managed to squat myself down in the bath," he whispered to me. "The fellow only opened the door and put his arm in to hang the coat up. All the same—"

"I never thought of that," I whispered back, even more appalled than before at the closeness of the shave, and marveling at that something unyielding in his character which was carrying him through so finely. There was no agitation in his whisper. Whoever was being driven distracted, it was not he. He was sane. And the proof of his sanity was continued when he took up the whispering again.

"It would never do for me to come to life again."

It was something that a ghost might have said. But what he was alluding to was his old captain's reluctant admission of the theory of suicide. It would obviously serve his turn—if I had understood at all the view which seemed to govern the unalterable purpose of his action.

"You must maroon me as soon as ever you can get amongst these islands off the Cambodje shore," he went on.

"Maroon you! We are not living in a boy's adventure tale," I protested. His scornful whispering took me up.

"We aren't indeed! There's nothing of a boy's tale in this. But there's nothing else for it. I want no more. You don't suppose I am afraid of what can be done to me? Prison or gallows or whatever they may please. But you don't see me coming back to explain such things to an old fellow in a wig and twelve respectable tradesmen, do you? What can they know whether I am guilty or not—or of *what* I am guilty, either? That's my affair. What does the Bible say? 'Driven off the face of the earth.' Very well. I am off the face of the earth now. As I came at night so I shall go."

"Impossible!" I murmured. "You can't."

"Can't? . . . Not naked like a soul on the Day of Judgment. I shall freeze on to this sleeping suit. The Last Day is not yet—and . . . you have understood thoroughly. Didn't you?"

I felt suddenly ashamed of myself. I may say truly that

I understood—and my hesitation in letting that man swim away from my ship's side had been a mere sham sentiment, a sort of cowardice.

"It can't be done now till next night," I breathed out. "The ship is on the offshore tack and the wind may fail us."

"As long as I know that you understand," he whispered. "But of course you do. It's a great satisfaction to have got somebody to understand. You seem to have been there on purpose." And in the same whisper, as if we two whenever we talked had to say things to each other which were not fit for the world to hear, he added, "It's very wonderful."

We remained side by side talking in our secret way— but sometimes silent or just exchanging a whispered word or two at long intervals. And as usual he stared through the port. A breath of wind came now and again into our faces. The ship might have been moored in dock, so gently and on an even keel she slipped through the water, that did not murmur even at our passage, shadowy and silent like a phantom sea.

At midnight I went on deck, and to my mate's great surprise put the ship round on the other tack. His terrible whiskers flitted round me in silent criticism. I certainly should not have done it if it had been only a question of getting out of that sleepy gulf as quickly as possible. I believe he told the second mate, who relieved him, that it was a great want of judgment. The other only yawned. That intolerable cub shuffled about so sleepily and lolled against the rails in such a slack, improper fashion that I came down on him sharply.

"Aren't you properly awake yet?"

"Yes, sir! I am awake."

"Well, then, be good enough to hold yourself as if you

were. And keep a lookout. If there's any current we'll be closing with some islands before daylight."

The east side of the gulf is fringed with islands, some solitary, others in groups. On the blue background of the high coast they seem to float on silvery patches of calm water, arid and gray, or dark green and rounded like clumps of evergreen bushes, with the larger ones, a mile or two long, showing the outlines of ridges, ribs of gray rock under the dark mantle of matted leafage. Unknown to trade, to travel, almost to geography, the manner of life they harbor is an unsolved secret. There must be villages —settlements of fishermen at least—on the largest of them, and some communication with the world is probably kept up by native craft. But all that forenoon, as we headed for them, fanned along by the faintest of breezes, I saw no sign of man or canoe in the field of the telescope I kept on pointing at the scattered group.

At noon I gave no orders for a change of course, and the mate's whiskers became much concerned and seemed to be offering themselves unduly to my notice. At last I said:

"I am going to stand right in. Quite in as far as I can take her."

The stare of extreme surprise imparted an air of ferocity also to his eyes, and he looked truly terrific for a moment.

"We're not doing well in the middle of the gulf," I continued, casually. "I am going to look for the land breezes tonight."

"Bless my soul! Do you mean, sir, in the dark amongst the lot of all them islands and reefs and shoals?"

"Well—if there are any regular land breezes at all on

this coast one must get close inshore to find them, mustn't one?"

"Bless my soul!" he exclaimed again under his breath. All that afternoon he wore a dreamy, contemplative appearance which in him was a mark of perplexity. After dinner I went into my stateroom as if I meant to take some rest. There we two bent our dark heads over a half-unrolled chart lying on my bed.

"There," I said. "It's got to be Koh-ring. I've been looking at it ever since sunrise. It has got two hills and a low point. It must be inhabited. And on the coast opposite there is what looks like the mouth of a biggish river—with some town, no doubt, not far up. It's the best chance for you that I can see."

"Anything. Koh-ring let it be."

He looked thoughtfully at the chart as if surveying chances and distances from a lofty height—and following with his eyes his own figure wandering on the blank land of Cochin-China, and then passing off that piece of paper clean out of sight into uncharted regions. And it was as if the ship had two captains to plan her course for her. I had been so worried and restless running up and down that I had not had the patience to dress that day. I had remained in my sleeping suit, with straw slippers and a soft floppy hat. The closeness of the heat in the gulf had been most oppressive, and the crew were used to see me wandering in that airy attire.

"She will clear the south point as she heads now," I whispered into his ear. "Goodness only knows when, though, but certainly after dark. I'll edge her in to half a mile, as far as I may be able to judge in the dark—"

"Be careful," he murmured, warningly—and I realized suddenly that all my future, the only future for which I was fit, would perhaps go irretrievably to pieces in any mishap to my first command.

I could not stop a moment longer in the room. I motioned him to get out of sight and made my way on the poop. That unplayful cub had the watch. I walked up and down for a while thinking things out, then beckoned him over.

"Send a couple of hands to open the two quarter-deck ports," I said, mildly.

He actually had the impudence, or else so forgot himself in his wonder at such an incomprehensible order, as to repeat:

"Open the quarter-deck ports! What for, sir?"

"The only reason you need concern yourself about is because I tell you to do so. Have them open wide and fastened properly."

He reddened and went off, but I believe made some jeering remark to the carpenter as to the sensible practice of ventilating a ship's quarter-deck. I know he popped into the mate's cabin to impart the fact to him because the whiskers came on deck, as it were by chance, and stole glances at me from below—for signs of lunacy or drunkenness, I suppose.

A little before supper, feeling more restless than ever, I rejoined, for a moment, my second self. And to find him sitting so quietly was surprising, like something against nature, inhuman.

I developed my plan in a hurried whisper.

"I shall stand in as close as I dare and then put her round. I shall presently find means to smuggle you out of here into the sail locker, which communicates with the lobby. But there is an opening, a sort of square for hauling the sails out, which gives straight on the quarter-deck and

JOSEPH CONRAD | 258

which is never closed in fine weather, so as to give air to the sails. When the ship's way is deadened in stays and all the hands are aft at the main braces you shall have a clear road to slip out and get overboard through the open quarter-deck port. I've had them both fastened up. Use a rope's end to lower yourself into the water so as to avoid a splash—you know. It could be heard and cause some beastly complication."

He kept silent for a while, then whispered, "I understand."

"I won't be there to see you go," I began with an effort. "The rest . . . I only hope I have understood, too."

"You have. From first to last," and for the first time there seemed to be a faltering, something strained in his whisper. He caught hold of my arm, but the ringing of the supper bell made me start. He didn't, though; he only released his grip.

After supper I didn't come below again till well past eight o'clock. The faint, steady breeze was loaded with dew; and the wet, darkened sails held all there was of propelling power in it. The night, clear and starry, sparkled darkly, and the opaque, lightless patches shifting slowly against the low stars were the drifting islets. On the port bow there was a big one more distant and shadowily imposing by the great space of sky it eclipsed.

On opening the door I had a back view of my very own self looking at a chart. He had come out of the recess and was standing near the table.

"Quite dark enough," I whispered.

He stepped back and leaned against my bed with a level, quiet glance. I sat on the couch. We had nothing to say to each other. Over our heads the officer of the watch moved here and there. Then I heard him move quickly. I knew what that meant. He was making for the companion; and presently his voice was outside my door.

"We are drawing in pretty fast, sir. Land looks rather close."

"Very well," I answered. "I am coming on deck directly."

I waited till he was gone out of the cuddy, then rose. My double moved too. The time had come to exchange our last whispers, for neither of us was ever to hear each other's natural voice.

"Look here!" I opened a drawer and took out three sovereigns. "Take this, anyhow. I've got six and I'd give you the lot, only I must keep a little money to buy some fruit and vegetables for the crew from native boats as we go through Sundra Straits."

He shook his head.

"Take it," I urged him, whispering desperately. "No one can tell what—"

He smiled and slapped meaningly the only pocket of the sleeping jacket. It was not safe, certainly. But I produced a large old silk handkerchief of mine, and tying the three pieces of gold in a corner, pressed it on him. He was touched, I suppose, because he took it at last and tied it quickly round his waist under the jacket, on his bare skin.

Our eyes met; several seconds elapsed, till, our glances still mingled, I extended my hand and turned the lamp out. Then I passed through the cuddy, leaving the door of my room wide open. . . . "Steward!"

He was still lingering in the pantry in the greatness of his zeal, giving a rub-up to a plated cruet stand the last thing before going to bed. Being careful not to wake up the mate, whose room was opposite, I spoke in an undertone.

He looked round anxiously. "Sir!"

"Can you get me a little hot water from the galley?"

"I am afraid, sir, the galley fire's been out for some time now."

"Go and see."

He fled up the stairs.

"Now," I whispered, loudly, into the saloon—too loudly, perhaps, but I was afraid I couldn't make a sound. He was by my side in an instant—the double captain slipped past the stairs—through the tiny dark passage . . . a sliding door. We were in the sail locker, scrambling on our knees over the sails. A sudden thought struck me. I saw myself wandering barefooted, bareheaded, the sun beating on my dark poll. I snatched off my floppy hat and tried hurriedly in the dark to ram it on my other self. He dodged and fended off silently. I wonder what he thought had come to me before he understood and suddenly desisted. Our hands met gropingly, lingered united in a steady, motionless clasp for a second. . . . No word was breathed by either of us when they separated.

I was standing quietly by the pantry door when the steward returned.

"Sorry, sir. Kettle barely warm. Shall I light the spirit lamp?"

"Never mind."

I came out on deck slowly. It was now a matter of conscience to shave the land as close as possible—for now he must go overboard whenever the ship was put in stays. Must! There could be no going back for him. After a moment I walked over to leeward and my heart flew into my mouth at the nearness of the land on the bow. Under any other circumstances I would not have held on a minute longer. The second mate had followed me anxiously.

I looked on till I felt I could command my voice.

"She will weather," I said then in a quiet tone.

"Are you going to try that, sir?" he stammered out incredulously.

I took no notice of him and raised my tone just enough to be heard by the helmsman.

"Keep her good full."

"Good full, sir."

The wind fanned my cheek, the sails slept, the world was silent. The strain of watching the dark loom of the land grow bigger and denser was too much for me. I had shut my eyes—because the ship must go closer. She must! The stillness was intolerable. Were we standing still?

When I opened my eyes the second view started my heart with a thump. The black southern hill of Koh-ring seemed to hang right over the ship like a towering fragment of the everlasting night. On that enormous mass of blackness there was not a gleam to be seen, not a sound to be heard. It was gliding irresistibly toward us and yet seemed already within reach of the hand. I saw the vague figures of the watch grouped in the waist, gazing in awed silence.

"Are you going on, sir?" inquired an unsteady voice at my elbow.

I ignored it. I had to go on.

"Keep her full. Don't check her way. That won't do now," I said warningly.

"I can't see the sails very well," the helmsman answered me, in strange, quavering tones.

Was she close enough? Already she was, I won't say in the shadow of the land, but in the very blackness of it, already swallowed up as it were, gone too close to be recalled, gone from me altogether.

"Give the mate a call," I said to the young man who stood at my elbow as still as death. "And turn all hands up."

My tone had a borrowed loudness reverberated from the height of the land. Several voices cried out together: "We are all on deck, sir."

Then stillness again, with the great shadow gliding closer, towering higher, without a light, without a sound. Such a hush had fallen on the ship that she might have been a bark of the dead floating in slowly under the very gate of Erebus.

"My God! Where are we?"

It was the mate moaning at my elbow. He was thunderstruck, and as it were deprived of the moral support of his whiskers. He clapped his hands and absolutely cried out, "Lost!"

"Be quiet," I said sternly.

He lowered his tone, but I saw the shadowy gesture of his despair. "What are we doing here?"

"Looking for the land wind."

He made as if to tear his hair, and addressed me recklessly.

"She will never get out. You have done it, sir. I knew it'd end in something like this. She will never weather, and you are too close now to stay. She'll drift ashore before she's round. O my God!"

I caught his arm as he was raising it to batter his poor devoted head, and shook it violently.

"She's ashore already," he wailed, trying to tear himself away.

"Is she? . . . Keep good full there!"

"Good full, sir," cried the helmsman in a frightened, thin, childlike voice.

I hadn't let go the mate's arm and went on shaking it. "Ready about, do you hear? You go forward"—shake— "and stop there"—shake—"and hold your noise"—shake —"and see these head sheets properly overhauled" shake, shake—shake.

And all the time I dared not look toward the land lest my heart should fail me. I released my grip at last and he ran forward as if fleeing for dear life.

I wondered what my double there in the sail locker thought of this commotion. He was able to hear everything—and perhaps he was able to understand why, on my conscience, it had to be thus close—no less. My first order. "Hard alee!" re-echoed ominously under the towering shadow of Koh-ring as if I had shouted in a mountain gorge. And then I watched the land intently. In that smooth water and light wind it was impossible to feel the ship coming-to. No! I could not feel her. And my second self was making now ready to slip out and lower himself overboard. Perhaps he was gone already . . . ?

The great black mass brooding over our very mastheads began to pivot away from the ship's side silently. And now I forgot the secret stranger ready to depart, and remembered only that I was a total stranger to the ship. I did not know her. Would she do it? How was she to be handled?

I swung the mainyard and waited helplessly. She was perhaps stopped, and her very fate hung in the balance, with the black mass of Koh-ring like the gate of the everlasting night towering over her taffrail. What would she do now? Had she way on her yet? I stepped to the side swiftly, and on the shadowy water I could see nothing except a faint phosphorescent flash revealing the glassy smoothness of the sleeping surface. It was impossible to tell—and I had not learned yet the feel of my ship. Was she moving? What I needed was something easily seen, a piece of paper, which I could throw overboard and watch. I had nothing on me. To run down for it I didn't dare. There was no time. All at once my strained, yearning stare distinguished a white object floating within a yard of the ship's side. White on the black water. A phosphorescent flash passed under it. What was that thing? . . . I recognized my own floppy hat. It must have fallen off his head . . . and he didn't bother. Now I had what I wanted —the saving mark for my eyes. But I hardly thought of my other self, now gone from the ship, to be hidden forever from all friendly faces, to be a fugitive and a vagabond on the earth, with no brand of the curse on his sane forehead to stay a slaying hand . . . too proud to explain.

And I watched the hat—the expression of my sudden pity for his mere flesh. It had been meant to save his homeless head from the dangers of the sun. And now— behold—it was saving the ship, by serving me for a mark to help out the ignorance of my strangeness. Ha! It was drifting forward, warning me just in time that the ship had gathered sternway.

"Shift the helm," I said in a low voice to the seaman standing still like a statue.

The man's eyes glistened wildly in the binnacle light as he jumped round to the other side and spun round the wheel.

I walked to the break of the poop. On the overshadowed deck all hands stood by the forebraces waiting for my order. The stars ahead seemed to be gliding from right to left. And all was so still in the world that I heard the quiet remark "She's round," passed in a tone of intense relief between two seamen.

"Let go and haul."

The foreyards ran round with a great noise, amidst cheery cries. And now the frightful whiskers made themselves heard giving various orders. Already the ship was drawing ahead. And I was alone with her. Nothing! no one in the world should stand now between us, throwing a shadow on the way of silent knowledge and mute affection, the perfect communion of a seaman with his first command.

Walking to the taffrail, I was in time to make out, on the very edge of a darkness thrown by a towering black mass like the very gateway of Erebus—yes, I was in time to catch an evanescent glimpse of my white hat left behind to mark the spot where the secret sharer of my cabin and of my thoughts, as though he were my second self, had lowered himself into the water to take his punishment: a free man, a proud swimmer striking out for a new destiny.

Carson McCullers

A Tree, A Rock, A Cloud

IT WAS RAINING THAT MORNING, AND STILL VERY DARK. When the boy reached the streetcar café he had almost finished his route and he went in for a cup of coffee. The place was an all-night café owned by a bitter and stingy man called Leo. After the raw, empty street, the café seemed friendly and bright: along the counter there were a couple of soldiers, three spinners from the cotton mill, and in a corner a man who sat hunched over with his nose and half his face down in a beer mug. The boy wore a helmet such as aviators wear. When he went into the café he unbuckled the chin strap and raised the right flap up over his pink little ear; often as he drank his coffee someone would speak to him in a friendly way. But this morning Leo did not look into his face and none of the men were talking. He paid and was leaving the café when a voice called out to him:

"Son! Hey Son!"

He turned back and the man in the corner was crooking his finger and nodding to him. He had brought his face out of the beer mug and he seemed suddenly very happy. The man was long and pale, with a big nose and faded orange hair.

"Hey Son!"

The boy went toward him. He was an undersized boy of about twelve, with one shoulder drawn higher than the other because of the weight of the paper sack. His face was shallow, freckled, and his eyes were round child eyes.

"Yeah Mister?"

The man laid one hand on the paper boy's shoulders, then grasped the boy's chin and turned his face slowly from one side to the other. The boy shrank back uneasily.

"Say! What's the big idea?"

The boy's voice was shrill; inside the café it was suddenly very quiet.

The man said slowly. "I love you."

All along the counter the men laughed. The boy, who had scowled and sidled away, did not know what to do. He looked over the counter at Leo, and Leo watched him with a weary, brittle jeer. The boy tried to laugh also. But the man was serious and sad.

"I did not mean to tease you, Son," he said. "Sit down and have a beer with me. There is something I have to explain."

Cautiously, out of the corner of his eye, the paper boy questioned the men along the counter to see what he should do. But they had gone back to their beer or their breakfast and did not notice him. Leo put a cup of coffee on the counter and a little jug of cream.

"He is a minor," Leo said.

The paper boy slid himself up onto the stool. His ear beneath the upturned flap of the helmet was very small and red. The man was nodding at him soberly. "It is important," he said. Then he reached in his hip pocket and brought out something which he held up in the palm of his hand for the boy to see.

"Look very carefully," he said.

The boy stared, but there was nothing to look at very

carefully. The man held in his big, grimy palm a photograph. It was the face of a woman, but blurred, so that only the hat and the dress she was wearing stood out clearly.

"See?" the man asked.

The boy nodded and the man placed another picture in his palm. The woman was standing on a beach in a bathing suit. The suit made her stomach very big, and that was the main thing you noticed.

"Got a good look?" He leaned over closer and finally asked: "You ever seen her before?"

The boy sat motionless, staring slantwise at the man. "Not so I know of."

"Very well." The man blew on the photographs and put them back into his pocket. "That was my wife."

"Dead?" the boy asked.

Slowly the man shook his head. He pursed his lips as though about to whistle and answered in a long-drawn way: "Nuuu—" he said. "I will explain."

The beer on the counter before the man was in a large brown mug. He did not pick it up to drink. Instead he bent down and, putting his face over the rim, he rested there for a moment. Then with both hands he tilted the mug and sipped.

"Some night you'll go to sleep with your big nose in a mug and drown," said Leo. "Prominent transient drowns in beer. That would be a cute death."

The paper boy tried to signal to Leo. While the man was not looking he screwed up his face and worked his mouth to question soundlessly: "Drunk?" But Leo only raised his eyebrows and turned away to put some pink strips of bacon on the grill. The man pushed the mug away from him, straightened himself, and folded his loose crooked hands on the counter. His face was sad as he looked at the paper boy. He did not blink, but from time to time the lids closed down with delicate gravity over his pale green eyes. It was nearing dawn and the boy shifted the weight of the paper sack.

"I am talking about love," the man said. "With me it is a science."

The boy half slid down from the stool. But the man raised his forefinger, and there was something about him that held the boy and would not let him go away.

"Twelve years ago I married the woman in the photograph. She was my wife for one year, nine months, three days, and two nights. I loved her. Yes. . . ." He tightened his blurred, rambling voice and said again: "I loved her. I thought also that she loved me. I was a railroad engineer. She had all home comforts and luxuries. It never crept into my brain that she was not satisfied. But do you know what happened?"

"Mgnccow!" said Leo.

The man did not take his eyes from the boy's face. "She left me. I came in one night and the house was empty and she was gone. She left me."

"With a fellow?" the boy asked.

Gently the man placed his palm down on the counter. "Why naturally, Son. A woman does not run off like that alone."

The café was quiet, the soft rain black and endless in the street outside. Leo pressed down the frying bacon with the prongs of his long fork. "So you have been chasing the floozie for eleven years. You frazzled old rascal!"

For the first time the man glanced at Leo. "Please don't be vulgar. Besides, I was not speaking to you." He turned

back to the boy and said in a trusting and secretive undertone. "Let's not pay any attention to him. O.K.?"

The paper boy nodded doubtfully.

"It was like this," the man continued. "I am a person
who feels many things. All my life one thing after another
has impressed me. Moonlight. The leg of a pretty girl. One
thing after another. But the point is that when I had
enjoyed anything there was a peculiar sensation as though
it was laying around loose in me. Nothing seemed to finish
itself up or fit in with the other things. Women? I had my
portion of them. The same. Afterwards laying around
loose in me. I was a man who had never loved."

Very slowly he closed his eyelids, and the gesture was
like a curtain drawn at the end of a scene in a play. When
he spoke again his voice was excited and the words came
fast—the lobes of his large, loose ears seemed to tremble.

"Then I met this woman. I was fifty-one years old and
she always said she was thirty. I met her at a filling station
and we were married within three days. And do you know
what it was like? I just can't tell you. All I had ever felt
was gathered together around this woman. Nothing lay
around loose in me any more but was finished up by her."

The man stopped suddenly and stroked his long nose.
His voice sank down to a steady and reproachful undertone: "I'm not explaining this right. What happened was
this. There were these beautiful feelings and loose little
pleasures inside me. And this woman was something like
an assembly line for my soul. I run these little pieces of
myself through her and I come out complete. Now do you
follow me?"

"What was her name?" the boy asked.

"Oh," he said. "I called her Dodo. But that is
immaterial."

"Did you try to make her come back?"

The man did not seem to hear. "Under the circumstances you can imagine how I felt when she left me."

Leo took the bacon from the grill and folded two strips of it between a bun. He had a gray face, with slitted eyes, and a pinched nose, saddled by faint blue shadows. One of the mill workers signaled for more coffee and Leo poured it. He did not give refills on coffee free. The spinner ate breakfast there every morning, but the better Leo knew his customers the stingier he treated them. He nibbled his own bun as though he grudged it to himself.

"And you never got hold of her again?"

The boy did not know what to think of the man, and his child's face was uncertain with mingled curiosity and doubt. He was new on the paper route; it was still strange to him to be out in the town in the black, queer early morning.

"Yes," the man said. "I took a number of steps to get her back. I went around trying to locate her. I went to Tulsa where she had folks. And to Mobile. I went to every town she had ever mentioned to me, and I hunted down every man she had formerly been connected with. Tulsa, Atlanta, Chicago, Cheehaw, Memphis. . . . For the better part of two years I chased around the country trying to lay hold of her."

"But the pair of them had vanished from the face of the earth!" said Leo.

"Don't listen to him," the man said confidentially. "And also just forget those two years. They are not important. What matters is that around the third year a curious thing begun to happen to me."

"What?" the boy asked.

The man leaned down and tilted his mug to take a sip

of beer. But as he hovered over the mug his nostrils fluttered slightly; he sniffed the staleness of the beer and did not drink. "Love is a curious thing to begin with. At first I thought only of getting her back. It was a kind of mania. But then as time went on I tried to remember her. But do you know what happened?"

"No," the boy said.

"When I laid myself down on a bed and tried to think about her my mind became a blank. I couldn't see her. I would take out her pictures and look. No good. Nothing doing. A blank. Can you imagine it?"

"Say Mac!" Leo called down the counter. "Can you imagine this bozo's mind a blank!"

Slowly, as though fanning away flies, the man waved his hand. His green eyes were concentrated and fixed on the shallow little face of the paper boy.

"But a sudden piece of glass on a sidewalk. Or a nickel tune in a music box. A shadow on a wall at night. And I would remember. It might happen in a street and I would cry or bang my head against a lamppost. You follow me?"

"A piece of glass . . ." the boy said.

"Anything. I would walk around and I had no power of how and when to remember her. You think you can put up a kind of shield. But remembering don't come to a man face forward—it corners around sideways. I was at the mercy of everything I saw and heard. Suddenly instead of me combing the countryside to find her she begun to chase me around in my very soul. *She* chasing *me*, mind you! And in my soul."

The boy asked finally: "What part of the country were you in then?"

"Ooh," the man groaned. "I was a sick mortal. It was

like smallpox. I confess, Son, that I boozed. I fornicated. I committed any sin that suddenly appealed to me. I am loath to confess it but I will do so. When I recall that period it is all curdled in my mind, it was so terrible."

The man leaned his head down and tapped his forehead on the counter. For a few seconds he stayed bowed over in this position, the back of his stringy neck covered with orange furze, his hands with their long warped fingers held palm to palm in an attitude of prayer. Then the man straightened himself; he was smiling and suddenly his face was bright and tremulous and old.

"It was in the fifth year that it happened," he said. "And with it I started my science."

Leo's mouth jerked with a pale, quick grin. "Well none of we boys are getting any younger," he said. Then with sudden anger he balled up a dishcloth he was holding and threw it down hard on the floor. "You draggle-tailed old Romeo!"

"What happened?" the boy asked.

The old man's voice was high and clear: "Peace," he answered.

"Huh?"

"It is hard to explain scientifically, Son," he said. "I guess the logical explanation is that she and I had fleed around from each other for so long that finally we just got tangled up together and lay down and quit. Peace. A queer and beautiful blankness. It was spring in Portland and the rain came every afternoon. All evening I just stayed there on my bed in the dark. And that is how the science come to me."

The windows in the streetcar were pale blue with light. The two soldiers paid for their beers and opened the door —one of the soldiers combed his hair and wiped off his muddy puttees before they went outside. The three mill workers bent silently over their breakfasts. Leo's clock was ticking on the wall.

"It is this. And listen carefully. I meditated on love and reasoned it out. I realized what is wrong with us. Men fall in love for the first time. And what do they fall in love with?"

The boy's soft mouth was partly open and he did not answer.

"A woman," the old man said. "Without science, with nothing to go by, they undertake the most dangerous and sacred experience in God's earth. They fall in love with a woman. Is that correct, Son?"

"Yeah," the boy said faintly.

"They start at the wrong end of love. They begin at the climax. Can you wonder it is so miserable? Do you know how men should love?"

The old man reached over and grasped the boy by the collar of his leather jacket. He gave him a gentle little shake and his green eyes gazed down unblinking and grave.

"Son, do you know how love should be begun?"

The boy sat small and listening and still. Slowly he shook his head. The old man leaned closer and whispered:

"A tree. A rock. A cloud."

It was still raining outside in the street: a mild, gray, endless rain. The mill whistle blew for the six o'clock shift and the three spinners paid and went away. There was no one in the café but Leo, the old man, and the little paper boy.

"The weather was like this in Portland," he said. "At the time my science was begun. I meditated and I started very cautious. I would pick up something from the street and take it home with me. I bought a goldfish and I concentrated on the goldfish and I loved it. I graduated from one thing to another. Day by day I was getting this technique. On the road from Portland to San Diego——"

"Aw shut up!" screamed Leo suddenly. "Shut up! Shut up!"

The old man still held the collar of the boy's jacket; he was trembling and his face was earnest and bright and wild. "For six years now I have gone around by myself and built up my science. And now I am a master. Son. I can love anything. No longer do I have to think about it even. I see a street full of people and a beautiful light comes in me. I watch a bird in the sky. Or I meet a traveler on the road. Everything, Son. And anybody. All stranger and all loved! Do you realize what a science like mine can mean?"

The boy held himself stiffly, his hands curled tight around the counter edge. Finally he asked: "Did you ever really find that lady?"

"What? What say, Son?"

"I mean," the boy asked timidly. "Have you fallen in love with a woman again?"

The old man loosened his grasp on the boy's collar. He turned away and for the first time his green eyes had a vague and scattered look. He lifted the mug from the counter, drank down the yellow beer. His head was shaking slowly from side to side. Then finally he answered: "No, Son. You see that is the last step in my science. I go cautious. And I am not quite ready yet."

"Well!" said Leo. "Well well well!"

The old man stood in the open doorway. "Remember," he said. Framed there in the gray damp light of the early morning he looked shrunken and seedy and frail. But his smile was bright. "Remember I love you," he said with a last nod. And the door closed quietly behind him.

The boy did not speak for a long time. He pulled down the bangs on his forehead and slid his grimy little forefinger around the rim of his empty cup. Then without looking at Leo he finally asked:

"Was he drunk?"

"No," said Leo shortly.

The boy raised his clear voice higher. "Then was he a dope fiend?"

"No."

The boy looked up at Leo, and his flat little face was desperate, his voice urgent and shrill. "Was he crazy? Do you think he was a lunatic?" The paper boy's voice dropped suddenly with doubt. "Leo? Or not?"

But Leo would not answer him. Leo had run a night café for fourteen years, and he held himself to be a critic of craziness. There were the town characters and also the transients who roamed in from the night. He knew the manias of all of them. But he did not want to satisfy the questions of the waiting child. He tightened his pale face and was silent.

So the boy pulled down the right flap of his helmet and as he turned to leave he made the only comment that seemed safe to him, the only remark that could not be laughed down and despised:

"He sure has done a lot of traveling."

Biographical Notes

ISAAC BABEL was born in a suburb of Odessa, Russia, in 1894. His first stories appeared in 1916, but not until after the Russian Revolution and the ensuing civil war did his talents fully emerge. By 1925, the stories in *Red Cavalry* and *Odessa Tales* marked him as one of the outstanding writers of his generation. But the increasing totalitarianism of the Soviet regime began to severely handicap Babel's work; the next fifteen years saw the publication of but a handful of stories. Arrested in 1939 for unknown reasons, Babel is thought to have died in a Siberian concentration camp in 1941.

JAMES BALDWIN was born in New York City's Harlem in 1924, and grew up there. When he was twenty-four, he went to Europe, and since then has alternated his residence between the United States and abroad. His novels, notably *Go Tell It on the Mountain* and *Another Country,* the essays in *Notes of a Native Son, Nobody Knows My Name* and *The Fire Next Time,* and the stories in *Going to Meet the Man,* show him not only to be a remarkable individual talent, but also one of the most eloquent spokesmen for black consciousness in America today.

JOSEPH CONRAD was born in Poland in 1857, and spent his young manhood first in the French, then in the British Merchant Marine. He was thirty-seven, and a ship's master, when he completed his first novel, *Almayer's Folly.* Retiring from the sea, Conrad went on to establish himself as one of the greatest masters of the English language with novels such as *Lord Jim, Victory, Nostromo* and *The Secret Agent,* and such shorter works as *The Heart of Darkness, The Nigger of the Narcissus, Typhoon, Youth* and *The Secret Sharer.* Conrad died in 1924.

WILLIAM FAULKNER was born in Mississippi in 1897. Though he spent time in Europe, New York and New Orleans, the bulk of his life and work was deeply rooted in the region of his birth. *The Sound and the Fury, As I Lay Dying* and *Light in August* are but the most prominent novels in a body of achievement second to none in modern American literature. Progressing from early obscurity to world fame without being unduly influenced by either, Faulkner numbered among his awards a Nobel prize, a Pulitzer prize and a National Book Award. He died in 1962.

IRVIN FAUST was born in Brooklyn, New York, in 1928, educated in the city's public schools, and graduated from the City College of New York. His book of short stories, *Roar Lion Roar*, and his novel, *The Steagle,* display a fresh and original voice, and a vision beautifully attuned to the sometimes grotesque realities of modern urban life.

ERNEST HEMINGWAY was born in Illinois in 1898. By the time he was twenty, he was an experienced newspaperman, had been wounded in World War I, and was ready to embark on a career of serious writing. Such novels as *The Sun Also Rises, A Farewell to Arms, For Whom the Bell Tolls,* and *The Old Man and the Sea*, as well as his forty-nine short stories, profoundly influenced writers of many countries, earned the author world fame and won him Nobel and Pulitzer prizes, while Hemingway's colorful, adventurous life made him a legendary public personality. Oppressed by physical illness and mental strain, Ernest Hemingway died by his own hand in 1961.

WILLIAM MAXWELL was born in 1908 in Illinois, and educated at the University of Illinois and Harvard. His most famous novel is *The Folded Leaf*, about the difficult passage from adolescence to maturity; other novels include *They Came like Swallows, Time Will Darken It,* and *The Chateau.* For over twenty-five years Mr. Maxwell has divided his time between his writing and his work as editor on *The New Yorker* magazine.

279 | *Biographical Notes*

CARSON MCCULLERS was born in Georgia in 1917. In 1936, she arrived in New York to study music, lost her tuition money in the subway, and turned to writing instead. She was twenty-three when her first novel, *The Heart Is a Lonely Hunter,* was recognized as an achievement of the first rank. This initial success was followed and enhanced by *Reflections in a Golden Eye, The Ballad of the Sad Café, The Member of the Wedding* (first a novel, then a play) and *Clock Without Hands.* After a long and gallant struggle against a debilitating illness, Carson McCullers died in 1967.

ALAN SILLITOE was born in England in 1928. He left school at fourteen, became a factory worker, then joined the armed forces. Returning to civilian life, he was encouraged by the poet Robert Graves to attempt a writing career. The result was the memorable first novel, *Saturday Night and Sunday Morning.* Sillitoe's other novels include *The General, The Death of William Posters* and *A Tree on Fire,* as well as two collections of short stories, all of which are informed by the author's savage candor and his anger at social injustice.

JEAN STAFFORD was born in California in 1915, raised in Colorado, and educated in the United States and Europe. Her first novel, *Boston Adventure,* won high praise, as did her subsequent *The Mountain Lion* and *The Catherine Wheel.* It has been with her short stories, however, that the author has enjoyed her greatest reputation—a reputation given added dimension by the publication in 1969 of her *Collected Stories.*

The
oners

ries About the